"There was no  having a meal

She gently revved the engine. "That may be fine for you, but not for me. I have to live among these people, and I'd really like to hold my head up again."

"And I'd like to do something for this town—for charity."

"Then I hope you will." She added, "Without me."

She moved to put the car in Reverse, but Dallas laid a hand on the open window. "What's changed, Lizzie? You weren't that eager to have dinner, I realize that, but you did. I thought we'd gotten to know each other a bit, laughed a little. You watched the PBR event when I know you didn't want to do that, either, but when I left your house, I felt good."

"I told you what changed."

"A couple of harmless comments?" His grip tightened on the window. "One neighbor gets nosy, and that's it?"

"I can't, Dallas. I can't go through that again."

Dear Reader,

From the minute Elizabeth Barnes first appeared in *Her Cowboy Sheriff* (book four of my Kansas Cowboys series), I knew I had to give her a story of her own. Certain characters almost demand their star turn at center stage!

Actually, Elizabeth *isn't* the demanding sort—she's newly divorced, on her own with three kids to raise and without even a job to help her get by. Dallas Maguire entered the picture in this series in *Twins Under the Tree* (book six). He's an injured bull rider who's in Barren, Kansas, to recover, and romance, much less a ready-made family, is the furthest thing from his mind.

The timing couldn't be more wrong for these two, but love doesn't have a season. I should know. Years ago, after college graduation, I moved from small-town Ohio to New York. I'd been there only a few days when I ran into a perfect stranger on Fifth Avenue—talk about taking a risk!—and decades later we're still married.

I hope you enjoy spending time with Dallas and Elizabeth. And if you missed the other books in this series, check them out. Happy reading!

Hugs,

Leigh

HEARTWARMING

The Cowboy's Secret Baby

—

Leigh Riker

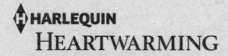

H HARLEQUIN
HEARTWARMING

HARLEQUIN®
HEARTWARMING™

ISBN-13: 978-1-335-88978-2

PLEASE RECYCLE
THIS PRODUCT IS RECYCLABLE

Recycling programs
for this product may
not exist in your area.

The Cowboy's Secret Baby

Harlequin Enterprises ULC
22 Adelaide St. West, 40th Floor
Toronto, Ontario M5H 4E3, Canada
www.Harlequin.com

Printed in U.S.A.

Leigh Riker, like so many dedicated readers, grew up with her nose in a book, and weekly trips to the local library for a new stack of stories were a favorite thing to do. This award-winning *USA TODAY* bestselling author still can't imagine a better way to spend her time than to curl up with a good romance novel—unless it is to write one! She is a member of the Authors Guild, Novelists, Inc. and Romance Writers of America. When not at the computer, she's out on the patio tending flowers, watching hummingbirds, spending time with family and friends, or, perhaps, traveling (for research purposes, of course). She loves to hear from readers. You can find Leigh on her website, leighriker.com, on Facebook at leighrikerauthor and on Twitter, @lbrwriter.

Books by Leigh Riker

Harlequin Heartwarming

Kansas Cowboys

The Reluctant Rancher
Last Chance Cowboy
Cowboy on Call
Her Cowboy Sheriff
The Rancher's Second Chance
Twins Under the Tree

A Heartwarming Thanksgiving
"Her Thanksgiving Soldier"
Lost and Found Family
Man of the Family
If I Loved You

Visit the Author Profile page at Harlequin.com for more titles.

For my boys,
Scott and Hal.
I love you with all my heart.

CHAPTER ONE

HER CHILDREN WERE GONE.

"Bye, Mom!" nine-year-old Jordan, her oldest, had yelled on his way to his father's car.

"Bye-bye, Mommy." A worried look from Stella, almost eight. "Will you be okay?"

"Why aren't you coming with us, Mama?" This last from six-year-old Seth, her shadow. For the first time in nearly a decade, she'd be childless for the next few months, and the summer promised—threatened?—to be one lonely day after another, which would only give her space to obsess about the recent changes in her life. "What am I going to do until August?" Elizabeth Barnes asked her empty house. It was only mid-June. Her kids had left less than an hour ago, and already she missed them terribly.

Elizabeth blew her nose. She'd used half a box of tissues and her reddened eyelids must look puffy. She should have been dancing for joy at the very thought of being her own person for a while rather than everyone's stay-at-home mom 24/7—but her initial euphoria when her ex-husband had offered to spend his summer with their kids had faded. Instead, she felt disconnected and a bit panicky.

A knock at her door predictably set her heart racing. Elizabeth, who'd been brought up on the belief that, above all, appearances mattered—*Thanks, Mom*—wasn't ready to see anyone this morning. Maybe she wouldn't answer. Today, in spite of her normally sunny outlook, she wanted to wallow in heartache—at least until tomorrow—before she finally went on with her life. The one she'd never wanted. The one that didn't include Harry and their family being together. The divorce had been finalized a month ago, and she'd certainly observed that day with what she could only call mad desperation—she'd done a very foolish thing. But Harry was out of her life, as much as he ever would be as the father of their children, and it was Elizabeth who, from now on, would do most of the heavy lifting while raising them.

The knock sounded again, and her mouth went dry. For months a rap at the door had meant another prying person in the guise of concern, even a nosy reporter from the local paper. Harry had been the town mayor, and his infidelity had put her in the spotlight right along with him. You'd think people would have had enough by now of prying into her life, tearing apart the last shreds of her privacy, but in Barren, Kansas, there were those who still talked. Elizabeth was torn between her desire to hide and a need for human company in this house that now echoed with silence, and solitude nearly won.

Elizabeth hated attention. She knew there were those in town who'd always called her Ms. Perfect and hoped to see her get her comeuppance. Although she'd been Harry's victim in all this, they blamed her. She couldn't think how to repair her former standing in the community as Elizabeth Barnes, "first lady"—how to get her legs under her again, so to speak. Goodness, she sounded like Dallas Maguire, the rodeo guy who'd moved in next door last January, renting the former Whittaker house while he recovered from serious injuries.

Fortunately for her, he'd been easy to avoid—especially after her divorce became final. Dallas had spent a lot of his time since then doing rehab, until he'd disappeared a few weeks ago. She'd finally stopped looking out her kitchen window, wondering where he'd gone. All for the best, she'd thought.

Elizabeth heard a third knock at the door, reminding her that—thanks again to her mother—she had manners. "Coming," she finally said, then opened the door. To her surprise, hands in his back pockets, Dallas stood on the porch assessing a pot of red geraniums, and after a quick glance at the back of his head, his dark hair, she looked away. Even in jeans and a faded T-shirt, he was an amazing sight, but since that day with him in May, she'd tried not to notice. "Dallas, I'm not in good shape today. Maybe you could come back later." Or not at all.

Dallas turned toward her. His electric-blue gaze drifted over her, probably seeing the remnants of her tears—seeing too much—and Elizabeth fought an urge to swipe them away. He was the gregarious type who'd probably never met a stranger, and the day her divorce was finalized he'd certainly pried Elizabeth out of her shell, the one she wanted to pull around her now like a cloak. An awkwardness nagged at her, an awareness of him that she couldn't afford to indulge again.

Dallas edged his broad-shouldered way into the house. He took only a few steps, but she could see he'd suffered a setback.

"You're limping again. What happened?"

The last time she'd seen him, he'd been doing so well with his recovery from that bad spill on the circuit.

He shrugged. "Tried a rodeo in Houston. Just to see if I could ride. The bull disagreed. Hurt myself again—nothing too bad, but my hip's unhappy this morning. Had to spend more time than I'd planned away from here."

"In a hospital?" Not long ago, he'd spent considerable time in one.

"Nah, resting a bit." She doubted that was the full story. "Then I paid my folks a quick visit. Sorry I haven't been around." His gaze strayed from hers. "You mad at me? I mean, because—"

The memory of that day in May was suddenly front and center again. "Dallas, I never did anything like that in my life. I never will again."

"Make love?" His mouth tilted in a smile

before he sobered. "I want you to know, I didn't intend for anything to happen that day."

"Yes, but we both know how that turned out."

"I came over to see if you were all right, that's all."

"I'm fine." She could feel her cheeks heat. She couldn't look at him either. The memory of that afternoon, in broad daylight while her children were in school...the warmth of Dallas's touch, at first on her shoulder to comfort when he'd come from next door, seemed very real again. But then she'd collapsed in tears—never prone to crying, she'd done more than her share this year—and found herself wrapped in Dallas's arms. And he'd kissed her...

"Dallas, I barely know you. I'm still mortified that I let things get so out of control. I acted like a...woman hoping to be rescued, but I'm not that person." She managed a weak laugh. "My mother saw to it that I know how to behave in every situation." She shook her head. "I still can't believe I did that—"

"*We* did that," he corrected her. "If you want me to be sorry, then I am. But let's leave that for now. You're divorced. You can start fresh, go on with your life and make whatever you want of it. Try something just for you."

"Like what?"

With the beginnings of another smile, he shrugged again. "I don't know. Take a trip, a cruise. Sign up for some course you've always wanted to take. Talk to a friend—meaning me." But even considering their onetime mistake together, she and Dallas weren't friends; they were neighbors, that was all, and temporary at that. He didn't seem to agree. "Let's have dinner tonight. My way of apologizing. I'll make reservations at the Bon Appetit. What time?"

"Food doesn't appeal to me. Go home," she said with a half smile of her own. "I'm in hiding. I may stay here all summer."

"Uh-uh." Dallas leaned in the doorway. "Not buying that, and—wow—" He glanced around the living room. Not a thing out of place. No toys scattered across the carpet, no children's books or games or art projects on view. Elizabeth's spirits sank even lower.

"I know," she said. "It's never looked this good." She'd spent the last half hour tidying up. And mopping tears.

"I saw them all leave." He slanted her a look. "You really okay?"

"No," she admitted, which seemed obvious. Elizabeth rolled her eyes. "And that's the same question you asked me in May." Which had started something she'd never be able to forget or overlook. The town gossips would have a field day with that. If they ever knew. "I'm overreacting, aren't I?"

"Yes, ma'am. Come for dinner with me," he said. "We'll have fun."

Her pulse jumped. "And most of Barren will somehow find out." As if the cheating mayor's ex-wife was also having an affair, destroying the rest of her reputation and endangering her children's welfare.

Dallas tilted his head to study her. "You aren't really going to stay in this house all summer while your kids are away, are you? You'll give people what they're looking for."

"And what would that be?"

"A chance to gloat."

"Why shouldn't they? Everything became so public Harry might as well have put up a billboard." She bit her lip. "Some would say I deserved that."

"You didn't, and you're well out of that

mess." Dallas sounded as if he knew all about that too. Just as he'd seemed to understand her pain the afternoon they'd…spent together. He'd been so understanding—way *too* understanding, as it turned out.

"Dallas, do I need to remind you? One of my dearest friends is now raising Harry's daughter, the one he sired out of wedlock." She nearly choked on the old-fashioned word, but Elizabeth had been raised in a world with definite social rules to be observed, and those lessons were deeply ingrained. What else could she call it? "In such a short time, tell me, *how* am I supposed to put that behind me? His child—Emmie—and my Seth see each other at school. They're practically the same age, which means—" She broke off, not wanting to think of that timing. "As you said, what a mess. Harry may be on his way to Colorado with our children, but I'm still here. Dealing with the fallout. The last thing I need is fresh scandal."

"And you think you'd create scandal just by having dinner with me?" Dallas glanced away, then turned and retraced his steps to the front door. His tone held an unfamiliar edge. "Your loss." He obviously had his pride, and Elizabeth had wounded it when he'd only been trying to apologize. He was on the porch and down the stairs before she could take back her hasty words. He wasn't to blame because, in a moment of weakness, she'd let down her guard or because her life had fallen apart. And she didn't know how to start over. All she did know for sure was that she had to safeguard her kids. They were her sole priority now.

Alone in the house again, she sank onto the sofa. Pillows plumped. Not a jelly smear in sight on the oatmeal-colored upholstery her mother had picked out. This wasn't Dallas's fault.

Neither was the other mess she'd made that did include him.

She was no better than Harry, really.

"WELL. HOW'S IT GOING, DALLAS?" his sports agent asked. There was a hidden message there, which Dallas tried to ignore. Lately, their conversations hadn't been going so well. Much like the one he'd just had with Lizzie.

It had been a long time since a woman deep-sixed him as she had. And yes, Dallas thought of her as Lizzie. To him, she wasn't an Elizabeth, and she could use some loosening up.

In his house next door to hers—the rental that had allowed him to stay in Barren while he recuperated, and closer to his brother than he'd been in more than twenty years—Dallas dropped onto the sofa with a stifled grunt. The persistent pain was a temporary inconvenience, a reminder that his right hip now had an artificial joint. He'd neglected—not forgotten—to take his cane across the yard, unwilling to rely on it or show weakness to Lizzie, but he had other things on his mind now.

"How am I doing?" he repeated for Ace. "Even better than expected. I'm almost a hundred percent." *Liar.* But he *had* to get back on the circuit. Better late than never, which had prompted his call to Ace O'Leary. The pressure was on and growing with each passing day. Except for Houston, Dallas had been off the road since before Christmas. He'd made a serious blunder by entering that event—and paid the price in a fresh round of pain—but he'd done it to show he could. He needed to boost Ace's belief in him, and all he would have to do then was conquer the anxiety he felt every time he entered the ring. Stage fright—he could feel the familiar edge of panic again now, the humiliating nausea before every ride, the certainty that his head was about to explode as the bull shifted under him. The tight grip on his rope that nearly broke the skin.

How many good years did he have left in a sport that made such physical, even emotional, demands? How long before his accumulated injuries would force him to retire? He wanted a world championship first, the perks that would follow and set him up for life. There were a lot of rodeos yet to come, prize money to win and lucrative endorsement contracts to hold on to. In the meantime, he didn't need Ace quitting on him, which Dallas had begun to suspect might happen. "Can't wait to get back," he said.

Ace muttered, "You lost the end of last year. This season's half-over." Dallas couldn't deny that. "Then you make that boneheaded decision to ride in Houston and wind up in rehab again. With every day you spend on the disabled list, Las Vegas—the big prize—gets further away. In fact, it's out of sight. You have no chance for the Finals, Dallas. I don't know what else to tell you."

Dallas flinched a little. The money he might have won there would have helped his adoptive parents, for whom he felt responsible. His mother hadn't been well lately—he'd recently stopped briefly in Denver to see her, but he had to check on her again soon. He owed the Maguires everything, and during his recovery he'd been sending part of his savings to them each month rather than some of his earnings. His accounts weren't growing right now, but at the moment his task was to keep Ace's spirits up. Rah-rah.

Ace wasn't talking now, a bad sign, and his silence was another harsh reminder that Dallas wasn't winning any prize money or points. His lack of status worried him. He'd been doing great, managing to conquer his nerves, until that bull tossed him clear across the ring in Lubbock late last year. More recently, he'd fallen off in Houston. Every cowboy in the business suffered injuries—sometimes bad ones—and Dallas had had his share even before this. "You can count on me, Ace."

"Any chance you can ride in Cody this

summer, then? A good venue for your come-back."

Comeback? He was that far out of the run-ning? The temptation to say yes made Dal-las's blood rush, quick enough to make him light-headed. If he didn't send Ace some signal that he was almost ready to compete again, he'd find himself without representa-tion.

"Cody," he repeated like a man stumbling out of a dream. It was the capital of rodeo, and the events there were already in full swing, including some fine bull riding. "I'd say sure, but—" Did he want to kill himself? The doctors had warned him—

"Don't push it," Ace said for him, though Dallas didn't quite believe his show of sup-port, which got thinner every time they talked, the tone of his voice cooler. For a long time, they'd been friends as well as agent and client, almost brothers, but he could tell Ace was about to hang up, move on to an-other client who was still making real money. "Thanks for checking in."

What was left of this year's schedule scrolled through his head. Calgary in July, another classic, beckoned to him like a siren's call. Not much time before that either, not enough to ease Ace's mind. But in the weeks ahead, if Dallas spent too much time alone— as Lizzie did—he'd only get down and dark.

Lizzie Barnes…with tears in her green eyes, that neat bob she wore without a dark hair out of place, the defeated slump of her shoulders. He'd hoped to cheer her up, but she'd made herself clear. *Not interested.* What was her deal? He couldn't deny his attraction to her or the fact they'd fallen into bed together once—*my bad*—but having dinner in the best local restaurant sure didn't mean he wanted anything more.

That wouldn't be fair to her, even when the particulars of that afternoon in May had lodged in his head. The sweet feel of her in his arms, her tears, their kisses… He'd certainly owed her that apology. Besides, what was he thinking? She had a family, and he was nowhere near ready for that.

When Dallas had first moved in, her son Jordan's eyes had lit up. He wasn't a ranch kid, like many of his friends, but having a rodeo cowboy next door gave him bragging rights. Lizzie's middle child, though—her daughter—had just as quickly distrusted him.

She seemed protective of her mom. The littlest guy Dallas didn't know at all. He wasn't good with kids. And for the next few years—God willing—he had to keep his focus. He wasn't about to complicate his life by getting involved with his pretty, vulnerable neighbor. *So, what's your brilliant idea, Maguire?*

He still needed to convince Ace he was really on the mend. And that he was using his off time more wisely than he had in Houston. He had to come up with something...

The idea hit him like that sudden swivel of the Brahma's hips that had ended his previous season. Dallas had a lot in common with the stubborn bulls he rode. "Ace? Listen. Don't know why I didn't think of this before. There's a rodeo coming up right here in Barren." He took a breath. "I'm not sure of the date but I could get back in the saddle then, so to speak, before I hit the road and we're both in the money again."

"I've never heard of a rodeo in Barren," Ace said, clearly doubting him.

"You probably wouldn't. It's a small one," Dallas improvised. "Not sanctioned, but I should stand a good chance. I could ride one of their bulls like I was sitting in a rocking chair."

"Well, if you say so…"

His mind was spinning. Ace had been right. There was no rodeo in Barren.

Dallas already felt guilty for the small lie he'd told. But at least he wasn't obsessing over Lizzie Barnes now, and he'd bought himself some time.

CHAPTER TWO

"MOM! GUESS WHAT?" Jordan shouted into the phone the next morning. "When we got to the resort, Dad took us to play miniature golf—and I won! Stella did terrible."

"Don't embarrass your sister," Elizabeth said at the same instant her daughter yelled, "I did not! I was good, right, Mommy?"

"I'm sure you were." Stella was her little worrywart and had suffered—if not as openly as Seth—during the divorce proceedings. She'd adored her father, who'd let her down last winter then all but disappeared from her life until he'd come up with the summer plan. Their children's sweet voices, even raised in typical sibling battle, flowed through Elizabeth like warm molasses. "I miss you," she said above the din, then in the background heard Seth's softer tone, his tears.

"Mama, I want to come home."

"He's such a baby," Jordan chimed in,

chanting, "*Baby, baby*... He almost threw up in the car. Again." Always eager to display a tough act, he'd become the self-appointed man of the family as if he felt he had to adopt Harry's role.

"Please. No more," Elizabeth said. "Jordan, get your father."

Seth was bawling now, hard enough to make her forget yesterday's encounter with Dallas Maguire and the apology she now needed to make.

"Sweetie, don't cry. Hey, I saw Emmie yesterday and she says hello." It was a reminder that wouldn't help, and Elizabeth immediately wished she'd bitten her tongue. She had nothing against the sweet child who'd become Seth's best friend at day care, and in September they'd be first graders together, but this was a sensitive issue for Elizabeth. For Seth too at the moment.

"I want to see Emmie! She's my sister! Like Stella!"

When that news had broken, Elizabeth had been honest with her children, not wanting them to get blindsided by someone's thoughtless comment.

Harry suddenly took the phone. "What's all this?"

"He's homesick," Elizabeth said. It should have been obvious.

Her ex used his best stern voice—he'd always considered himself the disciplinarian, although he'd rarely been around when such eruptions happened. "Stella, Jordan…stop fighting! Take your brother into the other room. I can't hear myself think."

"I can understand why Seth feels that way," she said, teeth clenched. "And you know he gets carsick. Are you sure you can handle this? Having the kids all summer?"

She heard him sigh. "Miniature golf yesterday was like World War III. At dinner last night, not a single thing on the menu was acceptable to them, including Seth—and of course, he spilled his milk all over the restaurant table."

"You know he only eats grilled cheese sandwiches when we—when he eats out."

He bypassed that. "What about Stella? I've seen her order pizza before."

"Only plain, no *stuff* on it."

"Then Jordan stuck his finger right in her macaroni and cheese, the only entrée she would eat." He paused. "Can I *handle* them? What kind of question was that?"

"Well, from what I just heard—"

He cut her off. "I am not going to debate my abilities as their father. What is this, Elizabeth? I hope you don't have some harebrained idea to get my visitation revoked merely because the kids are out of control. That's not my fault."

"I think it is—you're there, I'm not—but don't be paranoid. The court has spoken, your visitation is already mandated, including this summer, and this isn't getting us anywhere." She added, "Do you want me to come for Seth? I can bring him home—"

"He's fine with me. You coddle him."

Elizabeth's teeth clenched. "He's barely six years old, Harry. Stop treating him as if he were one of your aides at town hall who's expected to jump to do your bidding."

"As you well know, I'm not mayor any longer, thanks to this ridiculous turn of events. We could have made it work, if only you'd listened to your mother."

"No," she said, "you made your choice. Then, when everything became public knowledge about Emmie, I had to make mine. I'm still the town laughingstock."

He made a scoffing sound. "Aren't you imagining that? You have lots of friends. I'm sure they haven't abandoned you because of my little indiscretion."

"I don't see that as little. I had standing in this community and now I don't. My mother isn't the only one who thinks I should forgive and forget. Of course, that's due to her own broken marriage years ago..." She trailed off into a lengthy silence. Elizabeth felt tempted to pack an overnight bag and fly to Denver to rescue Seth, her baby, who was showing signs of distress.

"It's easy to see what I'm up against here," Harry finally said. "You've made *me* into the bad guy, encouraged the kids to take your side."

"I did not. Am I the one who took up with Sierra Hartwell, that poor woman?" After a bad car wreck, Harry's former girlfriend had died, leaving her daughter, Emmie, three years old at the time, with no guardian, and Elizabeth didn't blame Sierra anyway. The affair had been Harry's doing. In her view, Sierra was another of his victims. Thank goodness, Emmie lived now with the county sheriff and his wife, who were Elizabeth's good friends. Her voice trembled. "What kind of person are you? I don't know you anymore," she said. "It was your idea to take the children to Colorado. You're the adult in the room. Try to be there for them, will you?"

Harry took his usual logical stance. "I am here—in this condo with the Front Range of the Rockies in the backyard. They have everything they could possibly want. A playground, swimming pool, hiking trails, game room—"

"Will you ask Seth if he wants me to come?" Elizabeth didn't hear any commotion from the other room now, but that didn't ease her mind.

"No, I will not. He's fine, I told you." And to be fair, the shouting and tears had stopped. "They're all watching some movie about animated cars."

Yet she still couldn't relax. Sure, some adjustment to being away from home was to be expected, especially for Seth as her youngest, but not being able to comfort him hurt her even more, deep inside, than all the town gossip did. Her three children might as well have been on some distant planet… "Don't let them spend too many hours on their iPads," was all she could think of to say, but something else nagged at her.

Elizabeth could imagine him gritting his teeth too. "If I could run the town of Barren, I think I can deal with three children under the age of ten."

A thought blindsided her before she took her next breath. Were they quiet only because of their fixation on the movie? Or was there someone else in that room she couldn't see from her helpless place here in Kansas? Another woman to soothe her children? She hadn't considered that. She wanted to know yet didn't ask. And wouldn't Jordan, the tattletale in the group, have mentioned someone else on vacation with them?

"Trust me," Harry said in that cold tone she'd come to despise, and which reminded Elizabeth of her mother, whose moral authority was never to be questioned.

"Harry, you destroyed my trust."

HIS TALK WITH Ace O'Leary and the small lie he'd told continued to worry Dallas. As usual, so did his adoptive parents. Dallas had phoned them earlier, but on his way to the McMann ranch this morning to see about a temporary job, he didn't feel reassured.

"We're fine, honey," his mom had insisted from their suburban home near Denver.

"Don't worry about us," his dad chimed in, but underneath their expected reassurances, Dallas heard a note of what sounded like a cover-up.

"What did the doctor say?" he asked Millie Maguire. "How were your test results?"

"A touch of heart failure," she admitted, making Dallas's stomach roll. *A touch?* "She prescribed medication. I feel on top of the world again."

"Dad?"

"No, really. She does. You should see the pink in her cheeks. The swelling in her ankles has already gone down."

By the time the call had ended, Dallas suspected there was no telling what the truth was. Joe and Millie always tried to deflect his concerns, but Millie's health had been steadily declining in the past few years. Now, always fearing the worst news, Dallas dreaded every phone call, and he tried to visit them more often to gauge things for himself. But that wasn't his only problem.

He couldn't help his parents financially when their bills kept going up and he wasn't earning or saving any money. He was done sitting around. He needed a temporary job to tide him over.

The most likely place to get hired was Clara McMann's ranch, where his brother, Hadley, was foreman and would eventually become the owner. When Dallas got there, he found Hadley—tall, muscled, with a powerful build—saddling a horse. He barely glanced at Dallas, who got out of his truck then reached back inside for the cane he tried not to rely on. The ground here was uneven, and his hip felt cranky this morning. Which wouldn't help his cause.

"Glad I caught you," he said. Except for the brief wave he'd gotten, his big brother didn't appear to have time for him. Dark-haired like Dallas, but unsmiling now, he was already fastening the sorrel's bridle, checking the saddle girth. Dallas eyed him. "For a man who just got married, you don't look happy."

His blue eyes, the same shade as Dallas's, hardened. "We'll be checking fence today—

nothing new. A regular chore and I'm supposed to grin like some fool?"

The scowl on his face sure said otherwise. Ever since Hadley had told Dallas he was getting married for the second time, he'd rarely stopped smiling. Sappy enough to make Dallas look away. At the wedding two months ago, in which Dallas had served as best man, Hadley and his bride, Jenna, had gazed into each other's eyes with apparent adoration. Had something happened to change that? Dallas didn't like to think so any more than he wanted to believe his mom was truly ill. His only brother's life, most of it spent in foster care, had been a hard one. His first marriage didn't improve things, and then Hadley had suddenly become a widower, a single dad with a pair of newborns to look after. He doted on his now twenty-month-old twins and deserved only the best.

"Something's bothering you."

Hadley sighed heavily. The admission seemed torn from him. "Jenna's great with the babies—our twins—and it feels like she's always lived here on the ranch with me, but after I finished feeding horses this morning,

I found her in the house, in the nursery, crying. She won't tell me why."

This was a new side of Hadley, who'd once tried to overcome their grim boyhood by covering up his feelings and pushing people away. Jenna had softened his edges, but there might be a simple explanation for this. Dallas was reminded of something an old rodeo buddy had experienced when he and his wife were having a baby. "What if she's pregnant? Women get touchy, I hear."

Another reason Dallas was staying single for now—he wasn't ready to marry or become a parent. He liked his niece and nephew, but with Hadley's twins, once the temper tantrums began, Dallas could go home. He preferred watching rodeo tapes to walking the floor all night with a crying baby. He supposed he'd change his tune, though, when he had one of his own. Someday.

Hadley's mouth tightened. "Jenna can't have children."

"Sorry, I didn't know." It didn't surprise him that Hadley hadn't mentioned his wife's infertility before. He'd probably seen no reason to share that with Dallas. After the decades they'd spent apart, they weren't that close again yet. "Is she okay with that?"

"She has Luke and Gracie now," his brother said.

Dallas wasn't convinced that was the whole story, but he let it go. At the age of eight, years after their birth parents had dumped them on the state, Dallas had been shut inside a bedroom in the last foster home Hadley and he had shared. He could still remember the click of that door lock, the raw panic he'd felt at being alone, trapped. Because Hadley had robbed a store shortly after that, he had spent time in a detention center, then gone back into foster care. By then, Dallas had been adopted. The Maguires had tried to find Hadley but the trail had gone cold. Until last December, Dallas hadn't known where Hadley was, and vice versa.

Hadley's mood didn't seem to be improving now, but Dallas still needed to ask about a job. "So. Reason I came by—I'm, uh, looking for work."

Hadley glanced deeper inside the barn, where Dallas heard movement from a stall. A second later a tall, rangy guy with rumpled dark hair stepped out into the aisle leading a dun-colored horse, and Dallas realized Hadley had said *we* about the fence. "Calvin Stern," Hadley told him as the man approached, and Dallas's confidence took a nosedive.

"Hey." Calvin shook Dallas's hand, put the horse in the second set of crossties, then disappeared into the nearby tack room.

"I hear in town the ranch is doing fine." Dallas hurried on. "Rumor has it you've been buying more cattle." He watched Calvin come out of the room carrying a saddle. "Thought you might be able to use another cowboy." But obviously Hadley had already hired a hand, and the McMann ranch wasn't that big or, for that matter, likely profitable enough to support a bigger crew after years of decline. Or did he think Dallas couldn't do the work?

Hadley looked pointedly at the cane. "You're hurt, Dallas."

"I can still ride a cow pony," he insisted.

"Ours aren't the most reliable sort. I won't see you getting thrown."

Was that a crack about his big accident in Lubbock? The memory made Dallas sweat. "I'll sign a waiver if you want. I need to get outdoors, earn a few bucks. I can muck stalls, fill buckets, measure grain. Lift hay bales. Maybe I'm not ready to wrestle a bull, but…" He ran out of words.

Hadley knew what he really meant. "Your folks doing okay?"

Dallas shrugged. "Dad's all right. I can tell Mom's not feeling great."

The very week Dallas had been tossed from that bull, his adoptive mother had landed in the hospital, and, especially after their talk earlier, Dallas wondered when she'd be back there again. "Sorry to hear that," Hadley said. "I know you worry about them."

Calvin Stern had tacked up his horse then walked off into the sun with the dun gelding. Dallas saw his gaze flick toward Hadley as if to say, *Aren't you coming?*

With his sorrel between them, Hadley walked Dallas to the doors. "I'd ask you to ride with us, kind of a test drive, but we only have the two horses."

Dallas waited. Was his brother weakening? Hadley had his own way of getting to his point.

In the barnyard, he swung into his saddle and, with Calvin mounted beside him, their horses shifted as if in some equine ballet. Hides quivering, they shook off flies, and Dallas felt like an outsider. He missed the camaraderie of his rodeo buddies. High in the sky, the summer sun blazed toward noon, and he could smell the grass from a nearby field. It wasn't Vegas behind the chutes or Cody in the open-air ring, or even his imaginary rodeo, but it was still something Dallas yearned for as he turned toward his truck.

"Wait up. Don't run off." Hadley looked at Calvin. "Guess there's enough work here— a change from last year. How does half-time sound for now? Assuming I can rustle up another horse."

"It'll be enough," Dallas said, though Hadley's tone had seemed grudging. "Thanks."

As he drove off, he stopped the truck halfway down the drive to watch his brother and Calvin disappear over the pancake-flat land toward the horizon. He admired the easy way they rode at a slow lope, hands loose on the reins, and imagined himself on a horse again—or even better, the back of another ornery bull with murder on its brain, because Dallas had a score to settle there.

His nemesis, Greased Lightning, was still on the circuit, flinging other cowboys into the dirt with leaping twists and turns of the bull's powerful body. Just like Dallas in Lubbock, where he'd pitted himself against the animal so perfectly named.

But the sport was his passion, the love of his life. So far. His stage fright aside, he relished the feel of muscle and bone under him, the smells of hide and hair and horn, hearing the roar of the crowd when he stayed glued to the beast's back till the eight-second buzzer sounded.

Anxiety or not, Dallas couldn't wait to show Greased Lightning who was boss.

For now, those hours as a temporary cowhand on the McMann ranch—money to send his folks—would do, and he looked forward to spending more time with his brother. They had a lot of catching up to do. Win-win.

But he wasn't here only to recuperate or be with Hadley. Dallas couldn't stop thinking about Lizzie. He hadn't seen her since he'd asked her to dinner. Who did she think he was? An insensitive jerk trying again to take advantage? He could see how vulnerable she must be, how badly her husband's betrayal had hurt her, how fiercely she loved her kids. And he couldn't get the image of her out of his mind, the set of her shoulders yesterday as if she were waiting for another blow.

He knew what she wanted—to mend her reputation in her hometown, where everybody gossiped. She didn't need a transient man in her life who couldn't wait to ride bulls again. But maybe she did need *something* to occupy her time while her kids were away.

And that brought to mind the lie he'd told Ace.

What if…it wasn't a lie? What if that imaginary rodeo could really happen?

With his mind made up, at the end of the driveway he turned his truck onto the road, then headed straight to the Bon Appetit in town, where he ordered take-out food for pickup later. He'd talk to Lizzie again, and dinner tonight would be a start, a chance to make his pitch about the rodeo he'd decided to make a reality.

The summer was short. They could spend a little time together, becoming business partners in addition to neighbors.

As long as no one got hurt, what could be the harm?

CHAPTER THREE

"I HOPE YOU didn't send Harry off with a sour look on your face," Elizabeth's mother had said. At lunch earlier at the local café, Claudia Monroe's words had killed Elizabeth's appetite. At home now, in the near darkness after sunset, she didn't bother to turn on any lamps. Since Bernice, her neighbor across Tumbleweed Street, couldn't see in her windows, Elizabeth was enjoying a glass of blush wine to take the edge off.

The rest of her mother's comments, which often seemed to focus on Elizabeth's blame for the divorce, had shifted to include the kids. "I think it's admirable that he's taken the children for the summer."

Elizabeth had massaged her aching temple as she tried to come up with a response. "He feels he lost too much time with them while we were dealing with lawyers." Again, to Elizabeth's discredit and Claudia's disapproval, it was all Elizabeth's fault because she'd thrown him out of the house.

"No wonder," her mother had continued, brown eyes snapping. "Not many men would do what he has."

Elizabeth couldn't agree more, though her mother couldn't mean the same thing she did. For a while, after she'd learned about his affair, Elizabeth and Harry had tried couples' counseling, but she'd done most of the trying. And then last November she'd suffered another heartbreak. Losing the baby she'd wanted so badly to complete their family, and had viewed as a sign their marriage might survive, had brought Elizabeth to her knees. Soon after that, Harry's extramarital relationship had become public knowledge at last, and they'd finally separated. To be honest, she was still grieving.

And her mother was half-right. Harry had seemed eager to spend the summer months with the children. But the still-painful reality of his betrayal swamped her every morning as soon as she woke up. Her mother thought Elizabeth should have come to terms with all her losses by now. And she definitely thought that if Elizabeth had been a better wife, Harry wouldn't have strayed.

"I'm still appalled by your behavior, Elizabeth," her mother had said. "When you married, you promised for better or worse to stand by him." She didn't seem to realize she'd all but quoted the lyrics of a classic country song.

"I guess the worst became too much for me. Do we really have to talk about this?"

Claudia patted her carefully highlighted brown hair into place. She'd leaned across their lunch table. "Why not admit you've made a mistake? More than one, actually."

But "I have to go" was all Elizabeth had answered. Thank goodness her mother didn't know about her transgression in May with Dallas. Elizabeth had stood, tucked some bills into the folder that held their check, then left the café before her mother could voice another attack. Elizabeth would hear about her rudeness the next time she saw Claudia.

"The story of my life," she muttered now.

The front bell chimed and, expecting it was Bernice hoping to hear some dirt about Elizabeth's lunch with her mother, this time she hurried to answer. Elizabeth, who avoided confrontation, was in the mood to put Bernice in her place.

Instead, she saw Dallas waiting on the porch again, wearing obviously new, pressed jeans and a crisp white shirt with the sleeves rolled back over his strong forearms. The cowboy's version of dress clothes. He held a large bag from the Bon Appetit. "Dinner, as promised," he said. "Please don't say no again. This food's getting cold, and I have something to run by you. Please," he repeated.

With a wave of her hand, Elizabeth stepped back out of the doorway. Persistence must be his middle name. But she did feel guilty about how she'd treated him when he asked her to dinner yesterday. She'd definitely overreacted. This would be *her* chance to apologize—once she worked up to it. "All right, but don't expect brilliant conversation." Or anything else. "Frankly, I'm in recovery mode."

With a slight limp, he carried the bag into the living room with Elizabeth trailing after him. "Ah, yesterday you were in hiding. I'd see this as progress, but obviously you spoke to your mother and there's been a setback. You always look this way afterward." Elizabeth was surprised that he'd noticed, but in the six months he'd lived next door, she'd told him several times in passing about some meeting with Claudia, and Dallas was perceptive. He turned to assess her unhappy expression.

"I met her at the café for lunch, and we talked—or she did." Elizabeth half smiled. "All I had to do was murmur a few words. I'm never the one she's listening to."

"Herself, then. Not a conversation, brilliant or otherwise."

She hadn't intended to share but found herself telling Dallas what had been said during the meal she'd barely touched.

He held her gaze. "Bad day," he said, and as if to change her mood, he swiftly laid out their meal on her glass-topped coffee table, lining up plastic knives and forks beside paper plates, which would have horrified her mother.

"You don't eat on real china in your dining room?"

"It'll be like a picnic. Since you're not into talking, we can watch rodeo while we eat. A PBR event's about to start."

Oh, goodie. That didn't appeal to Elizabeth either—she wasn't a fan of the dangerous sport—but at least he didn't see this as a date. She gestured at the next box he opened, which was releasing a delicious aroma. "What is that?"

"Celebration." Dallas told her about working for his brother at the McMann ranch. "That's part of it," he finished, and Elizabeth wondered what else he meant to run by her. "So, Jack made us this chicken dish with some fancy French name." Jack Hancock was the owner and head chef at the Bon Appetit restaurant.

"Coq au vin?"

"Yeah. His specialty, he said." Dallas pulled a loaf of bread from the bag. "This too."

Her mouth watered. "A freshly baked baguette. That is worth a celebration." She added, "Congratulations on your new job."

"Thanks. We'll need butter." He took out another container of salad. "And I'd like some extra dressing."

"Me too." Elizabeth's stomach rumbled— her plate had still been full when she'd left the café. "I'm often starving after I see my mother," she admitted.

While she fetched the bottle of vinaigrette,

a crock of butter, and the salt and pepper grinders, Elizabeth put the scene with her mother on the back burner. When she re-entered the living room, Dallas had switched on the TV, and the room was suddenly full of light and sound. Soon, they were down-ing the most incredible meal she'd eaten in a long time, and Elizabeth was sharing the rest of the blush wine with Dallas because, without Harry in the house, she kept no beer in the fridge.

"Ugh," Dallas said more than once, his gaze glued to the television screen.

"If you don't like wine, I have—"

"Nah, don't get up." Shoulders hunched, he said little else, intent upon the rodeo action and giving Elizabeth space, she supposed, at the opposite end of the sofa. The event didn't thrill her. Even though she saw it on TV, she couldn't understand the appeal of the dust in the actual arena that would clog her nostrils, the smell of dirty animals, and then there was the danger, one cowboy after another risk-ing his life. As Dallas had done and would do again.

Finally, during a series of commercials, she said, "I thought rodeo was exciting, but *you* don't shout and jump out of your seat like Harry does during a football game. You've barely moved."

He slid her a glance. "I'm assessing my competition." He pointed his fork at the TV. "That last guy from Guatemala? He was good. Between people like him and those who've graduated from some college rodeo program—"

"There's a degree?" It couldn't be like majoring in English literature as she had.

"Yep. And a ton of other rodeo schools. Competition is brutal. Gets harder and harder to rise in the standings."

"What's your standing?"

He frowned. "I haven't ridden bulls this season except in Houston, where I didn't make even six seconds much less the end buzzer before I reinjured my hip."

She glanced around for his cane, but he hadn't brought it tonight. "Which is why you're still here in Barren." It wasn't a question.

"Yeah, to recover and to see my brother again. Without going into that right now, we have a lot to catch up on before I rejoin the circuit—and get off the injured list." He shook his head. "My parents need that prize money more than I do, so for them too, I need to ride."

A reminder for Elizabeth that he was only here for a short time, not that she wanted a cowboy in her life.

He refocused his gaze on the television. The ads were over and a rider in a gray hat was clinging to the back of a bucking bull with blunted horns. "See that? His balance is off. He'll be on the ground—" the rider flew through the air "—now," Dallas finished as the man hit the dirt. "No score."

Elizabeth shuddered. She refused to look at her neighbor's strong hands or broad shoulders, his taut overall fitness as a trained athlete. Even so, he couldn't be a match for such a huge animal. "I'd never let my kids try that." Not that her oldest didn't badger her relentlessly about joining the other boys in the local version of junior rodeo.

Dallas studied her. "My mother wasn't crazy about the idea either, but she and Dad are proud of me." He paused. "Which brings me to the other reason I'm here tonight." Not quite looking at her, Dallas told her about his vague plan to put on a rodeo somewhere in town, then asked for her help and whether she knew of a good venue.

"The old fairgrounds might work, but they've been closed for years. And, of course, you'd need some kind of permit. From someone."

"You know everyone in town," he pointed out.

"Where I am, at the moment, largely persona non grata."

"This could be your chance to fix that, Lizzie."

She rolled her eyes. "No one's called me Lizzie since I was…six years old. Please don't."

His gaze warmed. "Elizabeth, then. I'll try to remember. You know…we'd be good together—working on the rodeo, I mean. You have the contacts. I have the knowledge of the sport. There are a ton of guys in Barren, ranchers and cowboys. Some of them might enter." Again, he took his time before he went on. "Picture it," he said. "A summertime festival of sorts. Kids and parents outdoors on a sunny afternoon watching what really is a pretty exciting thing."

"In your opinion," she murmured.

"Okay, you're not wild about the idea yet. How about this?" He arched his dark eyebrows. "What if we make it an event for charity? You pick which one, I don't care, but all proceeds would go to that except for recouping the cost of putting on the rodeo, and we'd have to carve out some prize money. I'd be getting a chance to ride, you'd be gaining the respect of the people who got all bent out of shape and linked you to the scandal with your husband." He added, "Even your mother might enjoy the day."

"I doubt she'd attend. No, Dallas, I'm sorry, I can't help you."

She could see the disappointment in his blue eyes. Before Elizabeth spoke again, he changed the topic slightly. "I don't mean to pry, but why isn't your mother supportive of you?"

"Ask her. She'll be glad to tell you." Elizabeth didn't want to expand on that. "Are you ready for dessert?" From the bag, she drew a smaller box of profiteroles, the delicate pastry filled with whipped cream and dusted with powdered sugar. Jack had gone all out at the Bon Appetit. But she had to smile… "These don't look like a cowboy's choice to end a meal."

He looked skeptical. "You try one first."

She did and nearly swooned. "Yum. Outstanding."

Dallas reached for one, took a first bite. "Right you are," he agreed. For a long moment he stared at her. "Thanks for having dinner with me."

"Thank you for bringing such excellent food." She fumbled for the next words. "Dallas, I'd like to apologize—not only for yesterday but for, um, the day we—you know, when I…"

"I was there too," he reminded her. "No need to apologize."

And wasn't she being presumptuous? Why would Dallas want to repeat that onetime slip? Any more than she did? Still, she couldn't afford to lose control like that again.

She sure wasn't going to spend time with him planning some rodeo.

CHAPTER FOUR

"I'LL FINISH HERE if you want," Calvin said.

At the McMann ranch, Dallas hauled another bale of hay off the delivery truck. He and Calvin Stern had spent all morning unloading, and both had worked up a sweat in the summer heat, but that was physical, hard labor. Dallas's mind was miles away on Lizzie—Elizabeth—and the dinner they'd shared a few nights ago. When the heavy bale slipped from his grasp, he jerked his thoughts back to the present. Losing focus was a good way to get hurt.

He muttered something about having wet hands. "I'm okay. Let's get this done."

Dallas was determined to pull his weight, but his thoughts soon returned to Lizzie anyway. He could hardly blame her for refusing about the rodeo, and he understood that, but was he disappointed? Sure, and not only about the event that was still a fantasy. Although he'd avoided hashing over the past the other night, he knew all about being publicly shamed, and the last thing he wanted was to do anything that would put her back in the limelight. As a kid in foster care before the Maguires adopted him, he'd endured plenty of teasing and taunting from other boys—just as Lizzie had more recently in Barren from adults who should know better—and to this day he too felt he had something to prove. He also liked her. He wanted to spend more time with her, if not in a romantic way.

But had his pitch for the rodeo been merely his excuse to see her?

Calvin was staring at him again.

Obviously, Dallas was on his own with the rodeo. He'd counted on his charm to gain Lizzie's support, and he knew few other people in town except—the thought suddenly occurred to him—Calvin Stern, who wasn't working beside him right now without any experience. Dallas had to start somewhere, or his event would never happen.

"You ever do any rodeoing?"

Calvin heaved another bale off the truck, stacked it in the barn with the others, then came back for more, wiping his hands, which were chafed like Dallas's from the bristly straw, several strands sticking to his palms. "Tried calf roping *once*, and that's the operative word."

"Calf roping. Huh," Dallas said.

"You don't have to say it like that. I'm good on a horse, but you bull riders are something else. Daredevils. I'd never risk my neck on the back of one of those ornery critters. That's a death wish."

Dallas laughed. "Yeah, you got that right. It can be a rush, though."

"Well, I've had my share of excitement."

Dallas guessed Calvin must mean his years in the military or his run-in with the law several years ago. Hadley had briefly mentioned Calvin and two of his buddies rustling some cows back then, but Dallas was in no position to judge him.

Calvin grinned. "These days I get my thrills in another arena." His gaze grew softer, warmer. "My girlfriend's all I can handle. Most of the time," he added.

"Maybe one rodeo wasn't enough to get hooked," Dallas said, though it had been for him. He unloaded the last hay bale, its sweet, grassy scent filling his nostrils. "You should try again." He took a breath. "In fact, there's going to be a rodeo in Barren late this summer."

Calvin looked skeptical. "A rodeo here? Where would that be?"

He suddenly turned away as if he'd been given a cue, and at the same instant, from the back steps of the main ranch house across the yard, the dinner bell clanged. Standing there in her apron, Clara McMann rang it again to make sure the cowhands didn't miss the big spread she served every day at noon. Fat chance. Slender, with graying brown hair, she waved at them. "Hurry, now. My famous beef stew will get cold."

"If so, Clara would heat it up," Calvin muttered, "but she's right. That stew should be called famous." He started toward the house.

His stomach growling, Dallas followed at Calvin's heels. "I'm telling you, my rodeo's going to happen," he said, though he didn't yet know how.

Calvin stopped walking to gape at him. "*You're* putting on the rodeo?"

"You bet."

Calvin resumed his walk to the house. As if she'd known they would make a dash for the food, Clara had gone inside. "For one thing, you'd need livestock."

"I'll have to work on that." Dallas knew some contractors he might be able to talk into supplying calves, horses and bulls for a reasonable fee.

Calvin shook his head. "We're off the beaten track here. Who would enter?"

Good question. Dallas hoped a few of his rodeo pals would welcome the chance to show off their skills for a new audience. He had calls to make there too. As they climbed the back steps, he rattled off some other possible names. Local ones. "Grey Wilson, Logan Hunter and his brother, Sawyer, from the Circle H, Cooper Ransom, who's running the Sutherland ranch with his wife, even Finn Donovan, the sheriff, who I'm told has a small herd of cattle. My brother," he added.

"Hadley? Good luck with that. You'll need it."

Calvin had pulled open the kitchen door, and the smells of beef, potatoes, carrots and onions tempted Dallas's taste buds. Hadley was already seated at the table, scooping heaping spoonfuls of stew onto his plate. His toddler twins were banging their hands against the trays of their high chairs, barely missing the plastic bowls that contained their lunch. Hadley looked up. "You two talking about me?"

"Sure are."

"Behind my back," Hadley murmured, but he didn't look as unhappy as he had the morning Dallas had begged for a job. Maybe he and Jenna had settled their differences, whatever they were, although she was nowhere to be seen. Probably working at her interior design firm in town.

"I've got a proposition for you," Dallas began, heading for the sink to wash his hands.

Calvin snorted. "Wait till you hear this."

Dallas tensed. The remark wasn't the same as being bullied by a pack of eight-year-old boys on a playground, or knocked around in some foster home, yet the words sent him back there anyway, and he was still smarting from Lizzie's refusal to help. Ace's suspicions too. No one seemed to believe in him.

"I'm definitely putting you on the roster," he told Calvin, then launched into an explanation for Hadley. As he took his place at the table, one of the twins—Luke—lobbed a piece of bread at Dallas with a surprisingly accurate arm, making his sister, Grace, giggle then sweep her bowl onto the floor. Clara hurried to pick it up. Dallas had quickly learned that lunchtime was always an adventure.

"A rodeo," she said, sounding as if the idea appealed to her.

And to Dallas's surprise, Hadley grinned. "I wouldn't mind. That would keep you here for a while." He sobered. "But I can't see you in any arena soon, Dallas. That what you're thinking?"

Dallas ladled stew onto his plate. "I have to ride sometime, the sooner the better as far as I'm concerned." He remembered his last conversation with Ace.

"And risk damaging your hip again?"

His mouth set. "It's made of metal. I'm told it will last longer than the rest of me."

"Leaving the 'rest of you' vulnerable," Hadley pointed out. "One wrong move on your part or some bull's and you're lying in the dirt again waiting for the ambulance. You really want to throw away your career? You've spent enough time laid up to know how long it takes—longer with each injury— to come back."

"Which is what I need to do," he insisted.

"I'm fine. I'm doing the work here, aren't I? Call it part of my rehab, if you want." In fact, he had sessions most days after work at a facility in Barren and was making good progress. "Calvin and I unloaded that entire truck of hay for you today and I'm ready for more. After lunch we'll ride out to check on that sick cow you mentioned and all the spring calves, see how they're doing in this heat…"

Without looking, Hadley snatched another bread missile from Luke before the toddler could fire it. "Easy, pal." Was he only talking to his son? "That's not the same, Dallas. You know it. If you want to put on some rodeo, maybe that's not a bad idea. Things do get pretty quiet around here in summer since the county fair moved over to Farrier—which I reminded our former mayor more than once is not the county seat—but for you to actually compete in the event?"

He was still shaking his head when Dallas answered. "You're getting the cart ahead of the horse. I have to arrange the whole thing first. I'm thinking early August. By then, I'll be good to go." Which wasn't much time. Would six weeks be enough?

He could tell Hadley didn't quite believe

him either. His blue gaze nailed Dallas like a butterfly to a board. "Is this about your folks again?"

"No…it's not." Another small lie that Hadley would probably see through. But he needed to ease back into the game. Prepare for his comeback, as his agent called it. "Sure, I'm worried about Mom, but that's not the only reason. If I don't do something, Ace is going to cut me from his roster. The rodeo, like my job here, will allow me to be physically active." And he'd like to give something back to this town that had helped his brother find his place in life. "Maybe, as I heal further, I can even enter some minor events around the state, test my renewed fitness. I won't get into any more trouble," he assured Hadley. "You don't have to worry."

"Where you're involved, I always worry. That gung-ho attitude of yours does get you into hot water, little brother. I worried about you even when I hadn't seen you for years."

"I'm here now," Dallas said, "where you can keep an eye on me every day." He picked up his fork, then hesitated.

Across the table, Clara was eating at the same time as she cut Grace's meat with her free hand. Calvin was halfway through his first serving of stew.

Dallas said, "I won't ride anywhere or in Barren unless I know I'm up to it. How's that?"

Hadley heaved a sigh. "I'll leave you to the details, and I haven't ridden a bull since I was eighteen, but you might as well sign me up. Then I'll be right there to pick you out of the dust." He reached over to ruffle Dallas's hair, an annoying habit from the time they were kids. "I figure I won't have any real competition."

"You made my day, Elizabeth. Goodness, I haven't seen you in weeks," Jenna Smith said, coming around her desk at Fantastic Designs for a brief hug. "You missed the last meeting of the Girls' Night Out group, and we were all wondering why."

"I was packing the kids' stuff for Colorado then," Elizabeth said, though that was only half the truth. Since the divorce proceedings began, she'd missed other get-togethers with her friends, those who had stood by her. "I'll come next time," she promised.

By then she might not be in hiding, and

maybe she'd have enough energy to stay awake all evening. Elizabeth was having a hard time sleeping, and mornings weren't her best time either. She stifled a yawn.

While trying to stay awake earlier today, she'd cleaned her already tidy house from top to bottom. Again. She'd even assembled the new bookshelves for Jordan's room, which had been languishing in a box from Ikea in the mostly empty garage. Harry had taken most of the tools and garden equipment, including the lawn mower, though she didn't know why since he was living in an apartment. Then she'd tackled Seth's collection of stuffed animals and packed half of them away in the attic—in case he missed them, she wouldn't throw them away or donate them to charity. As she dusted, she'd tried to see Stella's point that her bedroom really should have at least one purple wall.

Now she was at Jenna's office because she needed a friend, one she could trust.

"I can't sleep. I miss the kids," she admitted. "Harry never had time for his own children before, but now he's got them for the whole summer. Part of me wants their bond to strengthen—"

"And the rest of you would like to kick him off a cliff," Jenna murmured.

Elizabeth's quick smile faded. "I worry especially about Seth, who doesn't seem to be adjusting to the summer with his father, but I don't know what else to do. He's in Colorado—I'm in Kansas. Harry's not the most patient person. He's always a bear when he doesn't get enough sleep, and if he's up all night with Seth..."

"He might be more likely to bring them all home."

"Which I'd actually prefer. You can't imagine how quiet the house seems."

"Yes, I can—well, except for the twins." Tall and slim, Jenna leaned against the front of her desk. "Hadley and I have only been married for a few months, but I feel as if I've always taken care of those babies. Yet sometimes I can't help wishing..." She trailed off. The expression in her blue eyes looked wistful.

"Jenna. I shouldn't have said anything." Elizabeth touched her hand. Jenna rarely talked about her infertility, which was a sensitive issue. "I didn't mean to rattle on like that about my kids."

"No, it's not your fault." Jenna played with a strand of her auburn hair.

"I'm still sorry."

"And like you, I'd probably be going stir-crazy without our twins," Jenna murmured. "At some point I'll have the chance to miss them too. I won't look forward to that." She studied Elizabeth for a moment. "It can't be fun for you alone in the house—how could it? Is that why you had dinner with Dallas Maguire?"

Elizabeth startled. Other than from a distance when she'd watched Dallas drive off early in the morning to work, Elizabeth hadn't seen him much since that night. And what other answer could she have given him about his local rodeo? It wasn't in her to brave more public scrutiny. She couldn't afford another disaster. Her spine stiffened. "How did you know?"

"Jack told Mom, who told my sister. Shadow told me over coffee this morning. I thought I should warn you."

Elizabeth felt the color climb in her cheeks. At least Jenna's sister, another member of their Girls' Night Out group, had kept the talk within their family. Jack, the chef at the

Bon Appetit, was now married to Jenna's and Shadow's mom. But word might soon get out somehow. Elizabeth toyed with the strap of her bag. Good grief, news traveled in this town, even among her closest friends, and in the past months she'd endured way too much gossip. She swallowed. "Dallas and I are neighbors, that's all."

Elizabeth wouldn't seriously reconsider his notion about a rodeo, even for charity. Besides, if his rodeo didn't work out, Dallas might be back on the circuit before her children came home. In either case, she'd made one mistake with him and wouldn't risk another. "Harry may be free now to explore a new relationship, but I'm not. Especially with a guy who spends most of his time on the back of a bull or in his pickup." The conversation with Jenna had gotten way too personal. "Why would I choose another man like that?" As if he wanted to be roped and tied. "Dallas loves rodeo. It's like he's married to the sport. I have no interest in spending my nights watching sweaty men try to ride nasty bulls on TV."

"Is that what he did? Watched rodeo?"

Elizabeth arched an eyebrow. "Don't you

know that too?" she teased. "Yes, he wanted to watch the bull riding, so what could we possibly have in common?"

But she couldn't help thinking of the time they'd shared after her divorce became final.

Until that afternoon, her natural reserve—even caution—had sustained her. She'd felt that reserve ever since her father left home when she was only six, the same age Seth was now. Elizabeth remembered the stares, the whispering and the finger-pointing years ago after her dad abandoned their family. Although Harry hadn't left like Elizabeth's dad had, Seth's obvious pain caught at her soul. She supposed she felt an even stronger need to protect him than she had Jordan or Stella when they were about-to-be first graders before the divorce. Today on the phone Elizabeth's heart had broken for Seth all over again.

Still, that remembered afternoon with Dallas troubled her—maybe that was why she couldn't sleep—and prompted her now to confide in one of her dearest friends. "Jenna, may I tell you something? I think I need to get this off my chest."

"Of course." She bent to catch Elizabeth's gaze. "What's wrong?"

She assumed her face showed every sign of remorse. "I did such a foolish thing." She told Jenna about her unplanned tryst with Dallas, her tears, his comforting touch and then… "We, um, started kissing and had…sex." The last word came out as a whisper.

Jenna's eyes widened.

"I know," Elizabeth said, "I couldn't have done anything more stupid. All my fault."

"I doubt that," Jenna murmured.

"And now, it's just…awkward seeing him, which I've tried to avoid."

"I hope you avoided something else." Jenna's sympathetic gaze held hers. "I mean, he's a great-looking guy, I can't blame you if you've noticed, and Hadley says he's a hard worker. He seems very nice too, but what if, all at once… How can I put this delicately? You find yourself about to become a mom again?"

Elizabeth's heart stopped. Her thoughts flew back to the day of her divorce, Dallas coming to see how she was coping, then Elizabeth going upstairs with him… "No, not possible. We were careful—at least about that."

Jenna's face cleared. "Then if I were you, I'd try to forget what happened. He won't be living next door for long, will he? You don't have to interact if you don't want to." She paused. "He's not a talker, is he? He wouldn't tell other people?"

"No. I'm sure he won't," she said. "And he knows how I feel about the gossip after Harry's affair became public." Elizabeth mentally crossed her fingers. Did she know him well enough to trust his silence? "The only time I'll probably see Dallas again is when he mows the lawn next door." He'd started to do just that yesterday, but then he'd stopped and gone back into his house. "We made an error in judgment. My kids are my focus now. Before they come home, I need to get myself in order."

For another moment, she considered her choices. She wasn't about to take a cruise or sign up for some course, as Dallas had suggested. With the divorce, though, her situation had changed, not for the better. Elizabeth had refused alimony. She didn't want anything personally from Harry, but even with him paying child support her financial outlook was now different. "Which means eventually looking for a job," she said.

Jenna studied her office layout. "I wish I could hire you, but I'm not at the point with my business yet where I can afford help."

Elizabeth was briefly tempted, against her better instincts, by Dallas's proposal about the rodeo, but she wouldn't mention that. Besides, that position would be unpaid, and she'd still have her own life to rearrange. Where to start? "You probably don't know this," she said, "but I was once Harry's administrative assistant. That's how we met, his first year as mayor. But as my children's main caregiver now, I couldn't do that for someone else. In any job I apply for, I'd need less stress and more flexible hours."

Jenna tucked some hair behind her ear. "But they'll all be in school this year. The next best thing to an empty nest. Your time will be your own most of the day. Just like this summer." She tapped one finger against her chin. "If you'd be interested, I heard Olivia could use help with her shop here and her women's cooperative overseas."

Elizabeth hadn't expected that. "I know that's become wildly successful, but didn't she already hire someone? And I'm hardly in a position to jet off halfway around the world to buy handmade rugs in Kedar. The Himalayas?" Her house might be empty, but it was probably far more comfortable than the medical clinic Olivia's husband ran in those mountains, and it was home. "That would be worse than working for Harry. I couldn't leave my kids."

Jenna sent her a look. "Come on. Like you, Olivia has…children, two of them, and that's not all her co-op does now. It's expanded to include help for the women there, like microloans to foster their start-up businesses. Whenever she's away, which she's going to be again soon, maybe you could manage the shop. Fill the online orders. You wouldn't need to travel."

Elizabeth felt herself weakening. "The rugs they make—that she sells—are beautiful. Certainly, the co-op's a worthy cause…" Elizabeth felt a burst of enthusiasm. Working for Olivia shouldn't have such a steep learning curve as planning a rodeo might. "But Jenna, I'm no expert on antiques."

"You'll learn. Are you trying to talk yourself out of a job at Olivia McCord Antiques?"

"No." That job could be exactly what Elizabeth needed to help support her family, and it wouldn't cause gossip as organizing the rodeo might. She and Dallas had shared one pleasant meal. He'd celebrated his good news about his job at the McMann ranch, and she'd apologized for her rudeness before. He'd seemed empathetic about her mother. They'd even briefly talked about their one afternoon together. But to help with his event when she'd just gotten *out* of the spotlight? Again, no.

And lucky for me, Elizabeth told herself, there'd been no need to put Dallas in his place the night of their dinner. He hadn't tried to kiss her. He'd asked her to walk him to the door, touched her shoulder, then strolled off into the darkness, saying, "See you, Lizzie."

"I'll talk to Olivia," she said to Jenna. "Thanks." She mentally crossed her fingers. At least for now, the fatigue she'd been feeling every day had lifted from her shoulders.

With a job, she'd no longer be alone in her empty house. The antiques shop suited her far better than a rodeo, and no one else need ever know she'd lost her head, once, with Dallas.

CHAPTER FIVE

DALLAS WAS HALFWAY along Main Street when he spied Lizzie's car parked in front of the building that housed Jenna Smith's firm, Fantastic Designs. He'd already spent a frustrating hour at the small complex in Barren that contained the mayor's office, that of the town council, the library and the senior citizens' meeting space, but he still didn't have the name of the person he needed to see about a permit for the rodeo. As he whipped his truck on impulse into the angled slot beside Lizzie's sedan, he saw her step from the building onto the sidewalk. He supposed he was about to get another polite brush-off from his neighbor, but he hoped she could help him this once.

"Oh. Dallas," she said on her way to her car, keys in hand.

"Got a minute? Sorry to be a pest, but I have a problem."

She glanced toward Jenna's office building. "With your lawn mower?"

Obviously, she'd seen him struggling earlier with the old machine that looked as if it had been in his rented garage for the better part of a century. Before the grass grew as knee-high as a cornfield by the Fourth of July, he'd been heading for Earl's Hardware when he spotted Lizzie's car. "Not only the mower," he said, but she didn't stop walking.

Her shuttered expression said that even these few seconds had tried her patience. Since dinner that one night, he'd had the feeling she'd been avoiding him again. Now, apparently, she couldn't wait to get away from him.

"This is about the rodeo—and I'm not going to twist your arm." Dallas used his best coaxing tone. "I promise, all I need is a name."

She cracked a faint smile and a weak joke. "You already have one—two, in fact. Your brother's wife told me you were once called Smith, just like Hadley."

"That was before I got adopted." He crossed his arms, unwilling to explain any further. Dallas didn't like to dwell on his years in foster care or the estrangement from his brother. He was a Maguire now, and that other life— the deprivation he'd suffered then—was behind him. "Have a heart, Lizzie. This afternoon I ran into a brick wall at city hall, trying to find the permit person for the rodeo." He added, "Is there a public works department somewhere?"

Lizzie actually snickered. "No, but there's a guy who maintains the lawn, trims the bushes, strings up the Christmas lights the Friday after Thanksgiving. He handles local events too, and maybe the county fair as well. We're not very organized here in Barren." She studied a passing car, then waved at its driver. Everyone knew everyone else in this town. Dallas might be a cowboy, but rodeo was big business today and one-horse burgs and lesser events like his here were normally a thing of his past. A small-town girl, a guy whose playground was in nationwide arenas? One more difference between them.

"I tried your town's website, but it isn't user-friendly. They still have Harry listed as mayor."

She winced. "Barren's website has been a dead space for years. They tried, but then the boy who set it up left for college and never came back. Nobody offered to take it over." Her gaze returned to his reluctantly. "I don't mean to rain on your parade, Dallas, but there are also other issues to consider, like insurance against liability for injuries…" Her eyes held his. "This event won't be as simple as you think. You'd be using town facilities. That brings up all sorts of complications— and I'm not involved," she insisted.

Dallas fought an urge to grit his teeth. "Lizzie—Elizabeth—I'm not trying to drag you into the rodeo. All I'd like you to do is get me that guy's name and number, a start, then I'll take it from there."

She slipped into her car. "I can try, but people talk, you know they do—my neighbor Bernice, for example. She might have seen you leave my house the other night—"

His mouth hardened. "There was nothing wrong with us having a meal together."

She started the engine. "That may be fine for you, but I have to live among these people. I'd really like to hold my head up again."

"And I'd like to do something for this town—for charity."

"Then I hope you will."

She moved to put the car in Reverse, but Dallas laid a hand on the open window. "Why are you rushing off? Is it me? I realize I invited myself over and convinced you to watch PBR, but it couldn't have been that bad, could it? What's changed?"

"I told you what changed."

His grip tightened on the window. He glanced at the street, the few people who were walking on either side between stores and one cowboy in fancy lizard-skin boots dyed red who went into Earl's Hardware. "One neighbor gets nosy, and that's it?"

"It's not just Bernice. Jenna told me she'd heard from her sister, who heard from their mother, who'd heard from Jack Hancock about our dinner. They're harmless enough, but…" She looked at her hands. "You see what I mean?"

"Not really." A muscle jerked in his cheek. He eased away from the car. "Is this about that afternoon in May? If you're still peeved, Elizabeth—"

"No, but I have been wondering…" She averted her face. Her voice sounded tight and the question finally came as if she'd opened her purse and the contents had spilled out all over the street. "When you ordered the food from the Bon Appetit, did you tell Jack you were planning to eat with me?"

Now he was getting mad. "Why would you even ask me that?" So, this was what had been on her mind. "I didn't say a word. I'm not one of your town gossips. The only thing on my mind is to pull off my rodeo—without your help—then take off for the circuit before I lose what's left of my career!"

She merely nodded. "I'm sorry. I shouldn't have asked."

But she'd just had to know. Dallas didn't respond. He started toward his truck and on his way made a split-second decision. Not that he was doing so just to get away from Barren. "In case anyone's *looking* at my house and sees my truck there for the next few days, you can tell them I'm not here anyway, okay? You have my permission. I'm going to fly to visit my parents."

"Dallas." He could barely hear her calling out. Her car hadn't moved before he was in his truck, slamming the door. "I really will try to get you that number."

"You're home!" his father bellowed the instant Dallas walked into the house where his parents lived in a neat suburb of Denver. After talking with Liz—Elizabeth—yesterday and letting his temper get the best of him, he'd welcomed this quick getaway to see his parents again.

"Surprise," Dallas said. But then, enfolded in his dad's familiar bear hug, instead of grinning he couldn't help but frown. Never a small man, sandy-haired with gray-blue eyes, his adoptive father felt lighter, less substantial in Dallas's arms. Had he lost weight?

Dad kissed his cheek. Joe Maguire was the most demonstrative person Dallas had ever known, always ready with a comforting hand on a shoulder, a kind word. He'd rarely raised his voice to Dallas, even when he'd probably deserved a tongue-lashing as a kid. "Why didn't you tell us you were coming? Call beforehand? We would have rolled out the red carpet."

Why? Because he'd wanted to see for himself, not hear some spin over his cell, what their true situation was without giving them the opportunity to prepare. "I decided spur of the moment."

His mom hurried from the kitchen, wiping her hands on a dish towel. And huffing, he noticed, with every breath. Millie pushed Joe aside to pull Dallas into her arms. "Welcome, honey. We don't see you enough."

Their hug went on until Dallas finally eased away to look into her eyes. He wiped a lone tear from her face. She wore a soulful expression. "You doing all right, Mom? Really?" His father hovered nearby, likely prepared to cover for her as he had on the phone.

She looked down. "Of course. I told you. I hope you haven't been worrying."

He grinned. "That'll be the day." Dallas dropped his duffel bag in the front hall, then moved on into the living room, which looked the same as the first day he'd stepped inside this house. A skinny boy carrying the sum total of his worldly belongings in a plastic trash bag. A boy who'd been torn away from his brother, fearing he'd never see him again, that Hadley might stay forever in that detention facility. Dallas barely took in the well-remembered gray chenille sofa and chair, the navy-blue-and-white area rug that anchored the furniture in front of the fireplace. He never stopped worrying.

Or had he merely exchanged one frustration for another? He wasn't sure Lizzie would supply that name and number he'd asked for. He'd let that—and his still simmering anger—lie for the next few days. While he was gone, he didn't have to see her coming and going next door. He didn't have to think about her accusation. *Did you tell Jack?*

He continued on to the kitchen, then dropped into his usual chair at the table. His parents took the end seats. The family routine should have comforted him. It didn't. His mother's face had a gray cast, and there were dark circles under her eyes, their normally merry brown missing their golden glints. When she pushed a plate of brownies toward him, he saw her fingers were swollen.

"Mom, talk to me."

She pursed her lips, stared at the tabletop. "What's new, you mean? Not much except—you'll remember Mrs. Thackeray, your fifth-grade teacher? Well, she—finally—met a man." A faint tinge of color rose in her cheeks. "Can you believe? If I ever knew a confirmed spinster, that was her. Still, you never know, do you? She actually fell in love with the geometry teacher at the high school—"

"And eloped," his father finished, jumping up to pour coffee for everyone. "He was a widower, been alone for some time." He plunked mugs in front of Dallas and Millie before taking his seat again. "It's the talk of the town since Christmas. What do you think of that?"

An obvious smokescreen. "I think it's fine to learn what everyone's doing, but you're avoiding the real subject."

His mother couldn't seem to meet his gaze. "Don't be silly, Dallas. If the only reason you left Kansas was to check on us, you wasted the long drive. And I'd be very disappointed."

"I flew," he corrected her. "I didn't want to leave my job for too long, so I cut out the drive. Hadley's a hard taskmaster but a fair one. He gave me some days off to see you."

"We're not children." Dad scowled. "If your mother tells you she's fine, then she's fine. And I'm telling you again, she is. I hope you won't spoil this visit by probing for some *truth* that doesn't exist. Now, try that coffee. There's a new shop in town. I bought their latest arabica today while your mother was taking her daily walk."

As if his mom were training for some Olympic track event. Dallas had seen her version of exercise, a lone spin around the block at a snail's pace. He'd have to go with her while he was here. Gauge for himself how bad the heart failure was. Maybe speak to her doctor himself.

For now, Dallas knew better than to press the issue. He'd only end up making them mad, and even more defensive, and he wouldn't learn a thing. "By the way, Hadley sends his regards," he said.

Mom brightened. "We can't wait to meet him and those darling babies. His new bride too, of course." Until last December, all four of them had been lost to Dallas. If Hadley hadn't finally located him through Dallas's website, he'd never have seen him again either. "Maybe we'll drive down to meet everyone later this summer."

"Sure. If you're up to the trip," he said.

His dad shook his head. "A wife and family. That's a far cry from way back when." He looked at Dallas, who looked away. "I can only imagine what your brother went through—"

Dallas murmured, as he had with Lizzie, "Let's not talk about this, okay?"

The bad memories threatened to crowd in again, to take him under. All those foster homes, the cold ones and the hot ones, where every day was a threat…and Joe already knew what had happened to Hadley, to Dallas.

He'd begun to sweat. *Stop thinking about all that.* But Millie didn't agree.

She laid a hand over his, her eyes steady on him. "Honey, you should talk. It's not healthy to bottle things up."

"You're telling me?" He eased his hand back to fiddle with his spoon. "You've spent half this visit so far avoiding your own health issue."

"That's not an issue," she insisted. "As we get older, who doesn't need a few medications to keep going?" She paused. "But Dallas, you're young. Turning thirty-one this year—where does the time go?—and still unmarried." Her features grew wistful. "Without the grandbabies I'd like to have, I might add. Sometimes, even now, I can't help but see that frightened little boy who's still inside you. The child who'd lived too long in foster care and came to us so damaged, so afraid." Her voice had quavered.

"You were beaten, neglected, even starved

in that last place," his father said. "You watched Hadley being taken away."

Yes, he thought. *Because of me.*

"What does that kind of thing do to a child? To both of you?" Millie's eyes had filled. "I don't mean to upset you, but some things need to be reexamined. There are times when I think you chose that rough-and-tumble career of yours not to be vulnerable like that again to anyone. We're proud of you, Dallas, but maybe you're standing in your own way."

"That's enough." He pushed his chair back, then left the kitchen, unable to sit there another second. Inside, he was shaking, cowering as if expecting another blow. His brother had been his protector. *Hadley, don't leave!* After he'd gone to detention, Dallas had finally found solace with the Maguires, and a boyhood that had been denied him until then. His parents—not his birth mother and father, who'd left their two kids to the state—had saved him. Millie and Joe were a united pair, and he loved them with all his heart. But they also drove him up a wall.

He'd watch his parents closely while he was here, then decide for himself how they were really doing. Unfortunately, safeguarding them wouldn't keep those old memories at bay. That night Dallas lay awake for hours, remembering. The first thing he'd done in this house, in his new room, was to ask Joe to please remove the lock from his door.

IN THE MIDDLE of the night Elizabeth roamed her too-quiet house. Without her children, these rooms echoed. Exhausted, she still couldn't sleep for worrying about the three of them while grieving the heart-wrenching memory of another who'd never been born. Trying to distract herself, she wiped sticky peanut butter off the underside of a kitchen counter, which she'd missed seeing before, then laundered Stella's comforter again because the remnants of a blueberry stain hadn't come out the first time. From attic to basement, the house looked spotless and, in the kids' absence, stayed that way.

Upstairs, she looked into each of their abandoned rooms. Then she stood in the doorway of the spare bedroom—the loneliest room of all. Arms around her waist, she hugged herself; on this still-warm evening, she felt cold. Last November, little more than half a year ago, she'd been glowing, shopping for baby clothes, trying to think where she'd stored the beautiful crocheted blanket her grandmother had made for Jordan, used by each of her own babies in turn.

"This time," she'd told Harry, "I'm hoping for another girl."

"You don't want three boys to chase around?"

"No. Two of each." A girl would complete the neat life she'd expected to live with him and their children. Together she and Harry would learn the baby's sex at her next appointment. They'd stood in this same spot that other night, his arms around her, his cheek against her hair.

"I think we should buy a new crib and dresser, don't you? After the first three, everything looks a bit worn. So, maybe a changing table and rocking chair too," she'd said. Harry hadn't uttered a word. When Elizabeth turned in his embrace, she caught a look on his face that he quickly tried to mask.

"Is something wrong?" she asked.

"No, nothing." Harry had pressed a quick kiss to her lips. "What could be wrong?"

"Aren't you as excited as I am?"

"Sure," he'd told her. "Sure."

The tragedy of miscarriage had soon shattered her dream, and all along he'd been lying. Not long after that she was living a very public nightmare, and Elizabeth not only knew about his past affair but about his other daughter. He'd already had two of each. Without the last baby she'd yearned for, then abruptly lost, her body still felt empty, hollowed out.

She, Jordan, Stella and Seth were their own little family now, and maybe forever, but always for Elizabeth there would be someone missing. Not Harry—although, the possibility of her taking him back was her mother's favorite refrain. Elizabeth was still young, Claudia claimed. She also suggested that if Elizabeth didn't find a way to forgive her ex, which wouldn't happen, perhaps in time she'd meet someone new. A flash of thought made Elizabeth weak in the knees.

If she were looking, which she was not, Dallas did make a great first impression. Tall, well-built, broad-shouldered. Nice, as Jenna had said. It was the first thing that came to mind about him, but Elizabeth wouldn't go there. Could not. The memory of that one afternoon, in bright daylight, in the room near this barren nursery, was enough. There wouldn't be another day like that either, and besides, soon he'd likely be gone, out of her life. That message had been plain enough. *The only thing on my mind is to pull off my rodeo...then take off for the circuit before I lose what's left of my career.*

In fact, he was gone now to see his parents, he'd said.

Unlike Elizabeth, Dallas had no other strings; in her cherished children, she had three of them. She didn't—shouldn't—want what he might offer, though, of course, he hadn't even tried. Neighbors, that was all, as it should be.

Lost in her nighttime misery, she leaned against the door frame. It was as if her kids had left her to these forlorn spaces, to silence, to the shadow of a sister, a brother...a ghost.

She yearned for their laughter and fights and weeping, their beautiful faces so peaceful in sleep. Sometimes, she crept in to check on them at night, simply to watch. Jenna said Hadley did that too with their twins.

Elizabeth dashed at the sudden wetness on her face. She'd loved being pregnant, filled with life, knowing she was loved.

Was that the reason she'd let Dallas hold her the very day her marriage officially ended? Because she couldn't stand the thought of everything being over? Of being left loveless in the aftermath of miscarriage too? She'd felt so lost. It seemed she still was. A dangerous state of affairs with someone like Dallas living next door. Or, it would be if he hadn't set her straight.

"This summer will last forever," she said aloud.

Elizabeth pushed away from the door frame. Enough self-pity. She went downstairs, opened a pint of rum raisin ice cream and ate the whole thing. Cold comfort.

She really needed to get that job she and Jenna had talked about.

CHAPTER SIX

"HEY, DALLAS," LOGAN HUNTER called over his shoulder.

Dallas raised a hand in greeting. He didn't know Logan well, but he'd met him and his brother at a cookout at Clara McMann's once. "Five minutes," his brother, Sawyer McCord, added, "and we'll be done here."

At the Circle H, Dallas had found them working side by side in the outdoor ring, where a flashy chestnut colt made circles in the dust, urged on by the lunge line playing out from Logan's hand and the light whip that Sawyer held. The adult twins, like Dallas's niece and nephew, seemed to be in sync, their movements coordinated without the need for verbal cues. But Dallas knew it hadn't always been that way. Their family rift, if not the same as his separation from Hadley, had been enough to make Sawyer change his last name.

Dallas felt his insides start to unwind. His

few days in Denver had turned into a week, but the visit only increased the concern he felt for his folks. As he'd suspected, his mom wasn't doing as well as she and his dad had tried to tell him, and Dallas had come back to Barren feeling even more tense. In spite of their loving nature, and the recent attempts they'd made to talk about the damage from his childhood, his parents could be masters of deception.

But he could see that his mother's color was as bad as before, if not worse. And how she tired so easily that even going out for an early-bird dinner—his treat—had sent her to bed before eight o'clock.

This morning, as a distraction, he was making a tour of area ranches, trying to drum up interest in his rodeo-that-might-not-happen-after-all.

Dallas didn't have much time, so he had to multitask and find riders, a venue and the necessary stock for the events all at once. If the thing didn't work out and there was no rodeo after all, the cowboys wouldn't have to pay their entry fees. No risk.

Sawyer gestured with the whip at the colt. "What do you think of this guy?"

Dallas, who seemed to be a temporary local celebrity, climbed the four-board wooden fence and surveyed the horse, but mostly he watched the two men. Both athletic-looking with deep blue eyes and dark hair, they were identical rather than fraternal twins like Hadley's two, Luke and Grace. He wouldn't be able to tell one from the other except that now Sawyer wore a shirt and tie, probably because he'd soon head into town for his other job as a family physician at the office he and old Doc Baxter shared.

Watching the sun gleam off the colt's sleek hide, Dallas finally said, "Good lines." The Circle H kept its stock in prime condition, including the bison herd the twins' grandfather ran on this land. In the distance, Logan's newer Black Angus grazed on rich summer grass, the warm air filled with the sounds of their shifting hooves and, from a solitary paddock, the occasional bellow of the lonely bull apparently longing for love.

Dallas couldn't smile. *He* wasn't in the market for romance, but an image of Lizzie, her neat dark hair and unhappy green eyes, slid across the screen of his mind anyway. A dangerous bit of woolgathering on his part.

Years ago Dallas had learned from his drug-addicted birth parents that marriage wasn't for him—and neither was a family—at least, not until he was financially secure and emotionally ready. A woman so recently divorced and with children—Lizzie had three of them!—should send up bright red warning flares. He'd already made one mistake with her, and the last time he saw her they'd quarreled.

"That all you can say?" Sawyer asked, the whip twitching toward the colt's backside to keep him moving.

"Horses aren't part of my skill set," Dallas said, although he could ride. "I leave that to you and the Circle H, but he's sure a fine specimen. Now, put me on that black bull out there and you'll see some action." Sawyer, always the doctor, sent him a skeptical look. "My hip's okay," Dallas said, then saw his opening. He already had his brother and Calvin on the roster. "I hear you two did some rodeoing back in the day."

Logan reeled in the chestnut colt, its hide showing damp patches from the workout. It stood blowing, head down, at Logan's shoulder. "What boy from Barren hasn't?"

Dallas couldn't think of any, but he was new to the area. "I'm hoping no one," he said, "because I'm setting up a rodeo for later this summer and I need cowboys."

"Full rodeo? Not just bull riders?" Walking the colt around the ring to cool him, Logan grinned. "That being your specialty."

Dallas squared his shoulders. "All-out event. With a starting parade and everything, including barrel racing." That was if, other than the valuable specialty horses owned by those barrel riders, he could find other stock. During his stay with his folks, Dallas had made some calls but had come up empty with the contractors he knew best, and he was worried about that.

"Where? You aren't thinking of the fairgrounds, are you?"

Dallas shoved his hat back on his head. Everyone he talked to seemed to have the same opinion. "Well, yeah."

"Won't happen, Dallas."

"It will if I can come up with the right name to handle some permits."

Sawyer led the horse to the gate. "Have you been over to the site?"

"Not yet."

"You won't like what you see. Believe me, the place is a wreck. It hasn't been used in years. Bleachers are falling down, the arena footing's lumpy—no good even when it was in use—and what about the chutes? They don't exist, never did. Our county fair was always a kind of third-, no, make that fourth-class, event. Mostly for local kids to show their pigs and calves, and for people to display their best pies and homemade jams."

That part sounded good to Dallas. He hadn't considered such a competition to enhance the other events and draw in the crowd. "Guess the fairgrounds are my next stop."

He walked with the other men to the barn. Logan put the colt in its clean stall with a fresh bucket of water, and Sawyer slid the door shut. They both turned to him.

Logan wiped sweat from his forehead. "You're taking on a lot, you know that, right?"

"Nothing new," Dallas agreed. "I'm still going through with the plan."

"Just you?" Sawyer asked.

"So far." Thoughts of Lizzie filled his mind. Maybe instead of getting the name from her, he'd run into the person at the fairgrounds—or someone else would tip them off beforehand, and he—or she—would approach Dallas regarding the permit. If not, he'd find another way.

The Circle H boys were both trying to hide their grins. "Who's gonna ride?" Sawyer asked.

Dallas tensed. "Me. Calvin Stern. My brother."

"Really? You talked Hadley into that?"

"He volunteered," Dallas said.

"Next thing, you'll be telling us Finn Donovan has signed on." Which sounded like a private joke about the county sheriff. Maybe, with Finn's smaller ranch, they didn't think of him as a cowboy.

"I haven't talked to him. But I will." The sheriff might know about permits.

"No wonder you ride bulls. You guys are gluttons for punishment." Another common reaction that Dallas was used to. Logan's arms were crossed as he leaned against the colt's stall. He glanced at Sawyer, who stood in the middle of the barn aisle, tongue in his cheek, probably trying not to laugh. Well, let them. "What do you think, Tom?" Logan asked, the name another private joke between them, apparently.

Sawyer gave his brother the side-eye. "I haven't been in an arena except the one here since I was out of high school."

"Me either," Logan said. Dallas knew he'd led an interesting life. Rather than stay on the Circle H, Logan had become a test pilot, but he gave that up after he'd remarried to ranch with his twin and their grandfather. He'd recently added an airstrip to the property, just to keep his hand in, Hadley had also told Dallas, but more importantly as a safety measure. During a spring flood years ago when the ranch road had become impassable, Logan had nearly lost his first child, who'd been ill with pneumonia, and he wasn't taking that chance again.

Logan clapped Sawyer on the shoulder. "Let's do it."

Dallas blinked at them. "You want to enter?"

"Two for the price of one," they said in unison.

His roster was growing. Dallas left the Circle H wearing a grin.

THE DAY AFTER her pity party in the might-have-been-nursery, Elizabeth had talked to

Sawyer's wife, Olivia McCord, at her antiques store, and now, thanks to Jenna's suggestion, she had a job. On her first day here, she'd been training with Olivia's young assistant, but that didn't seem to be going well for Elizabeth or Rebecca Carter.

In the center of the showroom floor, Becca fussed over a Brussels lace tablecloth with an Olivia McCord Antiques price tag that could have bought Elizabeth a high-end salon treatment. Showing her the way to fold the cloth, Becca couldn't make the sides match up neatly. Olivia must have seen the girl's fumbling attempts, because she marched from her office. "This is delicate, Becca, so please be careful. One of my clients who collects lace, Bernice Caldwell, is coming in today to take a look at it. She'll be here any minute."

Elizabeth stood back with Becca while Olivia refolded then set the cloth on a wooden rack with bars that held similar items.

"Do you want us to inventory the glassware next from that estate sale last weekend?" Becca asked.

Olivia was now flying around the room, straightening things that Becca had shown Elizabeth before, her mouth set. She lined up some gleaming silver plates, then spun around. "I'll take care of the estate items. You can tidy up the front counter. When I came in this morning, there were papers scattered everywhere."

Becca sent Elizabeth a rueful glance. Blond ponytail swinging, she hurried toward the front desk. "If you need help, Mrs. Barnes, just call."

"Thank you, Becca."

Hands on her hips, Olivia gazed after her young employee. "I promised her poor father I'd instill a good work ethic in that girl, but I wonder," she whispered. "There are times— many of them—when even I despair."

"She seems to be trying hard, Libby."

She sighed. "Becca shows up on time, but she never quite grasps the truly important stuff. Like finding just the right item for someone. Rather than call me in to close a sale, she talks up the completely wrong chest of drawers or occasional chair to someone, and I lose money I could have made. Our numbers are down this month. I'm hoping you'll be able to help raise them."

Elizabeth studied the slender girl, who was now on the phone across the room, talking with her hands as she spoke to the caller. "Maybe Becca just needs more coaching," she said. *And I will too.* Had Olivia given Becca a job out of the goodness of her heart? The woman wasn't as tough as people thought. Had she felt sorry for Elizabeth as well?

"If only coaching would help," Olivia said. "Becca's had a number of jobs since she graduated from high school, but none of them stuck. She wasn't interested in college, still lives at home on the Carter farm outside of Farrier, and lately she's taken up with a man of whom her father doesn't approve."

Elizabeth felt sorry for the girl. "Once she settles in, she may be okay."

"She's been working here for six months."

"Olivia, I'm about to make a hundred mistakes. I can run my home without effort because that's my territory, my comfort zone—" *my refuge* "—but it's been a long time since I worked for someone else. I'd hate to ruin your business or our friendship."

Olivia shook her head. "No, Becca's different. She's a failure to launch. I've given her antiques books to read. I've spent hours trying to school her about our inventory, urged her to showcase the pieces that have been sitting too long on the floor so we can move them even at a discounted price, but Becca hasn't improved. Please don't ask her for advice. If I hadn't promised to take her under my wing at least until September, I'd let her go. She's certainly a challenge."

Elizabeth watched Becca skim through the store, straightening a lace doily on a nineteenth-century drum table, righting a ceramic figurine of a Parisian lady, running a hand over the top of a mahogany sideboard to check for dust. "Conscientious, though," she said just as Becca banged into the delicate-looking Louis XVI vanity chair in the center of the room and knocked it over.

Rushing to the rescue again, Olivia said under her breath, "Reminds me of my son Nick when he was seven years old."

Elizabeth refrained from further comment. Olivia could well have two subpar employees on her hands. It wasn't until later, after Olivia had left the shop to grab lunch at the café, that Elizabeth had an opportunity to talk to the girl alone.

"Let's take a break, Becca." It wouldn't hurt to get to know her, and as a mother Elizabeth had felt an immediate instinct to nurture her. Pretty and petite, with clear blue eyes and a satiny complexion, Becca struck Elizabeth as a rather wounded soul, with which she could empathize. They sat in Olivia's office with cups of tea. Becca curled her legs under her in one of the two chairs, and Elizabeth perched on the other. "Do you like working here, Becca?"

"My dad thought I would. Olivia doesn't like me, though."

Elizabeth's heart sank. "That's not true. She hired you."

"Because he talked her into it." That jibed with what Olivia had said, but Elizabeth was surprised Becca was that aware. "I've been a waitress at the café, a stock clerk at Earl's Hardware, an online customer service rep for a software company, a teacher's assistant at the elementary school. One summer I helped answer phones at Doc and Sawyer's medical office. But I never last anywhere. I guess I'll be putting this one on my list soon."

"Maybe you're trying too hard to please Olivia." Elizabeth smiled. "She can be…difficult. I was afraid of her myself years ago when we were in school. Olivia has her standards— though not as rigid as my mother's. And thank goodness, she's mellowed over time, especially since she married Sawyer and had a second child. You wouldn't believe how overly protective she was of her older boy." The aforementioned Nick, a friend of Jordan's.

Becca said, "Your mom is tough like Olivia?"

Elizabeth touched her hand. "Yes, and I'm obviously older than you. Thirty-three."

"I'm twenty-three."

"I shouldn't offer advice, but try to believe you can make it here, and that attitude could change everything. Goodness, I might be talking to myself." She paused, not wanting to belabor the subject. "Olivia mentioned that you have a boyfriend."

Becca's gaze turned softer. "He's the greatest, but my dad doesn't like him."

Elizabeth didn't want to pry. She wasn't here to become anyone's counselor, yet Becca's apparent vulnerability spoke to her as if it were her own. When Becca toyed with her spoon and remained silent, Elizabeth finished her own tea then started to stand. "I hope your boyfriend wins him over. We should both get back to work."

Becca dropped the spoon. The words burst

from her, and her chin quivered. "Calvin… has a record. He and two of his friends stole some cattle. The judge may send one of them to prison, but he gave Calvin community service, and he has a job now."

Elizabeth sank back onto her chair. There were few people in town who didn't know his story. "You mean Calvin Stern?"

"Yes, ma'am. Isn't he the cutest thing?"

He might be adorable, but there was more to any relationship than that. Elizabeth ought to know. She had a handsome ex-husband, and she'd certainly made a mistake with Dallas, not that they had any sort of relationship. Becca seemed immature. Perhaps, beyond befriending her at work, Elizabeth might do a bit of counseling after all.

SOON AFTER HER talk with Elizabeth, Becca drove home, but to her surprise, her father wasn't out in the fields. Their farm was nowhere near as big as the Circle H, for instance, and he still worked it himself, but he must have finished his chores. She found him in the garden, gloves on, spraying the roses. For years, her mother had nurtured them, but since last fall he'd taken over the task.

Becca fretted about him. Poor Daddy, kneeling as if to pray for a different outcome to his life rather than the loss of the woman he loved. She slipped up behind him, wrapped her arms around his too-thin frame, then kissed the top of his head. His hair was the same flaxen blond as her own.

He turned to her and beamed, as he did whenever he saw her. The apple of his eye, he always said. "You're home early."

"Olivia didn't need me." Becca had thrown out those papers by mistake, thinking they were duplicates of charge slips, but instead they'd been store copies. She'd left Olivia, just back from lunch, red-faced with anger. "I thought I'd spend the afternoon with you. Need help with the flowers?"

She knew better. He wouldn't let anyone else care for them. They were like children, spoiled with attention, but that didn't surprise Becca. As his daughter, she received similar devotion. If only her mother hadn't gotten sick, but now it was only Becca and her dad. That hadn't been a problem in itself until a few months ago.

"I'm fine, baby." He rose, knees popping. He'd always been a big man but looked as if he'd lost height while she was in town. "How was work?"

"Fine. Great. Olivia says I'm learning more every day." Olivia had said no such thing. "Let's make lunch. I haven't eaten."

Mentally, she crossed her fingers about her job. Becca didn't want to let her father down. He worked so hard to provide for them, even when she guessed he'd rather spend his days in bed with the covers over his head. Sometimes the sadness in his eyes made her want to cry. Yet she'd rarely seen him shed a tear. He held his grief inside, so as not to upset her.

In the kitchen, Becca spread mayonnaise on their bread, then tore freshly washed Bibb lettuce from the garden into pieces. "The corn's already up to the fences," she said, watching her father turn bacon in the skillet. "Maybe we can sell some here, open the farm stand again this summer. These tomatoes would be awesome too, Daddy. What do you think?"

"I don't have time to work the stand. Neither do you."

If she didn't start doing better at Olivia's, she might have all the time they needed. She'd try to take Elizabeth's advice, but still felt she was in over her head. She liked Elizabeth, though.

Her father drained the bacon, then set a plate of it on the counter. Becca assembled their sandwiches, added fruit she'd cut for breakfast and poured tall glasses of milk. At the table, she tried another topic, hoping to make him happy. Her daily assignment. "Did you answer that lady's message? She sounded nice."

He took a bite of his sandwich, chewed and swallowed, then pushed the BLT aside. "Becca, doesn't matter if she's nice or a raving lunatic. You should never have signed me up on that website. I don't need a date—or a second chance. No, I didn't answer and I'm not going to. Now eat."

The firm note in his voice ended that discussion. Well, she'd tried. Maybe in a few weeks, another month, he'd change his mind. The thought of his being lonely made her feel like a traitor. It wasn't right for him to spend so much of his time alone. Always, her father had had Mom waiting when he came in after evening chores. Her dad would smile, bend his head to kiss her mother's neck and the two of them would laugh, looking into each other's eyes with all that love they'd shared. The kind she wanted for herself. Becca couldn't wait to get out of the house to see Calvin tonight.

She said with a familiar lump in her throat, "Think about it, Daddy. Really, you need someone, maybe not right now, but Mom would want you to be happy."

A line appeared between his brows. "Becca. I was happy. Nothing can take that away from me. I don't need anyone new. That would be sacrilege to your mother's memory."

She disagreed but didn't say more. Her main goal was simply not to add to his sorrow.

Her dad took a slice of apple from his plate, then stood. One slice, when he used to eat several apples at once, would have had two sandwiches and another glass of milk. "Back to work now. I need to spread manure on the east pasture squash and melons."

Becca wished they ran cattle like her friend Willow's family did. In her view the crops took too much care and effort, sapping what little energy her dad seemed to have. Couldn't cows take care of themselves? Even the roses required work.

"I'll thaw steaks for dinner. How does that sound?" Becca wanted to eat early and felt a small thrill of anticipation then guilt. "Five thirty today?" Usually they ate after seven or even after dark, whenever he finished evening chores. His gaze homed in on her, his mouth set. She shouldn't have said that.

"You going somewhere tonight?" He knew Willow was away on vacation with her family.

"Um, I thought I'd see a movie in town."

He also knew what that meant. "You mean with Calvin Stern? Didn't I make myself clear? A boy with his history, no family I've heard of…not to mention the company he keeps."

"Kept," she murmured. "He has an uncle in Farrier. Fred Miller. You know him, don't you? Calvin doesn't see those other guys anymore."

"Yeah, well, people may say his pal Derek Moran's a reformed sinner, but what about Cody Jones? He's still awaiting trial. He'll soon be in prison, Becca, where they all belong. They're a bad bunch." He took a breath. "I'm telling you again to break it off with Stern. He's not welcome on this property and he's sure not going to take my little girl away from me."

Becca wanted to curl up in a ball. This had been the worst day, except for meeting Elizabeth, who might make life easier for her with Olivia. Tonight's movie wasn't going to happen. She'd have to call Calvin and tell him their date was off. She didn't dare mention to her father the fact that she wanted to move in with him.

CHAPTER SEVEN

"Mom, I'm borrred."

Elizabeth's daily phone reports from Colorado had changed like the weather, and this latest seemed to be another omen. Outside her windows the Kansas sky had darkened, thick leaden clouds closing in, followed by the occasional rumble of thunder. Seth's homesickness was still there, but this morning it was Jordan who was verbally pouting in her ear.

"There's nothing wrong with feeling bored now and then," she said. "That's part of life. You have to learn to entertain yourself." After her first few days on the job, her talk with Becca Carter remained in her mind if not at its center just now. She didn't want her oldest son to reach his twenties without feeling better grounded in himself. Watching Becca fumble her way through her days at work could be painful enough.

"Dad spends too much time on his computer," Jordan was saying. "Yesterday he dropped us at the kids' club for the *whole* afternoon. I'm too old for that silly stuff, Mom. I don't need a sitter. All we did was make lanyards out of beads and string—a baby thing, like, for Seth," he added. "I wanted to go canoeing."

"Jordan." He couldn't be serious about boating on his own.

"Then Dad ordered room service for dinner and while we were eating, he holed up in his own place—he has the upper floor— and we watched movies. Do you know how many times I've seen *Paddington*? It's Seth's favorite but not mine! And Stella? She still likes *Frozen*, the first one, so we had to watch that too. Dad won't let us see *The Avengers* because Seth might get scared." He groaned aloud in frustration. "There's nothing for me to do here."

Make that two out of three. Only Stella, her middle one, hadn't complained. Elizabeth stifled a yawn. She couldn't seem to wake up, and her energy level was down. What would happen once the kids came home with school activities to fit into the schedule? Plus, her job? "I'm sorry to hear all this. Your father doesn't get much time with you during the year, and now—"

"We don't even see him!"

Elizabeth would address that later. Surely Jordan was exaggerating. Lightning flashed, illuminating the backyard, with another grumble of thunder. The storm would break soon and right overhead. This time she couldn't hold back the yawn. "I hear you, honey, and I wish you were having a better time. Have you started your summer reading? You have three book reports to do before school starts. Make use of the time when you're not on some outing with your dad."

"Didn't you hear me? We don't have outings. He says there's the whole resort to run around in, the great outdoors, and Seth shouldn't worry about the bears—"

Elizabeth's throat seized. "Bears?"

"Not grizzlies, black bears," Jordan explained as if that made a difference. "We didn't see any. I could be home, Mom." He paused, and Elizabeth could hear a sly note enter his voice. "I could rodeo with Nick and the other kids on Saturdays. Wouldn't that be safer?"

Elizabeth didn't think so. She remembered

watching rodeo on TV with Dallas, seeing the cowboy who'd flown off the bull onto the dirt. For a few too-long seconds, he hadn't stirred or gotten up. Even the kids' event each weekend made her shudder.

Jordan's voice gained strength. "Nick's already riding. Why can't I? He'll be better than me while I'm wasting my summer here." His best friend did have an advantage. Nick was Logan and Olivia's son. His parents were also divorced, and Nick divided his time between the Circle H with his dad, Logan Hunter, and Wilson Cattle, where Olivia, who'd married Logan's twin brother, Sawyer, lived. Nick was a real ranch kid, twice over, when Jordan only dreamed of such a life. Elizabeth suppressed a flash of guilt. Frankly, she'd been almost relieved when he left home with Harry and was no longer around Dallas. She didn't want the cowboy to become her son's idol.

Elizabeth yawned. "Put your father on." And Jordan went off to find him. Most of her conversations with the children ended with another quarrel between Elizabeth and Harry. What was he doing on the computer when he should be bonding with their kids?

Jordan returned. "He says don't bother him. He's busy."

"Doing what?"

"Finding a new job, he says." She could imagine Jordan's shrug. Elizabeth barely had the energy to deal with Harry herself.

"Please tell him I need to speak to him. Now." When he finally picked up the phone, she spoke through gritted teeth. "Your job at the moment is taking care of three minor children. We've talked about this before. Jordan, Stella and Seth need your full attention."

"I've tried, Elizabeth. Have you ever taken them to the Buffalo Bill Museum? No," he said. "The gondola ride up the mountain? An evening powwow by a campfire with Native American dancing?" He didn't wait for her answer. "Well, I have. I've busted my..." He took a breath as if to calm himself. "None of that was more successful than our miniature golf adventure or swimming in this resort's Olympic-sized pool." He scoffed. "With Jordan, there's always something wrong."

"Yes." He was angry with his father. "What's the common denominator?"

"Three spoiled kids," Harry said.

"No, it's you. I don't want them to be spoiled, but instead of firing off résumés—"

"You'd better hope I find a new job or there won't be any support payments coming your way. What will you do then?"

"Don't threaten me, Harry. I've already found a job myself. Just live up to your obligations, preferably with a smile on your face." As the storm broke outside, Elizabeth felt the beginnings of a headache. *What is happening to my children?* She'd never felt this worn-out or utterly helpless. *What can I possibly do to make things better for them from so far away?*

AT THE FAIRGROUNDS on the edge of Barren, Dallas surveyed the abandoned site surrounded by a rusted chain-link fence. Logan and Sawyer had been right. There wasn't enough money in this world, or enough time, to make the fairgrounds suitable for a rodeo this summer. His usual positive outlook took a nosedive. He could have saved himself the effort to see the place. A permit was the least of his problems.

He glanced at the falling-down grandstand. *So, now what?*

"I've got a bunch of riders with no place to ride."

"Broaden your horizons." Finn Donovan, the county sheriff, shifted from one booted foot to the other. As usual, he wore jeans and a Western-style shirt instead of a uniform. Finn preferred a more casual approach. He liked to fit in with the community, not to play up his position of authority. "The rodeo's a good idea, Dallas. With a charity aspect, even better. This town needs something to get people excited again. There's been a dark cloud hanging over Main Street ever since Harry Barnes resigned as mayor." Finn pulled off his trademark aviator sunglasses to reveal earnest hazel eyes. "I'm glad he's away this summer. His family went through a bad time last year. His three kids were confused, as was Emmie. His *love child*, some of the older residents call her." Finn half smiled. "I just call her my daughter.

"Nobody gets to that kid," he added with a proud grin. He and his wife, Annabelle, were now Emmie's adoptive parents, and Harry Barnes had given up any claim to her. Dallas figured she'd lucked out, like him with the Maguires.

He walked with Finn across the dusty fairgrounds, which contained more ruts than even ground. "My brother tells me Emmie couldn't have a better home than she does with you and Annabelle. At least some good came of all that."

Finn frowned. "I wish I could say the same for Elizabeth. I know Annabelle worries about her," he said. "Having to see Harry all over town again this fall, the walking reminder that her marriage went down the tubes…" He didn't go on.

And not to call attention to himself, Dallas didn't respond. The day of her divorce he'd only made things worse for her. Fortunately, as far as he knew, no one else had learned about that.

"You're living next door, aren't you?" Finn asked. "In the Whittaker house?"

"Yep. I don't see much of Liz — Elizabeth. Not that I need to," Dallas added.

Finn's gaze sharpened. He'd obviously noticed the near slip of her nickname, as if she and Dallas were more than neighbors.

The sheriff studied him. "Elizabeth could use some kindness. There are people in this town who've been showing their dark sides.

Calling her names like Ms. Perfect, hoping she'll give them something more to talk about when she hasn't done anything. She doesn't deserve to take any blame for what Harry did."

Dallas couldn't agree more. "She seems like a fine person." Not that she needed his endorsement.

He was still thinking about that when he reached the Sutherland ranch, his next stop. He didn't know Cooper Ransom, who'd been Finn's partner in the Chicago PD before they both ended up in Barren, and he'd never met his wife, though he knew her reputation. But Nell, the granddaughter of the NLS's owner, didn't seem like the tough cowgirl he'd expected. When Dallas pulled up in his truck, he found her draped around Cooper by the outdoor arena, arms looped around his neck, sharing a kiss that Dallas probably wasn't supposed to see, and which made him squirm.

Cooper broke the kiss, then stared at him as if Dallas wasn't quite of this world. After a long moment, his gray eyes cleared. "We're still on our honeymoon," he said. "And you are...?"

Dallas introduced himself. "Hadley gave

me some local ranchers' names. Thought I'd see if you have interest in a rodeo I'm planning." He briefly explained, then added, "I thought getting a permit to use the old fairgrounds would be a hurdle, but turns out I need to look for another venue instead. Once I find that…"

"I did some rodeo as a kid—" Cooper hadn't finished the sentence before Nell piped up.

"You are not going to ride some wild bronc or bull." She was tall, though inches shorter than her husband. She glared up at him. "Haven't you had enough danger in your life?"

Dallas knew from Hadley that in Chicago Cooper had been ambushed by a vicious gang.

"You almost died!" Nell said. "No more hot-dogging. Your rodeo days are over too, Ransom."

Cooper only smiled and ran a hand through his sunny hair.

Nell kept sputtering. "I mean it. Buck me on this, and I'll…get your mother after you."

Cooper grinned. "Who wouldn't love this woman?"

"I'm not touching that," Dallas said, but she sure held her own.

Nell tucked a strand of light brown hair behind her ear. "If I can run this ranch—which I can—I can handle one ex-cop who still, need I remind you, Cooper, wakes up feeling stiff in the morning."

His grin widened. He turned to face Dallas as if to hide the expression. "About your rodeo...there might be some open land available in the area. Talk to the realty people at the office on Cottonwood Street. Maybe whoever owns acreage might like to rent it, see it used for a good cause."

Which for Dallas would also mean putting up fencing, building bleachers...

"I'll look into it." He avoided Nell's green eyes and tried to deflect her disapproval. "When I come up with something, would any of your hands care to compete?"

"Clete might, but especially Dex. He's younger—" Cooper began.

"I was practically born on a horse," Nell cut in. "Put me down for—"

"Oh, no, you don't." Cooper's mouth tightened, and Dallas realized he'd somehow stumbled into an argument. "You know why."

Her cheeks turned rosy. "That's not an issue. I ride every day—just ask Bear."

"I can't. He's a horse—"

"And I grew up knowing how to rope. So, what's your problem?" she asked Cooper.

"You are, Nell."

Dallas had an urge to turn around and hop in his truck before he got any deeper into their domestic quarrel, but before he could move, Cooper gently turned Nell toward the nearby barn. "We'll talk about this. Later."

She dug in her boot heels. "We'll talk now, and don't you dare treat me like some helpless female. If you even think of telling me I can't compete against a bunch of cowboys—"

Cooper told her mildly, "I have other means of persuasion that will be far better for your health." He slung an arm around her shoulders. "For now, would you mind feeding that orphaned calf for me? Please? Then we need to get into town." He raised an eyebrow. "One o'clock appointment, remember."

Her shoulders relaxed. "I forgot about that."

"Well, Sawyer won't. He'll be waiting."

Which caused Nell to head toward the barn, a smile on her lips.

Cooper watched her go. "Wouldn't trade

her for the world. She *is* my world," he said, staring after her with a goofy look on his face that reminded Dallas of Hadley with Jenna. "Nell's not going to be part of your rodeo, no matter what she said, but I'll compete. No matter what she said. Add me to the roster."

"Thanks." Dallas didn't envy those two the fight that was sure to continue later, but he did envy the obvious love they shared. Not that he was ready to find his own.

His gray gaze serious, Cooper turned back to Dallas. "About the fairgrounds not working out… I'd offer the arena here at the NLS, but we already use it on weekends for local kids who think they're going to be the next superstar on the circuit—like you—when they grow up. We have age-appropriate events, a bit of calf roping for the older kids, a few lassos get thrown…usually missing their mark. They're cute to watch, but that's enough disruption for the ranch. Your neighbor's boy Jordan would try his hand, but his mom won't allow that."

I'd never let my kids try that, Lizzie had said.

Dallas didn't want to talk about her. "I'll see what the Realtor can tell me. Ask your cowhands if they want to enter. I'll let you know when I've got a venue and a firm date. Should be soon." It had to be, or he'd run out of summer. And his time here.

Cooper stuck out his hand. "Welcome to the neighborhood, Dallas."

After a few words about keeping in touch, Dallas headed for his truck. He spent so much time on the road for his next chance to ride bulls, he'd stopped thinking about a place to call home. He lived out of his pickup or in hotel rooms. The house he'd rented in Barren was the only anchor he'd had in years, certainly since he'd left his parents' home in Denver to make his mark in the world of professional rodeo. And people still called his rental the Whittaker house. But he was meeting neighbors, making friends here, and his long-lost brother was nearby…good people, except for those who criticized Lizzie. And yeah, he still thought of her as Lizzie.

He could almost think about sinking roots in this flat Kansas ground.

Too bad Dallas didn't intend to stay.

He still had places to go. A gold buckle to win. He didn't want anything to tie him down.

As soon as she realized Dallas was home from Denver the next morning, Elizabeth carried a peace offering to his house. After her talk with Jordan, she'd wondered if she was being fair to her son, and that had just made her think about Dallas. She'd had to work up her nerve to cross the yard, and when he opened the door, he gaped at her, his eyes hooded, his posture taut. She hadn't seen him since before his trip. She shouldn't expect him to welcome her now.

She handed him a slip of paper, which Dallas glanced at. "Who's this?"

"The man you were looking for," she said. "His number. How were your parents?"

"Not that good. You mean the guy who mows the lawn at city hall? Handled the fair too?"

Dallas didn't seem particularly receptive, and Elizabeth had one foot on the top step to leave. Maybe he was holding a grudge. "I had to do some digging to find his phone contacts. I don't know whether he can be of help."

"Thanks for making the effort." Dallas folded and unfolded the note. "But the fairgrounds are out, so I may not need a permit."

She could hear the disappointment in his voice. "What will you do, then?"

"Try to find another arena." Then, as if he'd changed his mind about her unannounced visit, he said, "Come in. I want to show you something too."

Elizabeth hesitated. She had never been inside the house, even when the Whittakers lived there, and what else was there to say? As promised, she'd brought him that name. If she were lucky, Bernice wouldn't be watching from her window, which had a clear view of both homes, but Elizabeth had already exposed herself on the walk between her house and his. "I can't. I was on my way out when I realized you were home," she said, then felt the need to explain. "I'm working today. In town."

Dallas crossed his arms. "Glad to hear you're getting out more. What's the job?"

A new sense of pride made her smile. "I'm helping at Olivia's shop—she's leaving the country soon so I'm to pick up the slack while she's gone." She glanced toward Bernice's house, then took another backward step.

"I see." Dallas had followed her gaze. He caught her arm just before Elizabeth would have fallen down the stairs. "You really think people have their faces pressed to the glass?"

"In this case, I'm sure she would." Elizabeth cleared her throat. "Dallas, I'm sorry. After I asked you about Jack—if you'd told him about our dinner—it didn't take long for me to see the truth. Bernice Caldwell often has lunch, even dinner, at the Bon Appetit, so she talks to Jack all the time. She probably saw you pick up the food then come to my door later with the bags from the restaurant, put two and two together, and had to spread the news."

He continued to stare at her, but the hard look had faded from his eyes. In fact, they held both sympathy and a glint of challenge. She should pull her arm free.

Dallas said, "I'm also sorry. I shouldn't have shoved my rodeo career in your face." He held the door open for her. "Five minutes, in and out. Even Bernice can't be sitting at her window every second of the day."

Curiosity and his light grasp drew her inside to the cool dimness of the entryway. She looked around, then followed him into the living room. And stopped. There wasn't a lot there.

"I rented a furniture package, the basics."
He gestured at the plain, masculine-looking
sofa, matching chair, end tables and a coffee
table with a glass top. The dining room they
saw next was empty, so no wonder he didn't
eat there, but his kitchen held a small bistro
set with two French-style chairs. Elizabeth
wouldn't think about the second-floor rooms.
Maybe he slept on his couch. Dallas motioned
her to one of the seats, then took some papers
off the table.

Elizabeth watched the concentration on his
face as he scribbled something. Then, with a
satisfied nod, he handed her a list. "My riders
so far," he said. "Just added another. Cooper
Ransom. Too bad the fairgrounds are a no-
go." He looked into her eyes. "I'm curious.
What did you say to that guy I asked you to
find?"

"I told him I needed my lawn mowed and
I'd give him a call." Her gaze wandered toward the other room, the front door. "It's too
bad the fairgrounds didn't work out." She
stood and gave back the list of local ranchers she'd barely glanced at. "Now I do have
to go—"

He charmed her with the smile she hadn't

seen in too long, and some of the awkwardness that had been between them seemed to dissipate. "I haven't shown you my new mower yet." Teasing, he waggled his eyebrows. "Leased for the summer," he said, which only reminded her of his temporary status in her hometown. "It's a beauty, and you don't need that guy. I'll cut your grass for you—if you want me to."

The warmth in his eyes made Elizabeth wonder if he'd really meant something far more personal, a temptation she couldn't indulge. "That's a nice offer, but..."

"Friends and family discount."

At the door she turned and found herself mere inches from him, Dallas's lean body and his broad shoulders too close for her comfort. He smelled good, of a pine-scented soap and fresh air. She had to tilt her head to look up into his face. "I'm not family and I already have friends. Not all of them stood by me, which you know, but the ones who did are my lifetime friends. I don't mean to sound harsh or unwelcoming, but you're only here for a few weeks, and everything about you says so." She knew she was talking too fast, saying too much, but couldn't stop herself. "I shouldn't depend on someone who rents his furniture, even his lawn mower, and will be leaving Barren as soon as the rodeo is over."

"I'm here now," he said. "I realize you've been burned and have reason to be wary."

"Three of them, yes. Ages six, seven and nine." The awkwardness was back.

"All I'm saying is, when you see me, you don't have to run the other way. End of story."

"But it's not, Dallas." She gestured at the street outside, the houses in the neighborhood. "Yes, you're here now, you can enjoy Barren, and let's say your rodeo's a big success— the charity that hasn't been chosen yet gets a nice donation, and you look like a hero— but you're not *local*. I am. As you also said, you'll soon be on the road again, and I'd be suffering any fallout. I had enough of that with Harry."

"I'm not Harry," he said, his tone flat. "I didn't ask you to make a lifetime commitment." He reached out to tuck a strand of hair behind her ear, and without warning, Elizabeth's eyes filled. Dallas's voice turned husky. "I wouldn't do anything to harm you—or your kids. As for being local, I'm not, but Hadley is, and believe me I'd never get out of line with him around. Not that I would anyway."

And there, all at once, was the elephant in the room again. *I was there too*, he'd said.

"I swear, when your divorce came through, I wasn't trying to take advantage of you when you were feeling so down. Let me put all my cards on the table here," he said with a faint lightening of his expression. "I think you're an amazing woman... I like you, Lizzie."

"Please don't call me that." It sounded too...intimate.

He sighed. "Elizabeth. Would I hope for something more this summer? In theory, sure," he admitted, "because I'm human and I remember us in May, together. I know you're still hurting, but you can't hide from people, from what happened with your ex, even from *me*, forever. That's not good for your kids, and it's certainly not good for you."

She shook her head. "This, from a guy who never met a stranger. Yes, I know I can seem too 'buttoned up,' but I've always been an Elizabeth. We're very different, Dallas, and as you pointed out, my family, not just me, suffered real damage this past year." *I lost my baby too, another piece of my heart, and*

I'm still mourning that loss. "I'm not ready to fully take part in the world yet. When I do, it will have to be on my terms, no one else's."

"You've already made a start with that job." He paused. "Maybe I should have said this first. I've had my dark times too, and I want us to be friends, that's all. You could use another friend."

Elizabeth blinked back her tears. He was one of the best people she'd ever met, but was just friendship even possible after that day in May? She had to hold her ground. She'd given him that contact information as her latest apology, and that was where their connection should end. Her hand shaking, she opened the door. "I have to run. I'll be late for work." But before she stepped outside, Jordan's distress yesterday on the phone came back to her, and she realized Dallas had a point.

She *had* made a fresh start with her new job. And if she juggled her work at Olivia's, she might be able to help Dallas a bit and lift Jordan's spirits too, at least when he got home. And because Seth copied anything his big brother did or wanted to do, two of her kids might end up happier because of this small treat. Stella wouldn't care about a rodeo, so maybe a mother-daughter day with her would be best, but…first, she'd have to eat a bit of crow.

"I have an idea." Her heart thumping, she held Dallas's gaze. "When you find that other venue, maybe I could, um, handle some publicity, PR…"

Dallas blinked. "You will?"

It wasn't as if Elizabeth would be putting herself out there, really. She'd stay behind the scenes and avoid any missteps. With any luck, though, this could also be her opportunity to prove herself again to the people of Barren. "I think my kids will love the idea of your event, and if it's held after they come home—" *If it's successful…*

"I know Jordan's keen on rodeo."

Elizabeth groaned. "I'm sure he and his friend Nick will be over the moon."

"Don't give in too much," Dallas said, his gaze holding hers, "or I won't know how to react. Thanks, Liz—Elizabeth."

"Don't thank me yet. I don't know how much help I'll really be but, well, it looks like I'll help with your rodeo after all."

CHAPTER EIGHT

LIZZIE HAD OFFERED to help! Reluctantly, to be sure, yet Dallas was still enjoying the victory when he pulled up at Clara McMann's barn the next morning for work. This coming weekend he'd agreed to show up for the kids' rodeo at the Sutherland ranch and provide some guidance before the fledgling cowboys, close in age to Lizzie's oldest, learned bad habits.

Speaking of... The dun-colored horse in the crossties here was straining to break free, trying to rear up. "Problem?" Dallas asked.

Hadley laid a calming hand against the gelding's neck. "Trouble's just being trouble. Temper tantrum, which he does better than my Gracie. I think he's jealous of the new mare I bought. I wouldn't trade my horse—Mr. Robert and I understand each other—but you and Calvin can fight over which of you gets this one or the other."

Calvin wandered from the feed room. "I'm used to Trouble. He's not a bad sort. Just ornery. Believe me, I've had experience with that." His statement seemed double-edged and Dallas remembered him talking about his relationship with his girlfriend.

"Three horses." Dallas felt his smile spread. "You're building quite the herd, Hadley. Guess you plan to keep me on, then." All summer anyway.

"If you don't work out," Hadley said, "or you decide to just up and leave, I'll have an extra mount."

Dallas refused to feel guilty. They still had time to know each other again, but Hadley also knew his plans. He untied the dun, then handed the lead rope to Calvin. "Put him out in the ring for a while, let him run circles. Otherwise he'll kick out the wall in his stall or crib until the door's like Swiss cheese."

Trouble apparently had the equine bad habit of chewing on wood, which wasn't good for his teeth either. Dallas asked what chores needed to be done today. Later, after his rehab session, he and Lizzie would meet to discuss her new role in his rodeo, and maybe by then he'd have an actual venue. "Calvin's cleaning tack," Hadley said. "I'm mending a saddle. You get to measure grain and medications for tonight. Then we'll all drive over to Fred Miller's place, see if he's serious about us trailering that stock for him to the new owner." Hadley and Clara had bought a big rig and were building a side business for when things got slow with the cattle. "Let's get going."

It was only later that Dallas had an opportunity to talk to Hadley. He explained about the fairgrounds. "At least Cooper Ransom's two hands are also on board now. I've got a pretty good roster of guys to ride, but I need an arena with enough space around for parking, a decent barn…"

"You ask Cooper?"

"Yep. He's involved with the kids' event there. Not interested in a bigger rodeo. His wife wants to compete in mine—"

"I bet she does." Hadley laughed. "Nell and I had our difficulties when I was her foreman there, and she rarely loses. What did Cooper say?"

"He tried to say no."

His brother laughed again. "Did you sign her up?"

"I'm letting them work it out." Dallas leaned against a fence post, his hat tilted against the late-afternoon sun. "Good news, though. Lizzie—I mean, Elizabeth—Barnes is on my team now, helping me put the event together. Part-time."

Beside him, Hadley crossed his brawny arms. "That's a surprise. She hasn't been doing her usual civic duty since Harry moved out. She used to be in the center of everything, appearing at town functions, organizing the annual rummage sale the seniors put on, running every charity raffle and fundraiser Harry could think of. He's the original glad-hander, always working a room. Elizabeth did the real work, but since they split up— How'd you talk her into that?"

"I didn't. I mean, I tried, but she kept saying no. Then yesterday she said she'd do it."

"What's in it for her?" Hadley frowned. "Or I should ask, what else is in it for you?"

Dallas's tone was flat. "What does that mean."

"I know when you're on the road, there are lots of women. Big rodeo star like you, it can't be hard to find female companionship. Elizabeth's different. She's fragile."

"I know that."

"See that you remember," Hadley said. "Dallas, I'm more than glad to have you here, you know that, and I savor the time we have together after all those years when you were missing. But I also know you'll be back riding bulls soon because that's who you are, even if I'd have you stay. Don't give that woman any more heartache."

"I don't intend to." Seemed to Dallas that more people in Barren supported her, cared about her, than Elizabeth believed. Which was a good thing.

Hadley appeared to sense they were heading for a full-blown quarrel. He pushed away from the fence, then stood gazing around the property, taking in the house across the yard, the dirt space in front of the barn. He turned toward the outdoor ring where Trouble was still loping around the circle, snorting and shaking his head. "Let me talk to Clara."

Dallas's inner alarm sounded. "About what?" Had he said something he shouldn't have? Did Hadley really think Dallas was chasing Lizzie? And he was about to let him go after all? "Hadley, I'll stay as long as I can."

"Long enough to put on that rodeo?"

"Yeah, sure, but I won't slack off here, if that's what you're thinking. I can do both." He followed Hadley's gaze at the ranch. "All I need is to find—"

"A venue."

Dallas couldn't think where that might be. "I already tried the NLS, the Circle H, Wilson Cattle…the fairgrounds." He'd reached a dead end in his phone calls with the local Realtors to lease some land.

Hadley clapped him on the shoulder. "Relax, little brother." He grinned. "What about the McMann ranch? You work here, why not play here? I think Clara will give us permission without any fancy paperwork. Let's rodeo."

ELIZABETH HAD PROMISED Jenna she'd attend their next Girls' Night Out group, and when they met later at Liza Wilson's new home, she went. That had meant telling Dallas she couldn't meet with him tonight about his rodeo, but the women's get-together had almost slipped her mind.

On purpose? Not only was she yawning— not sleeping any better—but her stomach now felt queasy. As soon as she knocked at the door, Jenna answered and greeted her, putting an arm around her shoulders.

Jenna's auburn hair gleamed in the light. "Congratulations. Before Olivia left the States for Kedar, she told me you've taken a job with her, sweetie."

"Yes." They walked into the living room of the sprawling house, where Jenna had done the interior design. "I haven't been here since you finished. This place is gorgeous. Olivia told me you used some pieces from the shop," she said, but Jenna had picked up on her tone, which lacked sufficient enthusiasm.

"You don't like the work there?"

"I like it, quite a lot actually, but I'm kind of under the weather tonight. Just sleep deprivation probably, and I'd be home in bed except I didn't want to disappoint you again."

"Still missing your tribe? How's Harry doing with the kids?"

Elizabeth took a seat on a sofa in front of the fireplace. From the kitchen she could hear the clatter of plates and an oven door slamming. Water gushed from a faucet. "It's more how the kids are doing with him," she said. "Seth's better—not as homesick—but now it's

Jordan. Stella's been so quiet, even stoic, that I can't read how she really feels. At any rate, Harry is Harry. I don't think he was present in the same room with us as a family more than a couple of times a week. Even then, he was always the mayor, looking at his phone, answering messages on his laptop. I'd hoped for better this summer. For them." She told Jenna he was looking for a job. "I mean, suppose he becomes mayor of some town in Iowa or Vermont?"

Jenna's blue eyes sparkled. "He'd be out of your hair."

"But also farther from the kids. I won't have them divided like that, spending summers here and holidays wherever…"

"Let's hope he chooses a position in the state. He's not entirely irredeemable, is he?"

"You're asking me?" Her question didn't need an answer.

The front door opened then closed, and Elizabeth welcomed the interruption. Sound drifted from the entry hall. The others were all here, but she felt too weary to say more than a quick hello to each one. She really should have stayed home, but at that minute their hostess emerged from the kitchen to hug everyone, which virtually said *Let the party begin*. Elizabeth took a deep breath. She loved these women who had stood by her, but the subject of her divorce, a rehash of the scandal, would likely be on tonight's agenda at some point. Unless she found an excuse to leave early.

She didn't get that chance. Food was spread on the dining room table, wine was poured and talk sprinkled with laughter filled the air. It was Jenna who noticed that Cooper Ransom's wife had chosen to drink water—and that Nell couldn't suppress her broad smile.

"All right, Nell. What's happened now?" The group had heard stories about her new marriage, and her love for Cooper, every time they met.

"We're pregnant," Nell announced. "Too early to tell yet, but Sawyer thinks it's a boy. Everything's fine, he says, right on schedule."

Her last words were wiped out by the chorus of congratulations, more laughter and another round of hugs. Elizabeth participated, yet inside she held back. She might avoid any discussion now of the divorce, but hearing about other people's babies wasn't her favorite thing these days either. Then she realized she wasn't the only one who'd moved back from the group and was seated on the sofa again, the huge ceiling fan whirring overhead to cool the room. Beside her, Jenna stared at her hands clenched in her lap.

"I'm so happy for them," she said with a glance at Elizabeth. "Really, I am. Nell and Cooper were meant to be together. Now they'll be a family too."

Elizabeth covered Jenna's hands with hers. She remembered Jenna's wistful expression the last time they'd talked.

"Oh, Jen. You wish you could have a baby of your own, don't you?"

Her face looked suddenly stricken. "It's that obvious?"

"Have you talked to Hadley? Maybe there's some way—"

"I'd be going back on my word. When he asked me to marry him, I said I was fine with the twins, and I am. You know I adore them, and it doesn't bother him that I'm infertile, but wouldn't it be lovely for them to somehow have a sibling before they get much older?"

Nell had turned from the rest of the group. "Private party?" she asked, still with that aura about her that reminded Elizabeth of a

Madonna. The way she'd felt during her last pregnancy until…

Nell interrupted her thoughts. "Liza's opening champagne. Join us."

Nell drank more water while the others toasted her and Cooper, and everyone fought to see who would hold the baby shower. Elizabeth set aside her wine. Her already nervous stomach kept rolling.

Shutting out the happy talk in the room, Jenna leaned close. "You sure you're okay? You look a bit chalky."

Elizabeth glanced at Nell. Amid the chatter and celebration, she kept feeling worse. Day by day worse, if she were honest. "I'd kill for a good night's sleep. I should go," she said. "I need to catch up before the kids get home. It's nothing, really, just this relentless fatigue and a bit of tummy trouble tonight."

"I noticed you didn't eat much." Jenna's gaze looked keen. "I don't mean to throw a hand grenade into your life here, but what if, instead of all that, it's something else?"

"What else could it be?"

"Elizabeth. What have we all been talking about nonstop this evening? Some of us more happily than others." She arched one eyebrow. "I know it's not a subject either of us feel comfortable with—my infertility, your miscarriage last year—but isn't it possible?" Her voice softened. "After Dallas Maguire, I mean."

Oh, God. She never should have said anything about that day with him. Elizabeth searched her mind for the pertinent details. "I told you, we used contraception. Why would you think I could be—?"

"Accidents happen." Jenna drew back. "Never mind, I didn't intend to say anything. Forget it. Wishful thinking on my part, perhaps."

Yes, but that opened a whole Pandora's box for Elizabeth, and she was quaking inside.

She now had her excuse to run. She said her hasty good-nights, on her way out the door promised to call someone—she forgot who—about having lunch one day, then sped home along the dark roads into Barren, her mind racing faster than the car.

In the house, she tore upstairs to her bedroom and scrambled through the nightstand drawer until her fingers closed around the box Harry had left there. While trying to conceive their new baby, the one she'd lost, of course they'd given up using protection. Then last May, she and Dallas had their one unplanned romantic interlude. Naturally he hadn't come prepared. She stared in shock at the date on the box of condoms in her trembling hand. July. Two years ago. Expired.

She groaned aloud. *Accidents happen.* She needed a test kit from the pharmacy, but by now it was closed. Her pulse kept skipping. She'd have to wait until tomorrow, but she'd already borne three children, lost another. She knew all the signs, including her last missed cycle and the one due days ago, which she'd blamed on other factors. Nerves, the divorce, missing her kids...

This couldn't be. But it was. Elizabeth was sure she was pregnant.

ON SATURDAY MORNING, Elizabeth was still reeling. She hadn't slept at all. She had gotten up at dawn, gone to the drugstore and bought three home tests. All of them had read positive. The day of her divorce she'd taken one misstep, and now look. And as luck would have it, Dallas had phoned minutes after she'd taken the last test, while Elizabeth was still trying to absorb the fact that she was, indeed, pregnant. His deep voice, sounding excited about the venue he'd found for his rodeo, had sent another rush of shock through her, along with an unwelcome wave of awareness. How to tell him that his world was also about to be rocked off its foundation?

No wonder she'd been so tired and, more recently, queasy. She should have known.

"What are your plans today?" Dallas had asked.

Trying to keep my eyes open and my breakfast down. "Cleaning my pantry," she said.

What else did she have to do besides search her shelves for expired cans of beans or tuna? Oh, yes. Let him know he was about to become a father. How would she ever find the right words knowing he probably wouldn't welcome the news?

"Can I change your mind? Today's the kids' rodeo. I'd like you to see this lesser version of events—not on TV. Show you firsthand what the fun is all about. If it's that important to you, we don't have to go together," he added. "You drive, I'll drive, but you really should see this."

Elizabeth couldn't think of a good reason to say no. Maybe they'd find the opportunity to talk later. As if she didn't already feel nause-ated again, instead of going back to bed, she changed into fresh clothes then searched her closet for a pair of boots. And here she was, half an hour later, parked several cars behind Dallas's truck on the verge of the driveway at the Sutherland ranch.

As she walked with him across the yard to-ward the outdoor arena filled with boys and girls all eager to ride, or whatever they did at a kids' rodeo, Elizabeth stayed several paces behind. Though she tried to hide her mis-givings, her disapproval sounded clearly in her tone. Dallas knew how she felt about the sport. "How long have the kids been doing this?"

His voice was low. "Don't know. I wasn't here."

And Dallas wouldn't stay longer than the end of this summer. She tried not to let that panic her. This was a first. She'd never been pregnant before without Harry to share the experience. What would Dallas say when she found the nerve to tell him?

In the ring, Logan from the Circle H looked harried without his brother, who was now in Kedar with Olivia, as he tried to bring order to chaos. Children clamored for his attention, shouted and laughed, and a number of parents crowded around, a few with the same uneasy expression Elizabeth was sure she must be wearing. And Jordan wasn't even here.

"Are the events the same as in professional rodeo?" she asked.

"Not likely," Dallas said. "There are no bulls."

On the other side of the ring, Hadley had Dallas's niece and nephew, the twins, by the hands and, his face intent, was showing them a calf. "That little Hereford is a surrogate steer for today, and last time I checked—" he glanced at a trailer rig parked nearby "—no one around here was raising sheep, but I guess Cooper must have found someone. I count two, three, four, no, five right there."

The side of the truck hitched in front of the trailer read The Carter Farm. That must be Becca's father's rig. Elizabeth didn't see Becca, though.

She glanced at Dallas. "What do they do with the sheep?"

He grinned. "Ride 'em. Instead of bulls or broncs. We call that mutton bustin'."

"Really." Elizabeth inhaled the gamy-smelling air, then wrinkled her nose. "No, thanks."

"You're glad your boy's in Colorado, right?" He was still smiling, but her lips had firmed.

"If Jordan was here, my day would be even more of a challenge."

"I'll make a believer of you." Striding in front of her, Dallas led the way through the throng of local ranchers and their families. She knew most of them and, when she stopped to say hi to Jenna, Dallas moved on to approach some men, many of them fathers with kids on their shoulders or in their arms.

"How are you today?" Jenna asked.

Elizabeth hesitated, wondering if she should tell Jenna, then decided against it. She needed to talk to Dallas first. "Much better. I didn't mean to worry you last night."

Jenna glanced toward Dallas. "Did you two come together? I can't imagine you at a rodeo otherwise. You must have been dragged."

"No, we…happened to park near each other. Jordan's been so insistent about this, I decided to see for myself while he's away."

"A bigger crowd today," Jenna said, "with our local celebrity here. Wonder if he'll sign autographs?" She fanned her face. "Um, I'm wild about Hadley, and Dallas is my brother-in-law, but that is one good-looking man. Must run in the family."

Dallas was also a happy force of nature, so different from Elizabeth, who fretted over everything, including what other people might be thinking. She worried about his reaction when she found the courage to tell him about the baby. It was a good thing she'd driven herself today instead of riding with him. "The kids look so excited," she managed. "I can't imagine my mother allowing me to play cowgirl. Different times," she said.

"Different moms." Jenna's gaze tracked Harry's daughter Emmie, who'd been lifted onto a calf's back and was being led around by Logan. "I saw your mother yesterday at the Bon Appetit having lunch with Bernice Caldwell. They play mah-jongg every week, they said."

Elizabeth rolled her eyes. "They're bosom buddies, aren't they? I don't know which of them is harder to deal with." *Or more critical*, she added silently.

Jenna took her arm. "The first event's starting. Let's get a seat on the fence over there."

The kids' rodeo was a casual affair. In the mutton busting, the competitors' time and score counted but hardly mattered—everyone got a prize. Elizabeth was relieved to see that even on this hot summer day, they all wore helmets, long-sleeved shirts and jeans for protection. Soon, she stopped thinking about the speech she had to give Dallas. Several boys went head over heels off the sheep, which stopped on a dime then ran off around the ring. Luckily, one parent was permitted to be in the arena to supervise and, if necessary, intervene so no one got hurt. Dallas stood nearby, observing, giving pointers and shouting encouragement.

He'd been right. It was nothing like the rodeo Elizabeth had watched on TV with him. The people here were noisy too, but there was a generally festive, good-natured air that didn't come across as well on-screen. Elizabeth cheered along with everyone else.

After the event, Dallas strolled over to the fence and said hi to Jenna too.

"You're a great teacher," Elizabeth said, a bit breathless. Beside her, Jenna shot her an interested glance, then focused on the center of the ring where the pint-size entrants had lined up and were taking bows, none of them in sync.

Dallas grinned. "Wait till you see the next event." It involved the adorable calves, all of which had bright red ribbons now tied to their tails. There was a lot of swishing of flies and some bovine bellowing as the sun climbed overhead into the noon sky, increasing the heat and humidity. And the smells. Elizabeth mopped at her forehead but couldn't look away from the action. As the first calf took off running, so did the first contestant.

After saying, "It's not calf roping or tie-down, but it'll do," Dallas left the fence rail to again monitor the goings-on in the ring.

Jenna explained, "The idea is to chase down the calf, then grab the ribbon. Each child who does wins a few bucks."

Elizabeth edged even nearer to Jenna as they watched the last boy—or, no, that was a girl—sprint like a gazelle the length of the arena then hold up her ribbon, clear triumph in her eyes. Elizabeth laughed. "Good for her!"

She'd joined in the fun, but she wasn't about to let Jordan ride sheep or chase calves, though nothing seemed as dangerous as she'd expected. She wondered if it had become more a matter of not wanting her son to have that connection with Dallas. She didn't want Jordan to feel disappointed when Dallas left. By the time the rodeo ended, she had to admit she'd enjoyed herself. Most of all, she'd liked watching Dallas sign autographs, taking time to bend down and talk to each child in the line just as he'd made each of them feel special during the guidance he'd given them about the events. The kids all gazed up at him as if he'd truly hung the moon.

As Elizabeth walked to her car, Dallas fell into step beside her.

"You're quite the celebrity," she said.

"Maybe I was. My star's not on the rise these days…but it will be again."

Another reminder she didn't need that he'd be gone soon, but she regretted having to walk with space between them now as if she were ashamed of being seen with him. That wasn't fair to Dallas. Neither was keeping her news from him, but now didn't seem to be the right place after all, and she needed time to get used to the idea herself, to rehearse exactly what to say. "Are you worried about getting back into competition?"

"It's not like mutton bustin', that's for sure. And unlike these kids," he admitted, "I get sick before I ride."

"You do? Really?" He always seemed so confident and in charge of himself.

"Every time."

"Know how I cope with stress? Ice cream," she said. Last night had been dulce de leche.

Dallas laughed, then changed the subject. "Did the kids help you see things my way about our rodeo?"

"It's not ours. It's yours," she insisted. "But this was really fun."

Dallas was undeterred. "Then what would you say to a junior rodeo to go with the adult version we're planning?" His slow grin warmed her clear through. "We'll make more money for charity, plus the kids will have a blast."

She sighed. "Since this rodeo is growing like Topsy, what about other competitions, even a chili cook-off—"

"Clara would like that."

"—maybe garden produce and baked goods too."

Dallas agreed that would make for a great

day. "Jams, jellies," he said. "Sawyer mentioned those."

Elizabeth hadn't planned on getting even more involved, and in spite of the good time she'd had, she was glad Jordan wasn't here.

Which didn't let Elizabeth off the hook with Dallas.

She had to tell him she was pregnant. Just not now.

CHAPTER NINE

"YOU WON'T RECONSIDER?" Dallas asked the guy on his cell phone on Monday morning. "It's for a good cause."

"But it's not a sanctioned rodeo." The stock contractor wasn't having any part of Dallas's plans, not that he should be surprised. Half a dozen previous calls, not just today, had ended the same way. Without cows and bulls, there wouldn't be much of a rodeo, sanctioned or not. "Sorry, buddy. Wish I could help but I can't. Besides, the date you have in mind won't work."

"What if I change the date? I'm not wedded to it." Except he knew Lizzie wanted her kids there. A surprise treat for them, if not her, at the end of summer.

"My stock's all spoken for," the guy said. "Hope to see you on the circuit, Dallas."

"Yeah," he said, "right. But I hate to disappoint the good folks of Barren."

"If I could fit you in, I would. I'm full up with contracts through December."

Dallas hung up, then studied the ground under his feet. He scuffed at the dirt with the toe of his boot, the oldest pair he owned because work at the McMann ranch was dusty.

His brother came around the corner of the barn. "You planning to get anything done today? Or just stand there, admiring your Justins?"

"They're not Justin Boots." Dallas lifted his gaze to meet Hadley's eyes. He couldn't wear any brand except the one in his endorsement contract. "They're Prestige."

Hadley snorted. "You've been on that phone all morning. Doing what? Moving stocks and bonds around? Making investments?"

"Trying to find rodeo stock," he said. "I've got a venue—at last—thanks to you and Clara, and some cowboys, but nothing for them to ride, rope or bulldog. Maybe this thing isn't going to happen after all."

"Huh. The sunshine boy sees a few clouds? I don't suppose any contractor's willing to ship stock to a place like this even for charity. I suppose you had the funds to pay but—"

"Hadley, you seem to think I'm a billionaire or something. I'm not. I had a good stash and have some investments, but they're not liquid, and a big chunk of what I saved is gone."

Hadley nodded. "Your parents, huh?" He knew they were Dallas's chief concern.

"Yep. I wouldn't change that." He massaged the lingering slight ache in his hip. At least the cane now lived in a closet, and he'd cut his rehab to twice a week. "I can't ride yet—even I know that—so I thought this would keep me from losing my mind until I can get back on the circuit." And after last weekend, he kept expecting Lizzie to bail on him, leaving him to plan this thing on his own. Sure, she'd had a good time at the kids' rodeo, even when she probably hadn't wanted to, but he sensed something else was bothering her.

Hadley frowned. "So, what, now you're a quitter? I almost drove away from this ranch not that long ago. I know how it feels to be down and out, deep inside yourself." He spread his hands. "Look at me now, with a wife and kids. You ever consider retirement? How many years, how many seasons are you willing to risk yourself like that? Even without the money you'd like to earn, you'll find a way to take care of your folks."

Dallas studied his boots again. "I'm not ready to retire. I'm not looking to get married or, heaven forbid, have kids." Which made him think of the children's rodeo. Between events, Dallas had kept his eye on Lizzie, and he'd seen her cheer more than once, heard her laugh, which was like the soft tinkle of bells. And yet, with him, she kept her distance. He'd thought the awkwardness from May had eased, but maybe it hadn't. "I won't quit before I've made my mark." He hesitated. "I'm never going to wind up like our birth parents—"

"You won't, Dallas. We never will, and you have the Maguires."

"I do," he said, but that didn't stop the memories he tried to ignore. In a heartbeat he was back there again, not with his birth family and their desperate addictions, but in that foster home, trapped in a locked room, hungry and afraid. Dallas drew a sharp breath. He didn't want to delve into that, and Hadley must have seen the pained look on his face.

"You can take care of yourself now." When

Dallas didn't respond, Hadley sighed. "What kind of stock do you need?"

"Everything."

"I doubt anyone has a bucking bull to lend you, but then again, there's my Angus out there in that pasture." Hadley pointed toward his pride and joy. "Any bull will buck, given the right encouragement."

"Yeah, and keep on bucking, come after any rider that dares to get on him. Rodeo bulls are specialists at payback." Especially his nemesis, Greased Lightning.

Hadley went on anyway. "What about Sutherland's new bull? He's a beauty. Mean as a snake—Ned, I mean, not his bull." Having made his little joke about Nell's grandfather, he slapped Dallas on the back. "Help me shovel manure out of these stalls, then we'll pay some calls."

ELIZABETH WAS JUST putting her tote bag in the office that morning when someone swept through the front entrance of Olivia's shop, banging the door against the wall. "We're not open," she called, but light footsteps kept coming across the showroom. Couldn't people read signs? She shouldn't have left the door unlocked. Unless… "Becca? Is that you?"

Her coworker had yet to come in, and she'd called in sick once last week. Elizabeth hadn't seen her at the kids' rodeo on Saturday. Although concerned by her own persistent nausea, she was also beginning to worry about the girl. Just then, her own mother appeared in the office doorway, her mouth pursed.

"Are you out of your mind, Elizabeth?"

Her mouth went dry. She pushed past Claudia into the main part of the store, not wanting to get trapped behind Olivia's desk. She wouldn't pretend to misunderstand. "No, and I'm not in the habit of attending rodeo." She should have known word would get around. No matter how far apart she and Dallas had kept, there couldn't be enough space in this world between them.

"I'm not talking about that silly business at the NLS. I could care less if every child in town, other than my grandchildren, wants to ride some ridiculous sheep or chase cows—"

"They were calves."

"—but I do care for your reputation. What were you thinking, Elizabeth, gadding about with that *cowboy*?" So this wasn't really about the rodeo.

Elizabeth tried for an equally icy tone. She wasn't her mother's daughter for nothing. "If you're referring to Dallas Maguire, yes, we were in the same place at the same time. That's all."

Claudia paced the floor, oblivious of the fragile items on the tables, sweeping out a hand to make her point. "I had coffee at the café five minutes ago, and every busybody in Barren must be eager to let me know that my daughter—after we were all disgraced less than a year ago—is apparently 'keeping company' with that man." She took a breath. "The source of that quaint term was none other than—"

"Let me guess. Bernice." The biggest gossip in town, except for Doc Baxter's wife.

"We're friends, which makes her comment all the more hurtful. Bernice was trying to warn me, and she meant well—"

"Warn you? Mother, there's nothing between me and Dallas Maguire." Well, that was a lie she hoped would not be uncovered anytime soon.

"Don't fib to me, Elizabeth." As if she

knew Dallas wanted to be friends, and he was already more than that, though *baby daddy* didn't seem to suit, even when it was true. Her mother spun around, nearly knocking a Tiffany vase off a table. "People are beginning to whisper. Do you have no regard for my position, if not yours?"

Claudia didn't know the half of it. But this was not a new strain between them. All her life Elizabeth had been the one to take the brunt of her mother's unhappiness. Claudia's own divorce had devasted her—she'd never gotten over the humiliation she'd felt then. Reputation was everything to Claudia. She tended to blame Elizabeth for every bump in the road, as if she had driven her dad away.

"I know how disappointed you are in me, Mom, for becoming a divorced woman with three young children to raise." She remembered Dallas's comment. *I wouldn't do anything to harm you—or your kids*. "But that's my reality." And it would only get worse once she spoke to Dallas. "I wish you could lend me support rather than this constant criticism of everything I do."

No wonder she'd been reluctant to leave her house. Bernice watching from across the street couldn't compare to Claudia Monroe under full sail, but her mother's rejection hurt worse. Still, the decision to let Dallas talk her into attending last Saturday's rodeo fell on her. And of course, so did that afternoon in May.

"My reason for watching the children's rodeo was in part because I wanted to see what attracts Jordan—or anyone else." Including Dallas. It was time to make her stand before this new pregnancy became yet another issue. "Also, in case you haven't heard, Dallas is putting on an adult rodeo for charity. Possibly, you could give us suggestions as to which organization would be appropriate. I've agreed to help him as much as I can."

"Help—how?"

"I might as well make use of the experience I gained with Harry. All those rummage sales, raffles, the work on his campaign." Elizabeth could see she'd shocked her mother. "I do know how to get things done. It's useless to try to keep my life as private as I'd like."

"The proximity worries me," Claudia said. "You're a vulnerable woman and he—"

"Is an attractive man. But Mother, I have

all I can do to get through my days right now, and once the children are home my hands will be even fuller. Believe me, a romance with anyone, especially Dallas, is the furthest thing from my mind. Or his," she added. "He won't be here long, so you needn't worry. I'll handle the back-office part while he attends to the actual event."

"And where would that be?"

"Clara McMann's ranch."

Her mother's face settled into deeper lines of disapproval just as Elizabeth saw Bernice Caldwell pass the front window. A quick check of the clock told her it was a few minutes after ten. The shop was now officially open for business, and she stood arguing with her difficult mother. But at least one silence had been broken.

"Mom, your friend is here. No doubt she'll have her opinions, but I wish you'd believe me as much as you believe her."

IN SILENCE, BECCA trailed Calvin through the rooms of a small bungalow for rent, but her footsteps dragged, and for days she'd felt incredibly weary. Today she'd missed work again. A sense of disloyalty followed her from the living room through the kitchen—much smaller than she was used to on the farm— then on into the first of two bedrooms.

Becca surveyed the room's layout. A big bed occupied the wall opposite the double closet, where she could almost imagine her clothes hanging beside Calvin's.

She'd never felt this way before about anyone, and his work at the McMann ranch, outdoors in the summer sun all day, had gradually replaced his former pallor with a tan. His dark hair had a few highlights now, and Becca resisted an urge to sweep a stubborn lock off his forehead. "Well?" he said.

She lowered her voice. The Realtor stood nearby, not that close but still able to hear their conversation. "It's cute, but I think we should keep looking."

"You don't like this house? I like it." He peered past her through the window. "Small but way better than my apartment above the hardware store. We won't have to buy much furniture, and there's a good-sized yard out back. We could fence it and get a dog."

Calvin slipped an arm around her shoulders. Becca automatically leaned into his strength, inhaling the scent of his aftershave, spicy yet not overpowering. He was her first real boyfriend, but were they taking things too fast? Only a short time ago, she'd thought she couldn't move out of her family's home quick enough to be with him, and now she was having second thoughts. "You were the one who wanted to do this," he said.

But was she ready, after all, to leave her father? The notion of his living alone broke her heart. Who would cook for him? Share cleaning chores and laundry? Sit with him in the evenings while they watched television and tried to figure out who'd really murdered the victim on *The First 48*? Every night, he'd be sleeping in the house without her there. She was already gone more than he liked. Would he feel abandoned? Or worse? She knew what he thought of Calvin.

He edged toward the hallway. "Let's talk outside." He glanced at the Realtor. "We'll be back in a minute. Want to take a look at the yard."

The woman wore a faint frown, as if she too sensed Becca's new hesitation.

The outdoor space was big, though there were bare spots in the lawn under the large maple tree. "There'll be good shade," she pointed out, "but the grass needs work."

"Becca, I thought you wanted to live together. Now I can tell you're not sure."

She drew a breath. "Calvin, let's not jump into this, okay? There might be a house closer to Clara's so you wouldn't have to drive as far every day to work and I'd be near my dad's."

His gaze sharpened. "Why? So you could run home to him whenever something's not going right with us?"

"I'm worried he'll feel lonely."

"Okay, but he doesn't like me. I know I made some poor decisions, but I did what the law required, Becca." His mouth tightened. "I may not be a big prize, and I don't have much, but if we pool what we each make, we'll have our start. Or don't you really care about me?"

"I love you, Calvin. But we shouldn't rush into anything."

"That's a mixed message. And I'm not good at reading those," he said.

Becca's stomach churned. "It's not as if everyone in Barren wants to rent this house. I like it okay, but let's wait a few days. See if we feel the same way about it then before we tell the Realtor we've decided." A dozen scenarios kept running through her mind. What if she moved in with him and they couldn't agree on anything? Like this place right now? And signing a lease with Calvin might send her dad over the edge.

Calvin looked at the ground. "You know what? You sound like Willow Bodine."

Becca's best friend. "That's not fair."

"But you know how she and Cody were. Her dad wasn't keen on him either, and that's partly why they broke up. Maybe that rubbed off on you. Fine," he said, throwing out a hand in defeat then starting back toward the house.

Becca stood there a moment before she followed, as if a dark shroud had dropped around her shoulders, weighing her down. A fresh bout of nausea threatened. She hadn't meant to ruin things, but this was a huge step and maybe she hadn't thought it through. Without his embrace, more exhausted than she'd been when he picked her up tonight, she felt cold, alone.

The Realtor was standing at the back door, gazing out into the yard. Calvin climbed the steps ahead of Becca. He muttered, "Let's not do this, then. I wouldn't want you to make the wrong decision."

CHAPTER TEN

"YOU OKAY?" AT THE picnic table in Lizzie's backyard she and Dallas were supposed to be discussing the rodeo—a business meeting—but she didn't seem to be paying attention tonight. Even in the dim light, she looked pale and wan, worried, and Dallas saw that same distance in her eyes as he had at the kids' rodeo.

She yawned. "Sorry, I never seem to get enough sleep. Becca and I spend the first hour at work each day trying to stay awake. And I talked to the kids this morning. When I mentioned cleaning house before they come home, Seth said, 'You didn't throw out my stuffies?' Then Jordan whined about spending his summer with the *baby*, and Stella wouldn't even speak to me at first." Lizzie moved her glass of herbal iced tea around on the table. "Then I made the mistake of asking about Harry. They all said he was downstairs but would be right back. There's apparently a Starbucks in the resort lobby." She sighed. "I was upset that he'd left them alone, but Stella finally said, 'We're big enough to take care of each other,' and all I could think was— without me."

She kept shooting looks toward her driveway, the street and the house on the other side where her nosy neighbor lived. Dallas didn't buy her explanation. "What else?" he asked.

Her unhappy gaze met his. "When I told Stella I disagreed about Harry leaving them alone, Jordan piped up, 'He doesn't care, Mom,' with an air of disdain that sounded remarkably like Harry. 'You're divorced,' he told me. 'Dad can do what he wants.'"

"Aw, Lizzie." She couldn't keep him from thinking of her that way, and he couldn't keep the name from coming out now. Dallas tried to take her hand, but she drew back.

Her mouth turned down. "Harry has too much time in a different state to indoctrinate them, turn them against me." Her eyes flashed. "I won't be his pawn to move around on the chessboard, giving him an advantage. The kids are vulnerable, open to suggestion, eager to please their father, who was largely missing from their lives last winter and this past spring, which doesn't give Harry the right now to subvert my role as their mother."

"I'm sure they don't see it that way."

She rubbed the frown line between her brows. "Why am I telling you my troubles? The worst part is, I almost ruined my surprise and told them about your rodeo as a bribe, which I've never done. I felt tempted, though. Jordan was greatly impressed when you moved in next door, and before he left for Colorado, I know he peppered you with questions."

"He did," Dallas agreed with a smile.

"I could have handled the call better, but on top of all that, last night I nuked a frozen meal for dinner—only to discover later it was well past its use-by date." He saw something else in her expression, and for a moment she paused. "I don't feel that well today, enough to put me off my game."

"If you're not up to talking business tonight, we can postpone the discussion." *Again*, he thought. Elizabeth had canceled before to attend her women's meeting.

"No," she said, "I'd rather be distracted." She pushed a sheet of paper across the table to him. "About your rodeo, I made this list of people to approach as possible sponsors, and because I couldn't sleep last night I drafted a press release to start the PR push."

"What else?" he asked, because obviously there was more that troubled her.

"My mother and I had words about the rodeo last week—about you, actually."

He glanced at the list on the table next to her untouched glass of iced tea. He'd read it later after he pried the truth from Lizzie. Was the problem tonight her ongoing concern about public exposure?

She inhaled sharply. "Dallas, there's, um, something I need to tell you."

His gut churned. "I can guess you're a breath away from saying you can't help after all. Leaving me to do all the planning. Don't. We still need to designate a charity," he rushed on so she wouldn't get the chance to pull out, "and everything doesn't happen at once."

Her shoulders slumped. "Do you ever get discouraged? You must be the sunniest person I've ever known," she mumbled, as if he wouldn't be once she explained some issue. "Dallas—"

"No, you're beating yourself up right now

because your mother doesn't approve of the rodeo or, especially, *me*." Maybe she was right about that. "What's the worst Bernice, or anyone else, can think?"

She briefly closed her eyes. "That we're doing more than talking, that we already—"

His voice tightened. "Well, let me tell you something. Most people aren't that concerned, or even interested, in what we do. They're too caught up in themselves. Why not look ahead instead of back?" He finished his tea then set the glass down.

"I'm trying," she said. "And, yes, I know I'm whining."

Dallas looked over his shoulder. "I don't see a crowd, do you?"

"No," she admitted, "but that doesn't mean there won't be once—" She broke off. "This town's full of people who *don't* focus on themselves. My mother is only too happy to let me know who's been talking."

"You'll have to confront that someday. Her, I mean. Why not now?" *While I'm here willing to act as a buffer?*

"I did try." Lizzie gazed at him for a long moment. "Why aren't you married, Dallas?

You'd make someone the best husband. And a good father—"

"Husband? Father? Me?" He ran a hand through his hair. "I'm not married because I had a lousy set of parents before I went to live with the Maguires. My dear old dad was a dealer, and I don't mean cars. My mom was an addict too—match made in heaven, right?—and I'm *never* going down the road they traveled."

"From what I've heard, you had a loving home with the Maguires. You're in no danger, Dallas, of falling into the same kind of life your actual parents led."

"That's what Hadley said." He looked away. Sometimes he worried about that, one reason he'd seldom taken the pain pills his doctors prescribed after his accident. "But they hurt people. They abandoned us." And then, for his brother, it got worse. "I was luckier than Hadley, yeah, and until I saw him again last Christmas, I thought I'd gotten past that early stuff." He shut off the about-to-gush spigot of memory, pressing his lips tight.

"Yes," Lizzie said, "your brother had a worse upbringing than you did—or, rather, no upbringing—yet Jenna loves him as much as he loves her."

He couldn't seem to help the flat tone of his voice. The subject of marriage, kids, made him twitch. "Yeah, well, I'm fine the way I am. Single. No dependents like Hadley has with Grace and Luke. And Jenna. Except, of course, for my folks. I'll be on the road again soon, and I'm not going to stop until I earn enough to care of them all their lives." And enough to take care of the family he *might* have *someday*, but Dallas didn't add that.

Lizzie only stared at him until he had to blink. "I understand—about your career too—but don't you also want a good relationship? For yourself? Whether or not that includes children?"

He wondered where this was going. He felt as if there were a sudden noose around his neck. He'd never been serious about a woman and wasn't going to start now, even if the woman sitting across from him appealed to him. More than she should. "Why do you care if I get married or not? Or have a family?" Dallas reached for the pitcher of tea. "I thought we were talking about this rodeo. You in or out, Lizzie?" He could virtually see her decide not to say whatever else was obviously on her mind and had been since the kids' rodeo.

"In," she said, and his bones turned to water. "You need me more than I imagined."

WITH A GROAN, Elizabeth rolled over in bed. Normally she had a cast-iron stomach. When the kids brought a bug home from school, she rarely caught it. Even Harry, who'd never tended to a sick child, had often suffered instead. Now her morning nausea had become an unwelcome friend with the fatigue that made her want to cover her head with the blankets and try to sleep it off. Which wasn't likely considering her pregnancy.

The doorbell's sudden chime made her feel worse. "No," she said aloud, "not this early."

Was Dallas at the front door again with more plans for the rodeo? His enthusiasm was contagious, and she'd certainly stepped into the event with both feet last night. The soft yearning she'd seen in his eyes, the obvious pain caused by his birth parents—and that must be only half the story—had done the trick. That, and her own cowardice. She wanted to do the right thing. She'd tried several times to tell him about this baby, but then Dallas had claimed he wasn't marriage material or a great prospect as a father, and she'd lost whatever nerve she had. He might not want a family, yet she guessed he needed *something*.

When the bell rang again, she flung back the covers, stood without thinking, and another wave of nausea rolled through her. Elizabeth clung to the bedpost until her stomach settled, then grabbed yesterday's jeans and tunic. Taking no time to comb her hair, she flew down the stairs.

Not quite to her surprise, instead of Dallas, Bernice was trying to see through the frosted side glass in the front door. Elizabeth unlocked then opened it. With bleary eyes, she studied the Pyrex dish in the other woman's hands before Bernice walked into the house as if she'd been invited. "I've brought my special breakfast casserole."

The very thought of food roiled her stomach again. "That was thoughtful of you, but I'm not hungry."

Bernice, brown-haired and brown-eyed, was already bustling down the hall to the kitchen. With a sinking feeling, Elizabeth went after her. *What do you want?* She could guess the answer to that. Several times this summer Bernice had shown up with such an offering, her way of getting into the house. *Who is the young man who just moved in?* she'd asked her first visit. And more recently she'd suggested, *With Harry and the children gone, you must be lonely.*

Bernice shoved the casserole into Elizabeth's microwave, found the coffee canister and set the machine to brew. While Elizabeth looked helplessly on, she pulled mugs from the upper cupboard, plates from the lower one, obviously familiar with the layout of Elizabeth's kitchen. "My appetite's never good before coffee either," Bernice said, assessing Elizabeth's pale face, "but I can see that with everyone away you're not eating well."

She couldn't deny that. She was trying to keep her last meal down right now. "You're probably right."

The microwave dinged. While Bernice poured coffee then served, Elizabeth did her best not to bolt for the bathroom. She refused the coffee, then nudged her plate aside. "Bernice, I'm in a bit of a rush today. I'll save these eggs—"

"With ham, onion, cheese, a touch of *fine herbes*…" As a longtime widow, and with no job, without grandchildren to spoil, Bernice likely had time on her hands, and Elizabeth figured cooking, when she didn't eat out, was better than Bernice watching out her window. Still, Elizabeth didn't care to become her latest project. Nor was Bernice alone. Her mother was part of that club.

Trying to remember her manners, Elizabeth rose. "I wish I could chat, but I really need to get to work."

Bernice touched her arm. "Before you go, I just want to say I think Harry did you a terrible disservice. Your mother doesn't agree, and I also used to think he was an outstanding mayor, a model husband and father, but…"

"That wasn't true." Elizabeth dropped into her chair again. *All right, let's get this out in the open.* After Bernice left, she'd have to call Becca to say she'd be late. "What's on your mind, Bernice? Mom says you mean well, but you've made a habit of crossing the street to probe about one subject or another ever since Harry moved out."

Bernice cut her portion of the casserole into ever smaller pieces. "I was happy to see someone rent the Whittaker house but… really, Elizabeth? I've seen Mr. Maguire cutting your grass. I heard voices only last night—"

"What?" Elizabeth said sharply. As she'd suspected, even sitting in her backyard with Dallas hadn't worked to avoid prying eyes. At Olivia's shop she'd tried to defuse such interest in Dallas from her mother, but Bernice needed the same line drawn in the sand. "It's not enough that my entire life turned upside down—because of Harry—or that, yes, I'm the subject of everyone's constant scrutiny, but it seems people aren't just talking. They're *spying*."

Bernice bristled. "I've done no such thing."

Elizabeth wouldn't dignify that with an answer. How often had she seen Bernice at her window, the draperies pulled back, peering out across the street? It was a wonder she didn't use a pair of binoculars. Perhaps she did. "I don't need to be watched—or minded like a five-year-old. If you have questions about me and Dallas Maguire, ask them. Bernice, please, go ahead. I'm sure my mother will hear a report from you before I leave for work."

Bernice's eyes snapped. "How dare you speak to me this way. This is a quiet neighborhood. Hardworking people, families, don't need such goings-on on this street. Near my own house!"

Elizabeth was shaking so hard her teeth threatened to click together. "I did nothing wrong, not when I was married to Harry and he was cheating behind my back, and not after our divorce. Last night Dallas and I were working together on his rodeo, a charity event to benefit this town. He doesn't have to do that. He could let his injuries heal until he's ready to go back to the rodeo circuit, spend time with his brother instead, but he wants to contribute—and I'm helping, which my mother already knows, so I can save you the trip to see her. Or did *she* tell you?"

Neither of them had eaten a bite of Bernice's casserole, and their two coffee cups were still full. "You would do far better to keep company with my son," Bernice said. "He's a respected citizen in this community and Barney's not going anywhere."

"Worse luck for him," Elizabeth said. Bernice's bachelor son, who'd been a vice president at the Barren Cattlemen's Bank for years, had quit to seek a different pursuit, but he still lived with his mother, who monitored his every action too.

And there was that phrase again. *Keeping company.* Ah, but at least now they'd gotten to the true reason for this morning's visit. "You may be my mother's friend, but that does not give you permission to insult me or Dallas." This time she rose from her chair and stayed standing, her pulse hammering hard enough to make her breathless. "I'm tempted to throw you out of this house and never open my door to you again."

In a huff, Bernice pushed past her, then down the hall. "I definitely will tell your mother how I've been treated here. I only came to caution you not to make a spectacle of yourself—but I was wrong to give you the benefit of the doubt. I now agree with her that you must be exactly the reason Harry strayed."

She charged out the door, leaving Elizabeth to wonder how much worse things would get once Dallas, then the whole town, learned she was pregnant.

"Do you want to take the rest of the day off, Becca?" Certainly, Elizabeth did. Bernice's first-thing-in-the-morning vitriol had made Elizabeth's stomach finally revolt and she'd gotten to work after ten, but she only got a shrug for an answer now from Becca.

"No, I'm just…tired."

Elizabeth could identify with that. She wanted to lie down on an antique sofa and sleep until closing time. She envisioned Bernice at her mother's house, venting her displeasure over Elizabeth's behavior. "Are you sure?" she asked Becca. At least one of them should get an afternoon off, though that was becoming a habit for Becca.

The girl shrugged again then went into the storeroom, where Elizabeth could soon hear her sniffling, but, with Olivia in far-off Kedar, Elizabeth shouldn't pursue the matter right now. She had to run the shop and deal with the rug orders for the women's cooperative.

Becca wasn't being helpful. Could Elizabeth manage on her own? Had she been out of her mind to keep on with Dallas's rodeo? Could she really handle what amounted to two jobs?

Finally, Becca emerged from the other room, her eyes red and puffy, a soggy tissue in her hand. She shot a look at the only customer in the store, who was reexamining for the fourth time an overstuffed Chesterfield sofa. Elizabeth sighed. Becca was going to be no help at all until she talked about whatever was troubling her.

Elizabeth walked over to their customer. "I'm going to take a short break." To deal with her coworker, though she wouldn't say that. "This sofa is gorgeous, and I can arrange delivery for you. We offer white-glove service. If I'm not back when you're ready to buy, rap on the office door." She read the tag. "It's a great price. I wouldn't pass this piece up."

The woman glanced at her. "Yes, but I'm still thinking. Hoping it will go on sale."

Elizabeth left her to ponder her decision. She led Becca toward the back but, at Olivia's desk, Becca remained silent. She picked at a hangnail, and Elizabeth's heart went out to her. From her first day, she had sensed a connection with Becca, an instinct to nurture as she would Stella or the boys.

"You're not worried about this job, are you?"

As the stand-in manager, Elizabeth didn't have the authority to fire anyone.

"Actually, without Olivia here, my stomach doesn't even hurt." Becca studied the ceiling. "But what do I know? I'm really no better at this than I was answering phones at the clinic or waiting tables at the café." She gestured at the outer room. "I tried to sell that lady the old sofa, which has a totally outrageous price, but you stepped in and made her think she was getting a bargain."

A few footsteps told Elizabeth the woman was still out there. "I don't mean to pry, Becca, and we haven't known each other long, but you're obviously troubled. I know things could become awkward if you feel you've said too much when we have to work together, but I am a good listener. I wouldn't repeat anything you say. If there's some way I can help—"

"I've never been friends with an older woman."

Elizabeth tried not to take offense. "Not that old," she murmured, "but all right. I do respect your privacy." Clearly, Becca didn't intend to unburden herself. "I'll get back to our customer then, see if I can sweet-talk her into the Chesterfield—"

She didn't finish before Becca held up a hand. "I shouldn't have said that, Elizabeth. It's not even the job." Tears welled in her eyes. "I lost my mom last year, and I miss her so much."

Elizabeth reached for a tissue on the desk. "Here, sweetie. Oh, Becca. That's hard."

"I can't even bear to think she's not here."

Elizabeth choked up too. "I think I know how you must feel. Last winter I had a miscarriage at four months. I wanted the baby so much, and I still miss it. I always will."

"I'm sorry, Elizabeth. My dad misses Mom all the time too. He doesn't have anything now except the farm and the roses, which were hers." Becca managed a watery smile. "A while ago, I signed him up on a dating site, but he won't respond to any of the women who liked his profile."

"Which you must have written," Elizabeth said, risking a weak smile of her own.

"I wanted to make him feel better, but I don't ever seem to do the right thing!" Fresh tears welled again, then started to fall. "And

I'm a total wreck today. Calvin and I kind of had a fight. I'm afraid we're going to break up." She began to sob.

Elizabeth hoped their customer couldn't hear. She patted her shoulder. "Let's try to find some perspective. Do you want to talk about Calvin?" She made a motion of zipping her lip.

A long silence followed. Elizabeth could hear the shop's customer moving around the display room, probably examining similar pieces and other price tags. Her footsteps returned to the area where the Chesterfield sofa sat in the alcove staged to resemble a Victorian drawing room. Elizabeth really should check on the potential sale. Yet Becca was talking now. She couldn't leave her.

"I love Calvin so much. I thought he loved me too. We were going to live together. We've sort of talked about getting married. Then we looked at this house to rent, and something went wrong. I thought we should look around more, and I worry about my dad being alone if I move out, but Calvin didn't understand how I feel. He said he didn't want me to make the wrong decision, but he sounded mad. I don't know what to do."

"I see. You've been under a lot of stress, Becca. Maybe you should talk to your doctor. You don't want that tummyache to come back—"

"It's not an ache, more like queasy, and I couldn't work the other day. It wasn't the first time. Honest, I was surprised Olivia didn't fire me before she left." She buried her face in her hands. "I'm such a mess—happy one minute, mixed up the next. I never used to cry." She sobbed harder. "And I just want to sleep all the time."

Elizabeth's pulse lurched. Yes, she was an *older woman*, at least in Becca's mind, but that gave her experience. She'd had three children and, only months ago, had lost another. Now Elizabeth was carrying the baby Dallas didn't know about. Possibly she was off base here, but this didn't sound like stress, grief or depression over a job Becca didn't love. The same signs Elizabeth had ignored were there in Becca. In this brief conversation, they'd moved from being merely Olivia's employees to mutual confidantes. The question had to be asked.

Elizabeth used her gentlest tone. "Becca, could you be pregnant?"

CHAPTER ELEVEN

ON THIS CLEAR, sun-bright summer day, under a cloudless blue sky, Becca drove home from Barren lost in a dense mental fog. She kept hearing Elizabeth's words. *Could you be pregnant?* Becca hadn't answered. Her heart in her throat, she'd gasped then rushed from the office through the store, nearly knocking over Elizabeth's customer as she ran. She'd ignored Elizabeth's calls to wait. Yet now she sensed the truth.

She was turning onto the driveway at the farm near Farrier when, instead, she pulled over. She couldn't go home yet; she couldn't face her father. He'd see the distress on her face, the tears that threatened to fall again. He'd *know*. Becca turned the car around and drove back through town toward Clara McMann's ranch.

Trying to think what to say to Calvin, she parked beside the barn. She saw him coming from inside, a lead rope in his hand, but he didn't see her at first. On his way to the corral, he had his back turned, and for a moment Becca simply watched as he opened the gate, his quick strides approaching the gray-brown horse that rested in the corner.

"Easy, bud, workday's over," she heard him say, one hand scratching behind the horse's ears. "Until the farrier gets here to replace that shoe, you're on vacation." He led the gelding out of the paddock past Becca, who was standing by the fence. Was he ignoring her? Still angry about the rental house? What would happen when she told him?

"Calvin."

He turned his head, and for an instant she saw his eyes warm. Was he glad to see her? Maybe he wasn't mad, and this wouldn't be that hard. "Hey, Becca. You get a chance to think about the house?" He thought that was why she'd come.

"I need to talk to you," she said. "Not about that."

His voice faded as he walked the horse into the barn. "I'm at work till five."

Becca followed. "Can you spare a few minutes? Please. It's important."

He opened a stall door, stood back while the gelding sashayed inside, then slid the door shut. "We can talk while I refill his water." He walked in front of her to the faucet, fetched a clean pail and turned on the tap. Over his shoulder he sent her a smile. "Now, what's so important you left the antiques place and drove all the way out here on a workday?"

Words failed her. He had no idea how important this was. As she'd done with Elizabeth, Becca burst into tears, which ran down her cheeks like the water flowing into the bucket. She shook her head, kept shaking it.

Calvin shut off the tap, put an arm around her. "Hey," he said again as Becca leaned into him, "you upset because we didn't agree about the house? I don't care where we live. You pick. If you've found another, better place—"

"No." Like her tears, the words spilled over. "Calvin, we're having a baby."

"We… What?" All expression had been wiped from his handsome face, which had turned white under his summer tan.

"I'm pregnant."

Calvin swore under his breath. He dropped his arm from her shoulders. "How do you know? Did you take one of those tests? See a doctor?"

"Not yet," she admitted. "I should have waited, I guess, to tell you. But I'm sure, Calvin." Her stomach had already begun to swell.

His eyes looked haunted. She could almost see his mind racing like a high-speed computer. "But we only...that one time..."

"Yes," she said. She told him about her conversation with Elizabeth, then explained, "But I missed my last cycle and the one before..." She trailed off, not to discuss her symptoms. Her body's changes embarrassed her, as if she had no control of herself. "I'm scared."

"You should be. So am I. What would we do with a baby?"

"What *will* we do," she said, starting to tremble.

"I don't know, and I don't know if I can take this on."

"I wouldn't have told you if I didn't expect you to—" Was he about to break up with her, as she'd feared?

"Your dad won't like this, but he'll bend to protect you. He'll expect us to get married. I don't want to get married, Becca. You shouldn't want to either. We're not ready." He hefted the water bucket, strode past her to the stall and hung it on the hook inside. The gray-brown horse stamped a foot, and Becca heard the water being slurped into its mouth. Calvin had his back to her again, but he couldn't ignore this. "I wasn't keen on our living together, you know that. You talked me into it. Then you chickened out at that rental, so don't try to tell me you can't wait now to have a ring on your finger. I barely make enough to support myself."

"You said we'd have enough if we put our money together."

"If what you're saying is true, this makes everything different. See? It wouldn't be just you and me. There'd be three of us." He turned to her. "What would we be getting ourselves into?"

"We're already in—I was shocked too when Elizabeth guessed about the baby, but we'll be fine, Calvin," she said. "We would have gotten married in time anyway."

"Would we?" Again, he had doubts far worse than hers. "Why are you so into this?"

The day they'd seen the rental house, she'd worried about her father, about sharing her belongings, her life, with Calvin. Now her decision seemed simple. "This baby is a product of our love, a happy change in our lives…"

"Happy for you." He strode past her toward the barn doors.

"I can't believe you're acting like this." She followed him outside and nearly ran into Hadley Smith.

Hadley stepped back. "Pardon, miss. Didn't see you there." His gaze fell on Calvin, whose face was set, his mouth a straight line. "I'm moving cattle from the south pasture. When you're done here, join me."

"Trouble threw a shoe. Dallas took the new horse. There's nothing to ride."

Hadley glanced again at Becca, probably sensing the tension in the air. "Guess I won't need you, then. When you're finished, find something to do. If you can't find anything, ask Clara. She might need help at the house till I get back." He tipped his hat to Becca then disappeared into the barn, where she could hear him saddling and talking to his horse.

"You heard him. I gotta get to work." Calvin took a step before she stopped him.

He looked pointedly at her hand on his forearm. His skin felt warm, almost too warm, but his eyes were cold. "You want me to lose my job?"

He waited until she released his arm, then took a few more steps toward the barn. Hadley was leading his horse out. As one hoof clipped another, the iron shoes rang like bells. Warning bells when she'd expected, hoped, even prayed that Calvin would shelter her, wrap his strong arms around her again and tell her everything would be fine. He loved her and they'd be a family. Instead, he seemed to be rejecting her and their baby. His voice was so quiet she barely heard him.

"I gave you time to make your decision, Becca. Now I need time to make mine."

PASSING BY OLIVIA McCORD ANTIQUES, Dallas saw the lights were still on. The closed sign wasn't on the door yet. He had good news to share, but couldn't wait until he and Lizzie got home. He was also still riding high on her agreement to stick with the rodeo. *You need me more than I imagined.* Their quasi friendship had changed. He'd change it more if he could, but, remembering their talk in her backyard, he shouldn't. She knew his plans to leave Barren for the circuit, to postpone any thought of a serious relationship. Dallas pulled into a parking space then walked into the store. He didn't bother with preliminaries.

"Guess what?"

Lizzie glanced up from the front desk. For a second he saw the same dismay in her eyes he'd glimpsed the other night. "What are you doing here?"

"Hello to you too," he said, undeterred. Nothing would spoil his mood. "Go on, guess."

"I don't know. You've won the lottery? You looked at your bank balance this morning and, what do you know, you're a gazillionaire? You just mowed your lawn, noticed a hump in the backyard grass and dug up a cache of sapphires and emeralds? Pirate gold in the middle of Kansas?"

He smiled. "No, but I wanted to tell you this in person." He crossed the room. "Some of my buddies are on for the rodeo. They're going to contact more guys. Everybody loves our charity aspect. Grey Wilson said he'd lend us some Angus calves for the kids' event, some horses for the adult rodeo. And Fred Miller's lending us a bull from the herd he's gradually liquidating. Hadley's going to buy it afterward."

"Slow down," she said, coming out from behind the counter. "I was just closing up." She flipped the sign around on the door. "Honest, I can't keep up with you."

He followed her around the shop as she tidied the displays and tallied the cash register receipts. "It's going to happen," he said. "And yeah, there were times I wondered if it would. I hope that didn't show." He caught her upper arms, drew her to him. "Confidence, huh?"

She laughed a little. "Your confidence makes me dizzy."

"Guess what else."

"Hmm." One finger to her chin, she pretended to think. "Let's see. You've won Cowboy of the Year."

She was teasing, a good sign. Maybe he hadn't said too much about his birth family in her yard. "National Finals aren't till December. Next year will be my year."

Her answering smile died. "I hope so, but that only reminds me you won't be here then. Which, of course, has nothing to do with me."

Obviously he'd said way too much about his career, though.

She lifted a hand to her forehead. "Actually, this hasn't been my best day. I already had a headache when you came in, and earlier I had a...difficult discussion with a coworker."

With Olivia out of the country, there was only one other person here. "You must mean Becca Carter."

Her eyes widened. "You know Becca?"

"I work with her boyfriend. Apparently, their relationship isn't all smooth sailing. He doesn't know how to deal with her."

"And you know how I feel about gossip. Becca confided in me and *I* can't tell you any more than that."

"It's about him, though, isn't it?" Dallas guessed.

"And does not involve his job." She began to pull away. "Thus, not your concern." She stopped and gazed up at him. "I'm happy about the stock you've found and your friends riding, but today has been hard for another reason besides Becca." Her mouth turned down. "I had a visit this morning from Bernice. She heard us talking outdoors and assumed the worst."

"You're kidding."

"I wish I were." Elizabeth replayed that

conversation. "I sent her packing, and I felt pretty proud of myself, but I'd hoped you and I had kept a low profile. It's one thing to help with your rodeo, another to cause speculation about you and me."

"If people want to talk, they'll talk. You can't keep them from it. Why let that throw you off base?"

"Because I have my children to think of. Maybe you can't understand that—"

"Because I don't want to get tied down before I'm ready? With anyone?" They were back now to last night, and whatever she hadn't shared after he'd set her straight. "I'm glad you stood up to Bernice, but you really think she should dictate how you live? Looking over your shoulder all the time? Slinking around in your own backyard?"

"Dallas, you knew how I am when you asked me to help with the rodeo. If I can't do it on my terms, maybe it really would be better for me to drop out."

"Uh-uh," he said. "You promised, and I'm holding you to it because I do need you," he added. "Forget Bernice." He took a chance and massaged her shoulders, warming her skin through her blouse. She felt cool, like the look in her eyes that bothered him all over again. "Working together, we're bound to get noticed. That doesn't mean we're doing anything we shouldn't. But I can't help feeling there's something else going on here."

She held his gaze for a long moment, then hers dropped away. "No," she said.

He could tell that wasn't all. "What is it, Lizzie?"

She only shook her head.

Whatever it was, she wasn't ready to delve into the subject. "If it's about your kids, with them away they won't be harmed by anything we do. For the rodeo…or otherwise."

"You're way too convincing. That's how I ended up here in the first place."

"Right here?" With her still in his arms, he tried a lighter tone, daring her rejection. "Tell me you're glad about my news. It won't kill you."

She deadpanned him. "I'm glad about your news."

He raised his eyebrows, teasing her now. "Tell me like you really mean it."

Her eyes met his again. "I do, but Dallas, after the night in the yard and, um, that day you came over to console me—"

"I realize you wish that didn't happen, but it did."

She gently pushed at his chest. "And I know the friendship you asked for is all we can have. I agreed to help you, but that doesn't come with benefits. I'd have to be far more daring than I am to let y—"

"Let me what?" In the dim light of the closed shop, he cradled her face in his hands.

"I know you like me, Dallas. I like you too, but—"

"Yeah, yeah, I know the drill. Your kids. Your mother and her friend don't have enough to do so they keep track of you, and you hate being talked about. Your ex is a jerk who betrayed your trust, but this is now, you and me…here…and nobody else is looking," he pointed out. "I won't take advantage of you. Just remember," he nearly whispered, "how good we were together in May."

She made a frustrated sound. "I was half out of my mind then. When you showed up, I had a piece of paper in my hand that told me my marriage was officially over, that the man I had loved would never love me again… I felt utterly alone, Dallas. That day I would have clutched at a lamppost."

"Gee, thanks." He held her gaze. "You weren't alone. I was there," he said. "Yes, I need you now, but I've been thinking..." He lowered his head. "You need me too."

He gave her another moment to say no before Dallas forgot his vow to himself, forgot his bull-riding career and everything he owed Millie and Joe. His mouth met Lizzie's, brushed across her lips, and in the same instant Lizzie's arms wound around his neck until she was clinging. To him, not some post.

For a few bedazzled seconds the kiss went on before she drew back. "I can't... I really shouldn't."

"Neither should I," he said, and, while Dallas was trying to tamp down his disappointment and get his head together, she slipped free of his embrace. Leaving him to wonder what she was still keeping from him.

THE NEXT MORNING Elizabeth drove out to the McMann ranch. She hoped Dallas wasn't around, or at least stayed out of sight, but he stood outside the barn, spraying a dark horse with a hose. His hat thumbed back on his head, blue eyes squinting against the hot sun, he looked up and merely stared at her.

Elizabeth lifted a hand—he didn't answer her wave—then went on to the house. She'd come to see Clara about the rodeo. She hadn't meant to lead Dallas on yesterday, if that was what had happened, but nothing could come of the kiss they'd shared except another personal disaster for Elizabeth. She'd already been left by one man and was trying to stand on her own; she wouldn't set herself up for another loss. Especially with someone so temporary. Even when he'd told her, *I wouldn't do anything to harm you—or your kids.*

On the other hand, she might hurt him. She'd come so close to telling him about the baby, only to freeze at the opportunity. He'd asked what was going on, but she hadn't come up with those exactly right words she needed to say. By now her first shock had worn off, and she'd realized this baby was truly a miracle—she'd never expected to get pregnant again. She just needed to find a better moment when Dallas might be more receptive to her news. Or not. And what if, before that…she could barely form the thought…she miscarried again?

"Good morning, Elizabeth." Clara met her at the screened back door. She cradled an apron full of eggs, which she was tenderly holding so as not to drop them. "Ten o'clock and the temperature must be in the nineties. Midsummer's not my favorite season of the year. My poor chickens are panting." She led the way into the big ranch house kitchen. "I have coffee, but it's been on since before dawn—the men have finished most of it—and I'd make a new pot—" she paused "—but I was about to leave for town."

"I'm fine, thanks. I've had my tea. I won't stay long," she promised. "I'm on my way to work, but I wanted to talk to you—I'll be brief—about some competitions for the town rodeo Dallas is planning."

She might have dashed his romantic hopes, if that's what they were, but she would at least play her low-key role in his rodeo. As promised. And he'd told her Clara would be interested.

Clara set each egg in a blue stoneware bowl on the table. The warm air smelled of something delicious, as it always did on one of Elizabeth's rare visits. Clara said, "Dallas has been working so hard on that event. After my husband died, this ranch wasn't a working spread for too long, and I'm going to enjoy seeing it full of people and animals again beyond Hadley's cows and those three ornery horses we bought. My, it seems forever since the county fair folded its tent and abandoned us for Farrier. What kind of competition, dear?"

"Dallas and I talked about jams and jellies, baked goods, whatever anyone wants to contribute."

"We'd need judges, of course." Having already included herself in the planning, Clara smiled. "I can imagine Bernice crowing over her usual lemon meringue pie. I admit, it's good, but not as good as she thinks it is, and—" this with a wink "—I'd be willing to bet someone will knock her off her throne. Possibly me." She named a number of other local women who were known for their baking. "A good thing Olivia's out of town," Clara finished. "She'd feel obligated to enter and support the community…but she's not the best cook."

Elizabeth, of course, knew most of those people. Unlike Clara, however, she didn't keep track of who baked and who didn't. And frankly, Bernice's breakfast casserole hadn't been that tasty. Clara looked at the back door, obviously drawn by the sounds of men working at the barn. "That is music to my ears, thanks to Hadley, his brother and young Calvin Stern."

The last alerted Elizabeth. Did Calvin know he was about to become a father? If, indeed, she'd been correct about Becca's symptoms. The girl had left the shop before answering her question. As hard as Becca's situation was, Elizabeth's was no better. At Olivia's shop she'd kissed Dallas but shied away again when he asked what else was troubling her. What if the unthinkable did happen again? Then there'd be no reason to ever tell him.

Elizabeth focused on the tabletop. "The stock events and the kids' rodeo are Dallas's to worry about. I'm excited over this baked goods competition, but the PR work is more my territory. I'm glad to have your input, Clara, whatever you'd like to do."

Clara carried the blue bowl to the refrigerator, then set the eggs inside.

"For years I lived in this house alone. I'm not one to isolate myself, so that was very hard for me until Hadley came home. I was his last foster mother." She blinked, then sniffed. "Really, it's my pleasure, Elizabeth, to be part of this event. I'm sure we'll make a good team. Oh, and we'll need a chili contest."

"Yes," Elizabeth said, "that was mentioned."

The next few minutes passed in a blur of ideas traded back and forth until, finally, Clara noted the time on the kitchen wall clock. Taking her cue, Elizabeth stood up. "I won't keep you any longer. Let's meet soon to sort out the details."

Clara walked her to the door. "More notions are buzzing in my head. I'll make the calls to see what sort of possible numbers we're talking about for entrants, and do you agree that all the entered goods should also be for sale?"

"Yes," Elizabeth said. "More money for the rodeo and for charity."

"Have you chosen one yet?"

"I need to talk to… Dallas about that." At Elizabeth's hesitation over the name, Clara sent her a look. "The first flyers should go out. Then we'll need other advertising, local radio, social media…" As she stepped onto the porch, Elizabeth trailed off. Dallas was walking this way, his gaze on the ground that ran slightly uphill. His mood seemed the opposite of yesterday. Did he regret their kiss?

Clara cleared her throat. "Oh, dear. What's happened? I hope no one's hurt." Accidents were common on any ranch, but Elizabeth doubted that was the problem.

"I believe he's headed for me, Clara."

"If you need help there too, let me know." With a wave toward Dallas, which he returned, and another questioning look at Elizabeth, Clara disappeared into the house.

Stopping at the foot of the stairs, frowning, Dallas removed his hat. "I just had a call. Dusty Malone, the foreman at Wilson Cattle, got injured trying to fix their hay baler."

Elizabeth touched her chest. "Clara must have had a premonition. How serious?"

"He's pretty mangled up. Not a young man either and his family isn't well-off. They're looking at some steep medical expenses." Probably remembering his own accident, and rehab, Dallas caught her gaze. "Looks like we may have found our charity."

"Oh, that's perfect, Dallas. Yes, let's do that."

"I think it'll draw in a lot of folks who want

to help." His gaze fell, and just when she'd thought he wasn't holding a grudge after all, he said, "That's not the only reason I came up to the house. I stepped over another boundary yesterday. Are we okay here?"

The uncertain look in his eyes took Elizabeth by surprise. He seemed always so sure of himself, confident, as she'd said. It wasn't the kiss, then, but she could still feel the pressure of his mouth on hers, his touch on her shoulders, the warm nape of his neck when she'd wound her arms around him. They did like each other. She knew he thought of her as Lizzie, a looser version of herself. Maybe she was a bit too rigid. But at the moment he was worried about Dusty Malone, and telling him about her pregnancy wouldn't happen now either.

She held his gaze. "We're okay as long as yesterday doesn't repeat itself." Like that first afternoon at her house.

"Right," he said, studying his boots again.

Elizabeth went down the steps. "Dallas, that may have been as much my fault as yours. You caught me in a weak moment yesterday, and I can't deny you're an attractive man. But this has to remain business, and a casual friendship, until you leave Barren, nothing more." She recapped her talk with Clara as a new part of the team. "She could see the tension between us," Elizabeth finished.

"I can keep my hands to myself," he said. "I don't need another lecture. Takes two people to be friends…but two for a relationship as well, which you know I'm not looking for," he added. Had he thought their kiss over, seen her view? Or was he saving his pride? He turned on his heel and stalked off toward the barn, his last words hanging in the hot summer air. "Which should mean no problem on either side."

Except for one. Thank goodness, it was early yet. She'd tell him about the baby…but later. When she was farther along, and the risk of miscarriage wasn't as great.

She still had time.

CHAPTER TWELVE

DALLAS STALKED INTO the barn and found Calvin sitting on a bale of hay, staring at his phone. Dallas tried to pull his mind from the words he'd just had with Lizzie. He was seething, not in anger but frustration. Had he been too harsh with her? As Hadley had said, she was different from the sort of women Dallas usually met. Disgusted with himself, he studied Calvin.

"You're supposed to be grooming horses."

Calvin looked up. "I'm on my morning break. Taking care of a few things." He held up the cell. "My—uh—truck payment was due."

"Hadley doesn't pay us to manage our finances during work hours, Cal. He's been lenient with you, but don't let him catch you."

Calvin slowly got to his feet as if the effort was too much. He started down the aisle toward the first stall. When the kid was obviously troubled, Dallas had taken his mood out on him. He called in a friendlier tone, "Something bothering you?"

Calvin pulled a lead rope off the hook beside the stall door. "My girl," he admitted. "Told you we have our differences and she's not easy to read. I sure got this message, though." He raised his head, his eyes bleak. "Becca says she's pregnant."

That news surprised Dallas. "Wow. What are you going to do?"

A look of horror crossed Calvin's face. "I never said I'd marry her."

Dallas held up a hand. "Whoa, too fast. I didn't mean to make things worse. How do you feel about the baby?"

Calvin shrugged. "I never know what to say about stuff like that, not that I've ever been in this position before. When she told me, I couldn't think how to react except to pack my gear and take off for parts unknown." He gave Dallas a weak smile. Not serious, then. Calvin was basically a good guy. He'd likely do the right thing by her. Western men were the protective type. Dallas's first instinct was to shelter Lizzie, not that she was his. She didn't want to be, and considering his temporary status here, his chosen career, she was right.

"Is Becca sure she's actually having a baby? Has she taken a test, seen a doctor?"

"That's what I asked her. Not yet, but she's pretty certain."

"She must feel panicked, then, too, Calvin. You intend to stick by her?"

"Don't know. I just found out, but what kind of father would I make? My mom didn't know who my dad was. I had a bunch of 'uncles' growing up, and she had two other kids but never married. Half the time I was raising myself—guess I didn't do that good a job, but then neither did she."

Dallas could relate to that. He'd had a bad experience in a different way. He could be a confidant for Calvin—he empathized with him. "You had a rough deal. If it makes you feel better, so did I early on. My adoptive parents are great, so sometimes I forget that our birth family was all my brother and I had before a bunch of foster homes. Too many of them were bad news." Locked doors and all that. He told Calvin instead about his real mom and dad, the addicts who'd left him and Hadley to fend for themselves. "Because of the Maguires, I was lucky to finally get out of foster care. My brother didn't till he was eighteen and struck out on his own."

"That may explain why he can be such a hardnose."

Dallas had to smile. "Yeah, I guess, but Jenna's fixed most of that. She's good for him and so are the twins. Now, about you and Becca. You'll need a plan."

"To be honest, I'm kind of hoping it's a mistake. Women," he added, shaking his head. "I should have stuck to grooming horses."

"You and me both."

Calvin misunderstood. He gaped at Dallas. "You have a girl? She pregnant too?"

"No way!" But he guessed in his misery Calvin craved company.

For a moment today, despite his promise to himself, Dallas had felt tempted to try to shift his relationship with Lizzie from being neighbors and friends to... But he'd obviously been wrong to even taste the sweetness of her mouth. The last thing she needed was to get dumped again at the end of summer by him.

"After I bring off this rodeo in Barren," he said, "my concern is getting back to the professional circuit." Or, as Ace had implied during their most recent phone call, he might lose his endorsements, his sponsors, which supplied a good part of Dallas's income. "I need you to stick around, buddy. Got you down for calf roping and the bulls." He hoped the change of topic might lift Calvin's spirits while he considered what to do about Becca and their baby.

But Calvin's voice held envy. "You must see a lot of girls on the circuit."

Dallas couldn't deny that. "Buckle bunnies everywhere, but like I said, my mind's on work." He recalled Lizzie had said no benefits, and if he wanted her continued help with the rodeo, which he did, he had to mind his manners.

"I don't know how you resist." Calvin's eyes lightened. "If I was a big-deal rodeo star, on the road all the time, meeting women at every Saturday night dance… Man, that would be heaven." Clearly, he wasn't ready to settle down, but did Becca have the luxury of time?

"Like it or not, you're in this situation too, Calvin. Becca didn't start this new life she's carrying—let's assume she is—by herself. You care about her?"

"I love Becca. She's the best thing that ever happened to me." Calvin switched the lead rope from one hand to the other. "I care—but for my whole life?"

"You're not painting a very likable picture here," Dallas muttered. *Ditto, Maguire.* He had the uncomfortable notion that this conversation, without the intention on Dallas's part, might encourage Calvin to run.

Calvin sobered. "I'm not really looking to sleep around. I didn't mean that. It's more that I'm scared I'll end up letting Becca down. What would you do in my place?" he asked.

Dallas didn't hesitate. "I'm not in your place."

"But if you were?"

A knee-jerk image flashed in his head: Dallas's gear bag, loaded then tossed into the bed of his pickup truck, the tires rolling, gathering speed from one rodeo to the next...prize money in his pocket for his parents, their future assured... He couldn't think beyond that. Lizzie didn't want what he'd seemed to offer briefly with that kiss anyway.

"Calvin, I can't tell you. I don't know what I'd do if..." *No, don't even consider that.* Dallas wasn't ready either. He might never be ready.

Before he could even think about a long-term relationship, he needed to repay his folks for all they'd done for him when he was a kid, try to show them the kind of love they'd always given him. Why had he kissed Lizzie, then? Ruined what they already had for this one summer?

He said to Calvin, "Talk to Becca again. Find out what's really going on. Then when you have all the facts, make your decision. Together."

"Our decision," Calvin said, half to himself. He opened the stall door. "Thanks, man. I'll let you know what we decide."

Dallas gazed after him. Where Lizzie was concerned, because of that kiss he'd been an idiot. But at least in May he and Lizzie had used protection. Dallas always did.

He didn't need to worry.

ELIZABETH WAS WRAPPING a Lalique vase for a customer when Jenna walked into the store. Elizabeth came around the counter to give her a quick hug. "Hey, you."

"I was in Farrier and thought I'd stop by

on my way to the office." Jenna's pretty face looked as troubled as it had during their Girls' Night Out meeting. "Do you have a minute?"

"For you, always." She turned to hand the package to her customer. "Thanks so much, I hope you enjoy it. Please come again."

The woman, a visitor from Texas, beamed. "This will be the envy of all my friends." She swept from the store, the bell above the door jangling.

When they were alone, Elizabeth said, "Olivia claimed summer is her slow time, but we've had quite a few tourists, plus the locals who come in to see what's new." Or were the regulars sniffing for gossip fodder? No one could have seen her kiss Dallas, though. She was being paranoid. "First thing this morning, I supervised the packing and loading of a pricey Chesterfield sofa." The indecisive customer had finally made up her mind. "The odds aren't favorable that I'll make another big sale today, but at least the store was hopping then." That was both good and bad news. Elizabeth was enjoying her job, but by five o'clock she'd be even further behind in filling the online orders in her inbox for Kedar rugs. She'd have to work late and next weekend to catch up.

Jenna strolled around the shop's main room. "Managing this place without Olivia must be a workout."

"I'm dragging," she admitted, "and today I'm shorthanded. Becca didn't come in this morning or phone to let me know she was taking more time off." Had she quit without notice after their conversation about Becca's possible pregnancy? Elizabeth bit her tongue. She couldn't mention that. "I haven't had an opportunity to call and see how she's doing. Now, about you…" she said, because obviously Jenna had come in for a reason other than to say hello.

Jenna stopped beside a table of antique snow globes. "Remember how much I love Luke and Grace? But I still can't get it out of my head that I'd like to have another child. I've tried to bring it up with Hadley, but I feel disloyal. The twins are my family now, but they weren't mine when they were born. I thought I was resigned to never holding my own newborn baby, but obviously I'm not."

Elizabeth knew Jenna's life hadn't been easy. Other people may not have seen that.

But after she'd left home, and her parents' dysfunctional family, for Kansas City, she'd married young. Her first husband, a successful lawyer, had provided well, and their life together, their expensive home in a fashionable suburb, had appeared to be perfect. But that had proved to be a facade. He hadn't been the most loving man, and the marriage had ended badly, in part because Jenna's infertility had driven a wedge between them.

Elizabeth felt a guilty tug at her heartstrings. Yes, she'd lost a child, but she had three others, and, like Becca, she was pregnant again. If Elizabeth didn't miscarry this time—a constant worry—she would have four children while poor Jenna would never hold the one baby she wanted so much. "Have you talked to a new fertility specialist?"

"I've seen them all, from Farrier to Kansas City. My ex and I even tried in vitro. Several times."

"Then, are you thinking adoption? I know you considered that once."

Jenna sighed. "That's why I was in Farrier today. I talked with the agency there, gathering information before I face Hadley again."

"You'd have your hands full with three kids under five, Jen. Are you ready for that?"

"With Clara's help, yes. She's a godsend with the twins." Her expression dimmed as if someone had turned out the lights. "Unfortunately, I'm told the local adoption pool has dried up. Either more women are keeping their babies—or, sadly, they don't go through with their pregnancies."

"That's a tough one," Elizabeth said.

"Tell me. As I said, my ex and I tried everything until I finally did get pregnant—wonder of wonders—but then I lost it right away. We didn't try again."

"I didn't know that. Losing a baby, no matter how that happens, is a tragedy." Elizabeth's heart ached. "I'm so sorry, Jenna. When I lost my baby last year, my mother actually kept telling me not to think of it that way. With Harry out of the house, our marriage on the rocks, how would I deal with *four* children? Another way, I suppose, for her to urge me to reconcile with him."

"You were right not to patch things up. How could you ever trust him again?" Jenna murmured, "I just wish I knew the right thing to do in this situation."

"You have to do what's right for you." Just as Becca would, as Elizabeth had done with Harry, as she still needed to do with Dallas. "Are you afraid Hadley won't support you in this?"

"It's not that. The ranch is coming along, but not out of the woods yet, and even though Fantastic Designs is doing well, I have to wonder if I'd be putting another burden on Hadley. He'd have a third mouth to feed, a child to put through college." She added, "The twins are already covered. The trust we set up for them with the money their mother left will be sufficient for their educations."

Elizabeth put an arm around Jenna's shoulders. As Jenna's friend, she wanted to help find the right answer too. "You won't know how to proceed until you discuss this with him," she said, knowing she should deal with her fear of miscarriage then take her own advice.

After that, their conversation took a lighter turn, and Elizabeth told funny stories about the kids' adventures in Colorado, and Harry's attempts to manage all three of them. Come to think, she hadn't talked to them in days. She'd felt swamped with work, and maybe they were off somewhere with their father. Jordan couldn't be right that they never saw him. "By now, I hope he's truly bonded with them."

Despite what Dallas had said at the Mc-Mann ranch, rejecting any notion of a serious relationship, they did have a problem. It wasn't only hers, and those moments with him hadn't made telling him about her pregnancy any easier. How would she ever find the words? And the courage?

BY THE TIME she got home, Elizabeth's daily bouts of queasiness had passed, but her last bit of energy had dripped through her veins. All afternoon the shop had been even more crowded than in the morning, Jenna's dilemma was still playing through her mind and Elizabeth had more work to do before bed. She also needed to call the local radio and TV stations—maybe they'd interview Dallas—and the *Barren Journal*, the town's weekly newspaper. Thank heaven she'd been able to turn the food competitions and chili contest over to Clara.

A sudden commotion from somewhere

close by shattered the remnants of her concentration, then Elizabeth heard—

"Mom!"

"Mommy!"

"Mama!"

The trio of sweet voices split the air from just outside the house. And Elizabeth's heart nearly stopped. Unable to believe what she'd heard, she hurried to the window. No, she wasn't hearing things. Her children were running along the front walk! Their footsteps pounded up the steps, then across the porch. They burst through the door—and her arms were suddenly filled with a bunch of squirming little bodies. *My babies.*

"What a surprise," she said, face buried in Seth's hair. She kissed one dear face then the next. She'd come home to her empty house, but the rooms reverberated now with sound as each child vied to share some aspect of their summer adventures. Her thoughts a jumble, Elizabeth flipped through her mental calendar. They'd left in mid-June, it was now July, and late August, when they were due home, was still weeks away. Why this change in the schedule? As if on cue, Harry appeared in the entryway. He gave the children a critical glance.

"Why didn't someone shut this door?"

No one answered him. Elizabeth disentangled herself from the four-way embrace, and the kids scampered off up the stairs to their rooms, but she didn't mind the noise they made. They were home… Although it wasn't exactly convenient timing all around, especially because of the secret she carried. "Harry, what is this?"

"What do you think? I've brought them back."

"Early," she said. "Their school doesn't start until—"

"I know when the fall term begins. Try to keep up, Elizabeth. The last time we spoke, I told you about job interviews. They're scheduled now, half a dozen. Did you think I planned to take them with me?"

Hoping the children couldn't hear, she kept her voice low. "I thought you planned to have them for the summer. I'm glad they're here, but really, how can they trust you if you're of one mind today and another tomorrow?"

He surveyed the room, as if he were conducting a meeting at town hall, his gaze focused in turn on each member of his administration, except that Elizabeth was the only other person in the room now. "Jordan was bored. Stella misses her dolls. I can never remember their names, a mark against me in her book. Seth is always homesick. Nothing I tried changed that enough, but surely you don't want me to miss an opportunity to quit being unemployed?"

"I didn't want you to miss this time with them—the whole time," she said. "Why didn't you tell me you were on your way? There's a lot going on here too, Harry. I'm up to my ears at the shop, with the upcoming rodeo in Barren—"

"A rodeo," he muttered. "Ah, I see," he said. "I'm interrupting *your* plans?"

Elizabeth tried to explain. "I promised to help my neighbor."

His voice oozed with disdain. "That *cowboy*?" He sounded like her mother.

"And Clara McMann. The kids will love it, which is a big part of the reason I agreed to take part, but honestly, I don't even have a babysitter who can fill in while I'm at work in the shop or for the event."

He smirked. "You're too busy to take care

of your own children? I can't imagine that would please Claudia."

Elizabeth ignored that. Harry had often tried to keep her in line by mentioning her mother. "Excuse me? You never had time to look after them yourself. You and I had an agreement. I expected to have the summer—" which she'd dreaded in June "—to fix my own life, which I've been trying to do, and now you've reneged. What am I supposed to do? Quit the job *I* just started so you can trot off to all your interviews? Abandon people who are depending on me?"

"Jordan, Stella and Seth depend on you."

"As they did on you, Harry. You let them down, which isn't new, and you keep changing the rules. First, you have an affair, and you father a child who is not part of this family. You betray me in front of this whole town, all my friends...yes, my mother too. You leave me to pick up the pieces of my life, then waltz out of here again now to pursue your own interests when you should be—"

"Apparently you've pursued yours, as well. Don't get on your high horse with me, Elizabeth. That was an issue from the day we got married. Maybe I looked for someone more giving, more interested in who I was…which means part of the blame for our ridiculous divorce falls on you. One person in a relationship doesn't get to supersede the other."

"I could say the same thing to you." She might not confront her mother as she should, like Dallas advised, but she'd put Bernice in her place, and it was time to stand up to Harry. "In case you've forgotten, you were home maybe one night out of five. When you were, you stayed in your den on the phone with people who obviously meant more to you than we did. Than I did," she said. "We both know how that ended. And it is over, Harry. I'll expect you to pay for the sitter I need to find." She walked to the door, making sure she didn't come near him. "Thank you for bringing the children home. We'll manage, as we did before. Good luck with your interviews, wherever they may be." Elizabeth would not ask. "Let me know when you want to see them again."

She held the door until he walked through, then slammed it shut, rattling the windows.

CHAPTER THIRTEEN

IN HER BEDROOM Becca huddled up in a ball on her bed. She shouldn't have talked to Elizabeth the other day. She shouldn't have told Calvin about the pregnancy. Becca had been hiding out since then. When she'd reached the house again late today, her dad had been in the kitchen, the telltale sizzle from a skillet telling her he was browning meat for supper. Tiptoeing past the doorway, Becca had gone straight to her room. Now, filled with dread, she waited for him to come upstairs.

The soft rap at her door startled her anyway. "Yes?"

His deep voice rumbled from the hallway. "May I come in?"

She couldn't say no, and he'd only try the doorknob if she didn't answer.

The door opened. With one eye she peeked out from beneath the arm she'd flung across her face, shutting out the light, the world, as if hiding might make things simpler. Now there he stood, eyes dark with concern, the coveralls he'd worn for work today—every day—smudged with dirt from the barn.

She wondered how he managed without help. They couldn't afford hired hands, and it wasn't as if the farm was big like the Circle H or Wilson Cattle ranches, or even Clara McMann's, but her dad worked too hard. Drove himself, really. Becca asked, "Did you finish fertilizing the fields?"

"Almost done." He edged into her room. "Anything you want to share with me, Becca?"

"No," she tried, hoping he'd give up and go away.

He stayed, of course. "It's not like you to come home yesterday without saying a word, and today you must have known I was in the house. You didn't even call hello or eat dinner." He crossed to the bed, then stood over her, Becca's solid, dependable dad. "If you dislike the job you have, then look for another."

"I'm okay. It's easier to work with Elizabeth than Olivia."

His face darkened. "Then what about that boy you've been seeing? If he's hurt you—"

"It's not Calvin." He was certainly part of the problem, an even bigger part now when she feared letting her dad know why. But Calvin hadn't taken her news—their news—in the way she'd hoped, and she doubted her father would either. "I...didn't feel good. That's why I left work early again." In fact, she'd never gone to the shop today. She'd driven around aimlessly. She'd gone once to Willow's house, but after her vacation her friend had stayed in Ohio to spend time with an aunt.

He sat down on her bed. She didn't want to lie to him. "I stopped at the pharmacy on my way home," she said. "I got some stomach medicine."

"Your stomach, Becca?"

"I think have a virus." Maybe that would make him leave her room. He wouldn't want to pick up whatever she had and lose time to run the farm, not that he would ever take a sick day. But he didn't move. He stayed seated beside her, gazing at her with concern in his already sad eyes.

"Why don't you make an appointment with Doc Baxter?"

He was right about the doctor but for the wrong reason. Sooner or later, she'd have to see Doc, who was semiretired. His younger partner, Sawyer McCord, whom she preferred, was in some foreign country this summer, and in his absence Doc was holding office hours again. For now, she'd take the test she'd bought at the drugstore.

He frowned. "I'm concerned, Becca. Don't sit on this, promise?" He must be thinking of her mother, who'd ignored her symptoms until it was too late. She hadn't wanted to worry him.

"I promise." Becca rested a hand on her stomach. Each day its soft swell seemed more noticeable to her. How long before everyone would guess the truth, her dad especially? Still, she'd buy time if she could. Once he knew, he'd see her in a different way. After that he might not love her, and he'd miss her mother's presence all the more. Even if Becca remained in the house, it wouldn't be the same. "I should rest. I've also been doing too much."

"Seeing Calvin Stern," he said, "when you

should have stayed home." His smile didn't touch his eyes. "You missed *The First 48* this week. *Forensic Files* was an old one."

"They're all old," she said. "I've been neglecting you, haven't I?" That, at least, wouldn't be a problem for now, because she hadn't heard a word from Calvin. The thought made her feel more exhausted than she had before. She'd let down everyone she loved, including the memory of her mother.

"You're not supposed to take care of me," her father said. "I'm the dad, you're the daughter. That's my job." His gaze fixed on the far wall.

"Daddy, I'll be fine, but I'd rather be alone right now. I don't feel like watching TV tonight." She faked a yawn, her hand still cradling her abdomen.

What if Calvin really didn't want her or their baby? She was terrified, afraid to think she might panic and do something drastic. Like not have it. She'd read about girls who hid their pregnancies, gave birth in some restroom stall, abandoned their newborns… She needed to talk to Elizabeth again. There was no one else she could trust.

"Rebecca, tell me the truth." A sense of betrayal threatened to make her cry. He'd lost her mother, the love of his life, and yet he got up every morning, tended the farm and her roses, tended to Becca, as he'd said. The truth wouldn't get easier to reveal over time, and her dad's eyes told her he'd already made a connection. "It's not your stomach, is it?"

"No, and I'm not that sick," she said quickly to reassure him. He wasn't going to lose her as they had her mom, but she *was* going to break his heart. Becca waited until his gaze moved from the wall to meet hers. She took his hand and drew it to her tummy but still couldn't speak. Finally, he said the words for her that would change them forever, his quiet voice filled with the realization and shock.

"You're pregnant."

The tears welled in her eyes, then streamed down her cheeks. "I'm sorry, Daddy." Through blurred vision, she watched disappointment take over his expression, and a sheen of moisture brimmed in his eyes too. Without another word, he rose from the bed and left the room, his head down and his steps slow. She heard none of the clatter he usually made going down the wooden stairs; he didn't make a sound.

Leaving Becca and her baby alone.

WHAT IS HAPPENING next door? Every light in Lizzie's house seemed to be on, the deep thrum of bass from a television reverberated through those walls into his, and from his side window Dallas glimpsed the shadow of someone moving past in an opposite upstairs room. A figure in the darkened rear yard bounced a basketball in front of the hoop on the garage. Lizzie was no longer alone. Was that Jordan?

Dallas had his boots on, was out the door and on her front porch in a flash. Their quick conversation that morning at Clara's wasn't enough, and he needed to restore their friendship, if that's all they could have. Should have.

He rang the bell three times. Lizzie had ignored him before, and again he feared no one would answer. He had to look down, way down, to see the small boy, overwhelmed by Dallas's bigger shadow, who opened the door, light spilling from inside onto the porch. In the distance he could hear voices.

"Who're you?" the kid asked, peering up at him. What was his name? Seth? He had a slight build, blondish hair and Lizzie's green eyes. Compared to Jordan, her youngest was a munchkin, and Dallas felt a flash of guilt.

When he had no right, he'd recently kissed their mother. And before that, the day of her divorce, he'd done a lot more. This put a new slant on his attraction to Lizzie, sharply reminding him of the family she valued above all else.

Dallas introduced himself. "Your mom here?"

The boy gestured toward the hall behind him. "Upstairs. Stella can't find her best doll."

"Well, I don't know that I can be of help there, but—"

"You don't like dolls? I don't like 'em," he said, and Dallas decided to test the waters.

"I like horses." He hunkered down to meet the kid's gaze. "How about you?"

"I never rode a horse. Jordan wants to but he says I'm too little." He stepped back, then said abruptly, "Bye. I'm not s'posed to talk to strangers." He began to shut the door. Lizzie was a good mother who'd taught her son about safety.

Dallas put his foot in the wedge of open door. "Hey, do me a favor first, okay? Can you call your mom? I'm a friend—from next door—and I need to talk to her."

His eyes widened. "The *cowboy*? Why?"

Dallas assumed he meant why did he want to talk to Lizzie, not why he'd joined the rodeo circuit. Before Dallas could answer, Jordan dashed around the corner from the rear yard, the basketball in his hands. His blond hair was a rumpled mess, his gray eyes lighting up when he saw him. "Dallas! Hi! I'm back from Colorado."

Ah, a possible ally. The question remained, why were they all here now? "Welcome home. Jordan, can you go get your mom?" During the winter, and before the kids had left for part of the summer, he'd had a habit of monitoring the driveway like Bernice Caldwell, appearing as soon as Dallas came home from work or rehab. Dallas had given him a children's book about the sport, and for that short time he'd become Jordan's idol. Dallas had kind of gotten a kick out of that. "We'll get together soon—like I promised—to watch those videos."

"The ones with you in them?"

"Sure. But you'll have to ask your mom first if that's okay." He knew Lizzie's opinion of his chosen career. She rarely missed a chance to imply her children weren't going to follow in his footsteps, to remind Dallas that he might damage his hip again if he took part in their rodeo. He liked to think that meant she cared about him a little. As a friend, of course. "Your brother says she's upstairs."

That didn't work any better than with the youngest kid. "She doesn't want to be disturbed," Jordan said, obviously a quote, then in an overly polite tone, he asked, "Would you like to leave a message?"

Dallas considered that. Maybe he should go back to his place, his own problems, but a strange new silence from inside changed his mind. "No, I'd really like to see her."

Lizzie's daughter, Stella, hurried from the hall to lay a hand on Seth's shoulder. Dallas was surrounded, two kids facing him in the doorway, one behind him, like palace guards. The little girl, dark-haired like Lizzie but with gray eyes, glowered at him just as, to his vast relief, Lizzie herself showed up. "The kids are home," she said, which seemed obvious. Was she asking him to turn around, to leave? Not to complicate her life more than he already had? He ought to take that advice.

Instead, Dallas took a second look at her. Lizzie was white-faced.

"I know you're busy, but I, uh, hoped we could discuss that charity we picked."

She gathered Stella closer, put a hand on Seth's head. "It's nearly bedtime and they traveled all day. Everyone's exhausted." The truth, or a convenient excuse? She must be the one in need of sleep; the kids looked ready to roll. "I need to tuck them in."

She didn't get the last word out before, suddenly, Lizzie staggered. If not for the kids on either side of her, she would have fallen where she stood. No, he was not going back to his place, leaving her to cope with these three alone, not when she looked that way. "*Everyone* includes you," he said, then eased past the other two in the doorway. Taking Lizzie under his wing as he went into the house, Dallas heard himself giving orders. "Kids, pajamas. Brush your teeth. Get to bed. Lights out."

They all gaped at Dallas.

"I'm afraid of the dark," Seth answered in a thin voice.

"Do we have to do what he says, Mom?" Stella asked.

Lizzie appeared ready to protest, but instead she leaned against Dallas. "Yes," she said. "You do. Please, Stella. I'm too tired to argue."

"Is there any more pizza?" Jordan piped up.

"No. We'll have to shop tomorrow."

"I had two pieces," Seth chimed in.

"Please," Lizzie said again.

Stella sent Dallas a death stare before she headed toward the steps. Obviously, she'd made up her mind about him last winter and it wasn't good. Jordan hung back, studying him with a fresh look of hero worship in his eyes. Seth twined his arms around Lizzie's leg. He wouldn't let go until she promised, "Yes, I'll try to find your green dinosaur."

"I can't sleep without him, Mama."

Reluctantly, Dallas released her. While they all trooped upstairs, he stood rooted to the spot in the front hall. He didn't move until Lizzie finally came down, one hand rubbing the bridge of her nose, her hair mussed. She heaved a sigh.

"Listen to the quiet. Yesterday that would have bothered me. Seth fell asleep while I was searching for his dinosaur. Stella's out cold with half a dozen dolls around her, worn-out from weeping because we never found her favorite. Jordan's plugged in to his iPad listening to weird music. He's my fighter. He won't give in to sleep until midnight." She sank onto the living room sofa. "God give me strength."

"You didn't expect them," he guessed, taking a seat beside her.

"No, Harry turned up around sunset. He has job interviews scheduled. He didn't think to make arrangements for the kids while he was supposed to be in charge. I'm the default parent." Blinking, lip quivering, she started to tear up. "What kind of mother am I? I'm thrilled they're home, but how am I going to do this? My job, your rodeo…" She covered her eyes with her hands. "He uprooted them again, which means Stella will probably be back to square one. She's felt so adrift since he moved out. And I said terrible things to him—"

"Whatever you said he had coming to him." Dallas dipped his head to meet her gaze. "You're the most tactful, responsible person I know—in fact, you're a superwoman."

"Really? If that was true, I would have been able to produce dinner. I've been living like a single person, eating stuff like that outdated frozen entrée. You brought me the best meal I've had all summer. There wasn't enough food in the pantry to feed four people tonight."

"You didn't know you'd have to." He ticked off points on his fingers. "You run this house, do your job, help me with the rodeo and still look drop-dead gorgeous." He paused. "Well, at this moment…maybe just drop-dead."

She leaned over, weakly punched his upper arm. And her soft fist met his hard biceps. "Wow, amazing. Talk about superheroes. You're like the Incredible Hulk."

"Without a green face, I hope. Or his hair-trigger temper."

"I hope not," she agreed, and kept leaning. A second later, her head was on his shoulder, tucked into the curve of his neck, her voice barely above a whisper. "I gave you a hard time, didn't I, at Clara's?"

He let his fingers sift through her hair, soft and silky under his touch. His guilt aside about their kiss, he wanted another. "I know your situation's way different from mine—"

Her voice took on a husky tone. "You're a good guy, Dallas." She sighed. "If I wasn't the newly divorced mother of three rambunctious kids, things might be *very* different."

That was the most encouraging thing she'd ever said to him.

He waited, unsure if he should say this. "Even if you are, Lizzie, things can change."

She smiled. "And if you keep calling me Lizzie, I just might get used to it."

He shouldn't say this either, but, "Maybe you've been Elizabeth long enough. Not my decision to make, though."

She pulled back to look up at him. Remembering her ex, who'd hurt her, and the mother who disapproved of her? "It's tempting. The kiss was nice too, Dallas. I didn't mean to let you think it wasn't."

His heart turned over. But he had to be honest. "I'm still planning to ride out of town."

"And I'm staying here." Their gazes held, and his pulse did another dance. God, she was pretty, even this way with her hair a mess, her eyes teary…a second away from crying and the need for comfort, which Dallas had provided before, and for which she'd never forgiven him. But it wasn't only how she looked that drew him. He'd meant what he said. He liked the person she was inside, even that starchy part. Maybe especially that side of her.

"Dallas…" She didn't go on. Her gaze slid away as it had several times before when he'd thought she was hiding or omitting something he should know. She opened her mouth as if to speak, then pressed her lips together.

Dallas wrapped his arms around her, rested his forehead against hers for another moment and inhaled her sweetness before he drew back to gauge her expression. Still dewy, still…warm. And he ignored the voice within that told him to back off. To think of the circuit, his responsibility to his parents and the ever-present memory of his early years, which had haunted him since he'd found Hadley again. Dallas didn't listen, and in that moment he didn't care. Without planning what came next, he lowered his head, his lips met hers once more and he was lost. He didn't just like Lizzie Barnes, and from the way she'd looked at him, he wondered if she felt the same way. Which could be bad news for both of them.

Gradually, he ended the kiss. "What are we going to do about this?" he asked.

Easing from his embrace, Lizzie gave him a sad smile. "I guess we stop right where we are." She added, "And remember we're not alone. Seth's a sleepwalker, and Stella is my self-appointed protector. I'm not a free agent, Dallas. So," she said, "about that charity we need to talk about…"

Dallas didn't hear another word she said.

He no longer wanted to simply spend time with her this summer, to be friends or business partners as well as neighbors until he had to leave. In spite of his promise to himself that he'd avoid any serious relationship for now, and his vow never to hurt her, he already wanted that something more.

CHAPTER FOURTEEN

"MAMA!" SETH CALLED from his room. "I don't have any clothes."

The next morning Elizabeth woke up feeling groggy. After Dallas had left last night, she'd tossed and turned before falling into a restless sleep. She couldn't afford to be a slugabed now. Her children were home. Reality had intruded. She needed to be here for them, not in Dallas's arms.

And yet, for a moment she didn't answer Seth. She was enjoying Dallas's temporary friendship, their mutual attraction, at the same time she was keeping a secret from him. She wondered if he'd seen that in her eyes last night. He hadn't asked again but the question had been in his gaze. She needed to tell him, but *how*? That answer never seemed to come, even when she couldn't hide the truth much longer. To be honest, she feared his reaction—not a good enough excuse. Feared losing that friendship, the only relationship they might have. Or was there something else, which couldn't end well, going on here?

Could she be falling in love with Dallas?

She moaned aloud. What was she thinking? And what if she *did* miscarry again? She would have told him about the baby for nothing.

Seth was waiting. Elizabeth hadn't helped her kids unpack yesterday, but obviously Harry had neglected to do laundry. He hadn't packed their belongings clean and folded as she would have done; as always, he'd relied on Elizabeth to pick up his slack. With another groan, she put her legs over the side of the bed, then didn't move.

A familiar wave of nausea held her still. "Come here, Seth." He bounded into her room, landed on her in bed and giggled as he smacked a kiss on Elizabeth's cheek. Her stomach rolled. "Honeybunch, Mama's not awake yet."

His eyes twinkled. "But are you happy?"

"You mean because you're here? Yes, silly. I love you to the moon and back. Shall we see what's for breakfast? I know there's cereal."

"At the ski village I had a humongous

breakfast every day. In the dining room. They had everything. Bacon, eggs, pancakes…"

"Delicious," she said, fighting nausea and trying not to further resent Harry. He'd made things easy for himself there too. "I'm glad you ate well. Let's make a list for the store— right after breakfast." And yet, she lay there, cuddled against Seth, as if she hadn't slept at all. She really needed to reestablish a better, more healthful routine now.

It wasn't until Jordan came in, followed by Stella, both demanding to be fed, that Elizabeth hauled herself from her warm bed and went downstairs. Feeling out of sorts, she fixed cereal with honey and milk for the kids, and brewed tea for herself. The quiet while Elizabeth nursed her first cup and everyone else ate seemed like heaven. The fighting didn't start until three stomachs were full.

"I did not steal your dragon, *baby*," Jordan said.

"Did too!"

Stella, bursting into tears, yelled, "Seth took my doll. Where did you hide Victoria?"

Seth gave her an impish grin. "Maybe I burned her in the backyard."

The firepit there had been Harry's gift to

the family last Christmas. The kids loved it. To Elizabeth it was an accident waiting to happen.

Stella wept even harder. "Mommy, make him stop!"

"Seth, don't tease."

"I did, I did—" he danced around the table "—and you can't get me!"

He charged off through the living room, up the stairs with Jordan and Stella, who was sobbing, at his heels. "I love Victoria. You're mean!" Then, "Ow! Jordan, you stepped on my foot."

Elizabeth stopped listening. As a mom, she had better selective hearing than Harry did. And to think, she'd missed their noise and constant questions, the sibling rivalry. She'd abhorred the echoes in every room.

She leaned her elbows on the counter and contemplated the house next door, envying the single man who lived there even when she wouldn't have traded her children for anyone else, and tried not to remember how well he kissed. She'd been grateful for his presence last evening, though, as the kids slept upstairs while she and Dallas discussed the charity for Dusty Malone. He was in the hospital after surgery following his accident with the hay baler. Elizabeth also liked the idea of the rodeo money going directly to Dusty's family, such a great cause. They expected a strong response from the townspeople. How could she fret about her own problems?

She'd taken a last swig of tea when her stomach finally rebelled, and Elizabeth ran for the bathroom.

"ELIZABETH?" A WOMAN'S voice called from the main room of Olivia McCord Antiques.

"Anybody here?" said another.

"Just me." Becca hurried from the office into the showroom, where Clara McMann and Jenna Smith had just stepped inside, fanning themselves against the rapidly increasing heat outdoors. Barren was having one hot summer. The shop wasn't busy this morning, thank her lucky stars, but she wouldn't know what to do if it was.

"Elizabeth hasn't come in," she told them. Becca didn't like having to manage the store. She wasn't much of a self-starter, except she'd had no trouble starting the new life she carried. *But we only...that one time...* Calvin had said. She pulled herself from the perplexing thought. "Can I help you?"

Clara held a sheaf of brightly colored papers, red and blue and yellow. "We've brought you some flyers about the rodeo. And are you a baker, dear? We'll be holding a competition."

Becca flushed. By necessity she'd learned to cook after her mom died, one way in which she tried to take care of her father. Oh, she'd done that all right last night. "I make a pretty good pumpkin pie, not a bad apple, but I like raisins in mine. Some people don't," she said. Her dad had always loved the raisins, having been her greatest supporter, past tense. He hadn't said a word since he'd guessed about Becca's baby.

"We'll count on you, then," Clara said. "Jenna and I are going to judge fruits and vegetables, so if you have a garden…" With a slight wince, she didn't continue. Becca's mom had raised world-class tomatoes and peppers. Once, her squash had taken second place at the Stewart county fair, her pumpkin a blue ribbon.

"My dad didn't want a big garden this year. We use everything we grow."

Becca skimmed a hand over her stomach, hoping the two women couldn't tell it seemed to be growing by the hour. She wouldn't dwell on the past, when her mom was still alive, her dad was happy and Becca didn't worry about boyfriends...or babies.

Now she was living on borrowed time, waiting for her dad to throw her out. He'd risen early this morning as he usually did, but he took his coffee and daily toast out to the barn instead of eating with Becca. He must have come into the house to have his full breakfast once he sensed she'd left for work. And she still hadn't heard from Calvin.

"What do you want me to do with these flyers?" she asked.

Jenna took a batch from Clara. "If you don't mind—I know Elizabeth wouldn't—we'll leave a stack by the front register. We're going to paper every store in town."

"Let's put one in this front window," Clara added. "The more people who become aware of the rodeo, the more successful it will be."

Becca hurried to the counter for some tape. While Clara tacked the flyer on the glass, Becca felt Jenna watching her. Her gaze moved from Becca's face, down her front, then settled on her abdomen before she quickly looked away.

"There will be a kids' event too," Jenna said. "If you know anyone who might be interested, please let them know."

"I don't know any kids," Becca murmured, thinking, *except my own*.

Clara turned from the window. "Thank you so much, Rebecca. We'd better go, Jenna, to the other shops. If I'm not back in time to feed three hungry men their lunch, there may be a riot." She laughed. "They're eating me out of house and home, though I could never manage without them." She and Jenna were at the door when Clara faced Becca again.

"Two men, I should have said." Clara's expression dimmed. "When I served breakfast, Calvin was nowhere to be seen. Hadley tells me the bunkhouse has been cleared of all his belongings. No notice," she said with a sniff, "just when we're going to need his help on rodeo day." Her voice was tinged with concern. "Calvin Stern seems to have vanished."

AFTER WORK THAT AFTERNOON, Dallas pulled into his driveway. Living in town wasn't really his thing, and at the McMann ranch, he loved hearing the soft lowing of cattle, smelling the sweet scent of grass, being outdoors all day. He'd never liked closed-in spaces. He liked living next door to Lizzie, though.

Still, kissing her was one thing. Making a commitment he wasn't ready for, and that she would shy away from, was another—even when he wanted something more than friendship. And where might that lead them? He had no clue. Maybe he'd simply lost his head with Lizzie, but he wouldn't apologize this time. She'd liked kissing him too.

Dallas went into the house, dropped his mail on the kitchen counter, then walked out the back again, where he'd heard a lot of taunting and name-calling from next door. He found Lizzie's kids chasing each other around the yard with big water pistols, or rather the two boys were chasing Stella, who was screaming at the top of her lungs. Dallas didn't hesitate. "Hey!" He whistled through his teeth. "Leave your sister alone!" He couldn't believe Lizzie would let them fight like this, not with Bernice keeping watch, ready to report anything amiss to Lizzie's mother, if not the whole town.

"You're not the boss of me," little Seth

threw back over his shoulder at Dallas as he ran. He spun around, then squirted Stella right between the eyes.

More bloodcurdling shrieks. "You got my hair wet! Brat!" she yelled.

Dallas considered confiscating the pistols, but they weren't his children. He had no right to discipline them. He sprinted from the rear lawn to the door, where he didn't bother to knock.

"Lizzie! There's a war going on in your backyard," he announced, but she wasn't in the kitchen. Where was she? There was another telling silence in the house like last night, but she would never leave her kids home alone.

He strode through the living room. Empty, yet cluttered again with debris that only three kids could create. There were candy wrappers strewn on the coffee table. A pair of Nerf rifles lay abandoned on the carpet alongside a one-armed doll with glazed eyes—as if there'd been a murder here. The area behind the chutes at a rodeo would look neater. "Lizzie?" he called again.

Now he was getting worried. This wasn't his business, and yet it was. If something was

wrong, he couldn't ignore it. What if there'd
been an accident, and Lizzie had been elec-
trocuted by a hair dryer falling into the bath-
tub? Slashed her finger while trying to fix
dinner and was bleeding somewhere? Upstairs? The kids wouldn't hear her cries for
help.

Trying to shut out the still-growing clamor
from the yard, Dallas took the steps two at a
time. The first bedrooms on either side of the
hall were clearly the boys' rooms, one in blue
with a mountain of stuffed animals on the
bed, which was shaped like a race car. Seth's,
most likely. The other had a space theme with
a large decal of a Starfighter blazing across
the wall. Jordan's room. Next on the right
looked to be Stella's—it boasted one purple
wall, three pink, and shelves lined with dolls.
The last room on the left had to be Lizzie's
with its door shut.

Dallas pushed it open. Dark, with the draperies closed, at first it seemed empty too. Then
he heard a soft moan, a shape moved under
the covers and his pulse shot up. "Lizzie."
Remembering how pale she'd been the night
before, he crouched by the bed. "You sick?"

"Um," she answered, then shifted the blankets enough to reveal one eye, dull and not quite aware. "I missed work. Didn't get to the store." She waved a limp hand toward the ruckus still coming from the yard. "Oh, God, what are they doing out there?"

"Torturing each other."

"So. Normal," she said but didn't smile. "My stomach's not good. I called Olivia's sitter. Isn't she with them?"

"No."

"What time is it?"

"Five thirty."

She groaned. "I should have known. Her boyfriend's always the priority. She never told me she was leaving. I could have phoned my mother instead, but you know how that would turn out."

He frowned. "Why didn't you call me? You have my cell number."

"When I came out of the bathroom for the third time—which I thought was the last— this morning, I saw your truck leave. I assumed you were on your way to Clara's."

He touched her forehead. "Fever?"

"I don't think so." She clamped a hand on his forearm. "Don't fuss, it's likely…some sort of flu."

He disagreed. He wouldn't let her light touch distract him, and he sure didn't miss her evasive gaze. First, food poisoning, now this, along with the way she kept avoiding some subject she might have told him about. Dallas had experience. His parents were forever trying to reassure him they were fine, not to worry, and the more they protested, the more serious the problem might be.

"I'm sorry the children bothered you," she murmured. "I really am a bad mother. I appreciate you coming over, but I'm getting up now, so you can go—"

Through the upstairs window, he heard the battle in the yard escalate. Seth cried out, Jordan yelled back, then Stella melted down again. Dallas could have throttled all three of them. And Lizzie still hadn't moved from bed. Under normal circumstances, nothing would keep her from tending to her kids.

"Don't worry about me," he finally said, "and you're not a bad mom." He hooked a thumb toward the window. "But your three running around like banshees? You falling on your face—like you almost did last night? Doesn't that tell you anything? You seem pretty sick to me."

She sighed. "By tomorrow I'll be on my feet again." Even she couldn't believe that.

"I think you should call Doc Baxter." He pulled out his phone. "No, I'll call him. But first—with your permission—I'm going downstairs to get control of the situation in the yard. That okay with you?"

She nodded before she laid a hand across her eyes. "I don't need Doc." Her face had turned green again. "Take the water pistols away..." She didn't go on.

"I'll handle them," he said. After that, he intended to handle Lizzie.

Better not give her any warning.

CHAPTER FIFTEEN

"JORDAN, CLEAN THIS UP." Hands on his hips, Dallas surveyed the mound of clothing that had spilled from the boy's bedroom out into the hall and shook his head. Seth had tripped over the pile and was lying on the carpet, clutching his knee and wailing as if he were being murdered.

"Mama! I broke my leg!"

While Lizzie was at the doctor's office this afternoon, Dallas was babysitting, which he'd been doing most of the past three days, juggling his work at Clara's ranch and canceling his rehab sessions. Lizzie had protested that she didn't need to see Doc Baxter, but at last she'd given in.

Gently, he probed Seth's leg. "Your mom's not home yet, buddy, but nothing's broken." Dallas should know. Once, after a rodeo outside Reno, he had in fact set one of his friends' arms. No doctor or medic had been around by then, no hospital nearby either, but the break had been simple. *Just pull on it*, the guy begged him. The rough-and-tumble world of rodeo, as his mom had said—not a story he'd share with Lizzie. "Probably bruised, pardner, or at most a sprain. Can you get up? Let's put some ice on that."

Dallas couldn't lie. Taking care of Lizzie's kids was not his area of expertise. In the past few days, he'd confirmed to himself that he was indeed better off staying single, honing his fitness to get back to the circuit, working on his local rodeo plans. His, and Lizzie's. Too bad he couldn't keep his mind on that while he waited for her to come home from the clinic, fearing, as he always did with his mother, that the news wouldn't be good.

As he started to help Seth to his feet, Stella emerged from her room to glare at Dallas. "What did you do to him!" A hard case if he ever saw one. She'd instantly decided Dallas was an intruder, not to be trusted, especially near her mother. Stella held out her hand. "Seth, come with me. You can stay in my room. We can play—"

"Not *dolls*."

Dallas assumed she'd tried that ruse before.

"Legos," she conceded, sending Dallas another death stare. To eliminate him from the scene, she would lower herself to fitting plastic bricks together with her baby brother.

Seth's face brightened. "The new spaceship model Daddy bought me?" He scrambled up off the hall carpet, plunged through the pile of Jordan's clothes and followed his sister with no limp to be seen.

Dallas poked his head into Jordan's room. At least Lizzie's oldest remained on his side, still entranced at having a rodeo star living next door. "Get moving, man. Don't let your mother see that mess in the hall—plus it's a hazard. When you've finished hanging up those clothes, you owe Seth an apology. He could have been badly hurt."

"He wasn't." Jordan's voice had an unexpected stubborn tone. A chink in the armor of his hero worship. "Not my fault he's clumsy and stupid and fell over his own feet."

"Jordan, don't call your brother stupid." Clumsy at six years old was a different matter. Hadn't Seth seen the mound in the middle of the hallway? Or had he been running helter-skelter like he did most of the time, not looking where he was going? Cute, though. The kid melted Dallas's heart—but not enough to make him want one of his own just yet. "Why did you throw your clothes out there anyway?"

"Most of 'em are too small. Mom can give them to baby Seth."

"Don't call him a baby, Jordan."

He ignored that. "The rest are not cool. Besides, I'll need new clothes for school and my closet was too full."

"Makes sense to purge your room, then, but get a plastic bag for the things you don't want." He paused, remembering the time when he'd carried all his belongings in such a bag from one foster home to another. "Pretend you're getting ready to rodeo. You know, when I'm on the road, everything I need is in my one gear bag. No extras. Just me, my truck, my rope and a dream of the next bull I'll ride."

Jordan's eyes widened. "I wish I could run away, be in the rodeo with you."

Not the right thing, then, for Dallas to have said. "Let's start slow, okay? When you're finished here, we'll put on that rodeo tape. You can see what I normally do every day. So, cowboy up, Jordan. Now."

With a grin, Jordan shot from his room down the hall to the stairs. "I'll be back with the bag. You can show me how to pack."

Dallas congratulated himself. He'd corralled Lizzie's children like a bunch of calves he'd roped. Not that he was winning any popularity contest with Stella, and as the front door opened downstairs, he stopped patting himself on the back.

"Hi, sweetie," he heard Lizzie say. "Did you guys behave for Dallas?"

Jordan said, "We were good, Mom."

Dallas grinned. That was putting a spin on things, but oh, well. Anything less would worry Lizzie, especially when she wasn't feeling well. He clambered down the stairs, pausing on the bottom step to simply look at her. Dark hair neatly in place today, better color in her face, but her green eyes avoided his. He was almost getting used to that touch of suppressed—was that guilt?—he kept seeing there. She held Jordan tight before letting him go with a kiss on top of his head, though he squirmed. "That's my boy," she said. "Where are Seth and Stella?"

"In her room," Jordan said, not mentioning the accident in the hall.

Finally, Lizzie glanced up at Dallas. Even then, her gaze landed on his shoulder. "No trips to the emergency room?"

"Nope."

"The water guns are still in the closet?"

"Yep." Dallas watched Jordan head for the kitchen. "Jordan's cleaning his room, getting some things ready maybe for charity."

Lizzie stared at him. "You must be a miracle worker."

He shrugged. "I managed. That's what the Hulk would do. What's the word on you?"

Her blank expression looked as evasive as the other. "Word? Oh. Doc Baxter, um, said I'm fine. No medicine or anything."

"What about the flu?"

"Another day or two, he said." She set her purse on the entry table. "I feel better already. Really," she insisted when he cocked his head. "Stop looking at me like that. I'm not dying. I am, however, eternally grateful for all the help you've given."

"I like looking at you," he said. And she was changing the subject. Again.

Jordan skimmed past them, carrying the plastic trash bag up the stairs. "I'll be done in a minute. Get the tape ready!"

"Which gives us a little time. While I was kid sitting, I made coffee. Want some? We can talk in the kitchen." Dallas added, "Then I promised Jordan we'd watch some bull riding."

"That's generous of you, but I hope you didn't mention the kids' rodeo. I haven't told them yet. If I say something too soon, they'll get overexcited."

"It'll be a lot of fun for them. Maybe Jordan will get to chase a calf?"

"Another reason to wait. I haven't decided. I don't want him hurt."

"You saw how safe it really is. How much fun it can be."

She smiled, then admitted, "I don't want you hurt either."

He tried to tease her. "Then I'll stay out of the calf event." He sobered. Her interest had pleased him, though. "I'm not looking for a fight about Jordan," he said. "The kids' rodeo is your choice, like anything else, but I am wondering why you want to avoid talking about what Doc said. Are you telling me the truth?"

She didn't answer. She riffled through the mail on the hall table, her back to him, shutting him out. She had the right to do that too—they weren't married or anything—and she didn't know how he felt about her despite his current commitment phobia, but her rejection stung. Made him worry more.

Lizzie reminded him of his mother, always covering up the true state of her health. That choice was hers too, but he wished she would talk, ease his concerns or simply admit the truth, whatever it might be. Obviously, that wasn't going to happen now.

But Dallas would bet every one of his bull ropes and belt buckles that she was lying.

"I SHOULDN'T HAVE trusted him. I guess Calvin made his decision."

At the defeated tone of Becca's voice, Elizabeth glanced up from the rug order she'd been processing in the store's office. With luck, she'd finally be caught up before Olivia returned, but Becca's statement made Elizabeth close the window on the computer. "He hasn't come back?"

Biting her lip, Becca shook her head.

"I'm sorry, sweetie," Elizabeth said, quelling the soft roll of nausea in her stomach. "Are you feeling better otherwise?"

She should ask herself the same question. Physically this morning she could at least function enough to work. Since her visit with the doctor, she was being more careful about what she ate, which included a few soda crackers before she got out of bed, but emotionally she felt awful. *Are you telling me the truth?* Dallas had asked. She hated keeping this secret, but finding the right time to tell him hadn't happened yet. Plus, after he knew, their friendship might well go up in smoke. The help he'd provided with her children, the kisses they'd shared, the easy comfort of his presence would end. What if, once he knew, Dallas couldn't get back to the circuit fast enough? He might even leave before his rodeo.

"I don't know how I feel," Becca finally said.

At least she'd had the inner fortitude to let Calvin know he was going to be a father. Because of Elizabeth, Dallas remained clueless, and for the past few days she'd been avoiding him. Of course, he had a right to know, but she could only hope Doc Baxter's wife hadn't overheard from the reception area during Elizabeth's appointment. If she talked, Dallas might hear before Elizabeth told him.

Becca dropped onto a chair. "I told you how my dad reacted. With Calvin gone, I'm in a worse spot. It's just me and…" Her gaze softening, Becca laid a protective hand over her stomach.

Elizabeth tried to choose her words carefully. "You wouldn't want to marry Calvin anyway, Becca, if he's not on board about this baby."

Again, Elizabeth could have been talking about herself. If only she and Dallas didn't live in such different worlds—if he wanted a deeper relationship right here in Barren, if a family other than his parents was on his mind…would she take that second chance? Or had Harry destroyed not only her trust but her faith in marriage?

"You mean a shotgun wedding?" Becca said, massaging her abdomen. "No, but I can't have the baby then keep living with my dad the way we are now, like strangers, either. He's so disappointed in me. That wouldn't be fair to an innocent child."

Becca sounded surprisingly mature. Weird that they were in the same situation. Becca faced a private scandal at home, while Elizabeth's own unplanned pregnancy would give those in town who considered her to be Ms. Perfect a field day. Also, there was her mother to reckon with. She didn't want to think about that. This conversation was for Becca, who, for once, seemed to be more in control than Elizabeth. Keeping her pregnancy a secret made them seem less than equals, which was unfair, as it was with Dallas. "Becca, if I tell you something, can you keep it to yourself?"

Becca's gaze sharpened. "Sure."

Elizabeth took a breath. "I feel that while Olivia's been gone, you and I have gotten closer. I do hope we're friends by now. So, I thought you should know. You're not alone in this, sweetie. I'm—uh—I'm pregnant too."

"Oh, that's lovely. Congratulations, Elizabeth. But why don't you want anyone to know?" Then Becca seemed to remember Elizabeth's divorce and thus that Harry might not be the responsible party. "Oh," she said again. "I hope your baby's father is happier about that than Calvin was."

Elizabeth had to overlook Becca's statement. "Remember when I told you about my miscarriage last year? Sometimes I still walk around the house at night, grieving." She saw Becca's eyes well with tears. "You know how I make myself feel better then? Ice cream," she said, hoping to make the girl smile. "Most recently, butter pecan. But I don't mean to make light of things. When I found out I was pregnant again, I knew what a blessing this is. My baby will be a welcome addition to the family I already have. It won't be easy, but I never considered any other option." Elizabeth held her gaze. "What do you see as yours, Becca?"

She shuddered. "I already love my baby too, but how could I take care of it when I can hardly take care of myself? That's what Calvin said. This job…the money I make alone would never support a baby. I'd be the worst single mom on the planet."

Becca faced a truly hard choice.

So did Elizabeth. Her work on the rodeo had already thrust her back into the spotlight she'd hoped to avoid. Dallas had been right, before her children came home, that any gossip wouldn't hurt them, but once the news of the baby came out, she'd feel humiliated again, even more personally this time. The speculation then would be world-class, worthy of the best paparazzi. And her kids would suffer. She doubted Dallas would commit to stay, commit to her, as if that were a viable solution. He had responsibilities to his mother, his career. And, still in her first trimester, what if she *did* miscarry again? That fear was never far from her mind.

"Have you thought about adoption?" Elizabeth asked.

"No," Becca murmured. "I mean, I have—I tried to think of everything—but I'd be giving up my baby. I'd never see him or her again, would I?"

"In an open adoption maybe you could, if that's what you'd want to do, but it could be painful seeing the child all the time yet not being a true part of its life."

"He—or she—would have a good home, though. I'd make sure of that."

Becca seemed to be growing up before her eyes. Adoption would free her of responsibility for a helpless human being she couldn't afford to raise on her own; the baby would live in a more secure, maybe even prosperous home. Which didn't take away from the heartbreak Becca would likely feel.

The bell above the door chimed in the front

room, interrupting Elizabeth's thoughts, and a customer walked in.

"Back to work. We can talk later or whenever you want," Elizabeth told Becca.

"Thank you." With a flush on her cheeks, Becca disappeared into the storeroom to take inventory of the newest rugs from Kedar. And probably to ponder her difficult, life-changing decision.

When she'd taken that first pregnancy test, Elizabeth had made hers. With every cell of her being, she would protect her unborn child. For the moment, she busied herself and blocked any other thought by dusting the knickknacks out front.

If she told Dallas about the baby now, she'd needlessly complicate their temporary relationship. She had a little time left before she began to show.

Maybe she would tell him right before he left town for good.

CHAPTER SIXTEEN

ELIZABETH WAS PULLING out of her driveway the next morning when she realized the same house lights had been on next door for the past several days, not that she was keeping track of Dallas. His mail wouldn't pile up outdoors because all the homes on this street had brass slots in the front door. His truck was gone. Where was he? They had PR issues to discuss, if not personal ones.

Elizabeth backed out onto the street and headed through town toward the McMann ranch. She'd planned to see Clara today anyway.

"Scads of people want to enter our baked goods contest," Clara announced, meeting her at the door, all smiles. "Some are interested in showing their melons and tomatoes too! I know there'll be others."

"You're doing a fantastic job," Elizabeth said, following Clara into the ranch office and taking a seat. Clara seemed to have found a new purpose in life even beyond her devotion to Hadley's and Jenna's twins. Elizabeth reached for a piece of chocolate from the box between them. "About the rodeo, I'm concerned. Do you know where Dallas is? I don't think he's here in Barren," she said with a question in her voice.

"He's not, dear. I'm afraid his mother's in the hospital again. As soon as he got the call the other day on Hadley's sat phone while they were in the field rounding up strays, he left for Denver to be with her." Clara selected a chocolate truffle. "I should have let you know."

Elizabeth tensed. "No, Dallas should have." They were supposed to be partners in the event, but he hadn't thought to tell her he'd be out of town. Or that his mother was ill. "I hope Mrs. Maguire is all right." But she couldn't keep from asking, "Will he be here for the rodeo?"

"We expect he will. Things are already beginning to heat up on this ranch."

"I've been focused on publicity this week." Elizabeth frowned a little. "The *Barren Journal*'s editor finally caved. She'll interview

Dallas for a weekend edition. If he's available," she added. "If not, I'll have to fill in, but they're really interested in him and, of course, the celebrity factor. I don't know what we'll do regarding the TV segment I booked in Farrier. No one will want to see me when they're expecting a rodeo star."

"If necessary, perhaps Hadley could do the interviews." Clara's lips pursed. "Not that I should burden him with another obligation. His mood hasn't been the best, and even Jenna won't bring up an issue if it can wait."

Elizabeth hoped that Dallas would come back in time. She thought of Becca, who was beside herself about Calvin, which made them kindred spirits. She tried to sound upbeat. "We'll manage, Clara," she said.

"Everyone seems excited, and Barren is alive with energy."

Elizabeth couldn't complain. The gossip she'd expected hadn't materialized so far, and even Bernice was keeping quiet, although, certainly with her sharp gaze she'd noticed Dallas's absence.

Clara chose another square of chocolate. "With the rodeo goings-on, the ranch could use help. I wouldn't have taken Calvin for a quitter. Hadley's been good to him, and Calvin was due his pay, which he didn't take. I'm sure he needed that. What on earth made him pack his things then leave without a word? Without Dallas here too, poor Hadley's doing all the work himself."

Elizabeth guessed why Calvin had left but, for Becca's sake, she couldn't say anything. They were in the same boat now, and she wished she'd told Dallas about the baby after all. Even when he must already have enough on his mind too.

DALLAS HATED HOSPITALS. He'd spent time in several of them, most recently because of his hip injury, and it didn't matter how well the staff did their jobs, how skilled the doctors, how kind the nurses were. He always wanted to be somewhere else. Especially now.

"Hey, Mom." Dallas leaned over her bed. "It's me again. How you feeling today?"

She framed his face. "Oh, honey. Your father should never have bothered you."

"Don't kid a kidder. Of course I came." Had she forgotten he'd also been here for the past three days? The night before that he'd driven rather than flown to Denver, not only to save money but because he might have to stay longer this time and would need his truck. Perched on the edge of her bed, he took her hand. Hers felt cool, as if the blood had left her body, and his throat closed. "You tell me one more time you're fine when I can see you're not, I'll take all your toys away."

At his teasing, she brightened. "Not my new vacuum cleaner." She smiled wanly. "Your dad bought it for my birthday, every woman's fondest wish for a gift, but I know what he really wanted—to give up his cleaning chore—and just between us, I'm all for that." Her other hand covered her forehead. "You should see that man bang into every piece of furniture, the wood chips flying." Then she seemed to run out of steam. Her grip weakened, small and fragile, and the lump in his throat grew bigger. "I don't know how he'd manage without me."

"You're not going to do anything foolish, are you?" *Like leave me and Dad?* He'd left his father downstairs with sorrow in his eyes, the fear that Dallas also felt. He worried about him too. She was right. Their house—Dallas's home—could use a good cleaning, and when he'd arrived, there hadn't been a scrap of food in the refrigerator. His dad had been spending all his time in this hospital, sleeping on a chair next to her bed at night. A half hour ago, Dallas had taken him to the cafeteria for a good meal, so at least he'd eaten today. But what would happen if they lost Millie?

"Don't be ridiculous, Dallas. I'm in here to rest a few days, that's all." She managed a grin. "My doctor looks about twelve years old, but then everyone does—including you. You'll always be my boy. Tell me what you've been doing since we saw you last."

Dallas had trouble talking around the ache in his throat. His parents were the best, a far cry from the two who had conceived him and Hadley. For a few minutes, he talked about his rodeo, his temporary alliance with Lizzie—he tried to make that sound like strictly business—and his hip, which had mostly healed. He was done at last with rehab.

Millie held his gaze. "When will you introduce me to your Lizzie?"

Dallas froze. "She's not mine." Had his mom seen the glint in his eye whenever he said Lizzie's name? Heard his husky tone of voice? "I knew I was your son from a different mother—" true enough "—but I never guessed you were a mind reader."

"Then you don't deny it. That's not all business. I could tell."

"No, ma'am." He brushed hair back from her forehead. "But don't start naming your grandchildren or, to get things in the order that would please you, planning my wedding." He explained about Lizzie's ex-husband, the scandal she'd endured and her three children. "She has to put her life together again, Mom." And leaving rodeo was probably the only way he might convince Lizzie that he was more than friend material, but he wasn't about to do that. "If I don't return to the circuit, which would mean never being in Barren for her, Ace will sign a new rider."

"Then you'd find another agent." Her steady gaze made him squirm. "You'd really let Ace O'Leary make your decisions?"

"I'd be out of business, Mom, lose the rest of my endorsements."

Dallas remembered his most recent talk with Ace, the same day he'd heard Millie was in the hospital. *Your contract's about to expire with Prestige Boots, and they've decided—in part because you're off the circuit—not to renew.*

Dallas said, "The boot people already canned me."

"There are others." She wagged a finger at him. "If you quit before you win that championship, your father and I will disown you."

Dallas grinned. "No, you won't. I'm not getting rid of you either."

She answered his smile. "I was joking. I know you won't stop. You'd never forgive yourself, but about your—Lizzie?"

He stopped smiling. "What does she need with a guy like me? I'm practically a nomad."

"A nomad?" His mother wouldn't let him off the hook. "That's part of your job and won't last forever. Make use of the time you have. Before I'm through, I want to see you settled with a woman who loves you and a family of your own."

"I'm not ready to get serious."

"I think you already are."

Dallas didn't welcome the notion that zipped, unfiltered, through his head. Most of his rodeo friends had wives or serious girl-friends. In Barren, during this summer of re-covery, he'd learned Cooper and Nell Ransom were starting their family, and they weren't the only ones. No, Dallas wasn't ready, yet the idea held an appeal it never had before.

As his mom had said, time was passing. The day he'd left the McMann ranch, earlier he'd surprised Jenna and Hadley having a quarrel. Later in the field, looking miserable, Hadley had told Dallas why. "It's not bad enough she can't have babies, but I didn't realize she was this unhappy." Then Dallas had gotten the call about Millie. He'd hit the road within the hour.

Dallas wasn't bound to anyone. Or was he wasting the best years of his own life? Refusing, in part, to grow up? He hadn't seen Lizzie since right after her doctor's appointment, when Dallas had guessed she was still keeping something from him. He'd stayed long enough that day to watch the rodeo tape with Jordan, and during the video Seth had crawled onto Dallas's lap and fallen asleep in his arms. Soon after, Dallas had gone back to his house. On his way across the drive he'd seen Stella watching from a window as if to make sure he was headed in the opposite direction. Would have made him smile—fierce little tigress—but he'd been too worried that Lizzie was far more ill than she'd admitted.

What did all that mean? Sure, he'd like something more than friendship with her, but he also knew they weren't free to go further than that. Dallas's heart ached. Or was his mom right? And he'd waded into deeper waters here? Could he be falling in love with Lizzie?

He forced his attention back to Millie. Her tired gaze had brightened. "Three children, you said?"

"Mom, cut it out."

"Tell me their names."

With a sigh, Dallas did just that, throwing in a couple of cute stories about his babysitting stint with Lizzie's kids, then stood up, patting Millie's hand as it lay on the covers. "I'd like to grant your fondest wish but not yet, and never mind me. You concentrate on getting well." He kissed her cheek, still afraid for her, and knowing he'd likely disappoint her about Lizzie. His job, his parents, had to come first. "I'll take care of Dad for you."

CHAPTER SEVENTEEN

AT THE RANCH two days ago Elizabeth had told Clara the shop was out of flyers, and today Jenna had brought a fresh supply. Unfortunately, she interrupted one of Elizabeth's ongoing discussions with Becca about Calvin and their baby. "He won't ever come back," Becca was insisting, "and I don't want to give up my baby but…"

Seeing Jenna, she trailed off. Becca's lips flattened and she smoothed the tunic she wore to cover her stomach.

Jenna's eyebrows rose. "Should I go out and come in again?"

"No, you're fine." Elizabeth took the flyers, then fanned them across a bare space on the front counter. Even she could feel the growing sense of excitement in town, as Clara had said. The rodeo was getting ever closer, yet Dallas was still missing. She hoped his mom was doing better but… "Things must be hopping out at Clara's. I hope the disruption's not overwhelming."

Jenna's eyes were shadowed. "Hadley says the barn was mostly empty anyway. Now it will be full of stock and so will the paddocks, the pastures, plus the tack room will be stuffed with equipment."

Elizabeth couldn't stop from asking. "Has Dallas told Hadley when he'll be back?" Maybe he was avoiding her too, slipping in and out of his house without her seeing him. The pattern of his lights hadn't changed, though, so probably not. And she had to admit she missed him.

Jenna said, "His mom's better but he's staying there as long as he can."

Elizabeth tried to downplay her concerns. "His prep work for the rodeo was mostly done—except for some interviews I don't know whether to cancel or find a substitute for—so that leaves Clara and me to finish the rest." She just hoped he'd be here on rodeo day. Elizabeth had decided it was time to tell her kids about that, and now her two boys couldn't wait, but she still hesitated to let Jordan compete. And Stella had asked to enter the baking competition with the cookies she'd learned to make at a Brownie troop meeting. Elizabeth was happy to see her involved in what would be a family outing.

Becca excused herself to eat lunch in Olivia's office. Jenna looked after the girl with a laser-focused expression. "Did she say 'baby'?"

"Yes." Elizabeth wished Jenna had come in a few minutes later instead of overhearing part of the conversation.

"I thought I noticed a bump the last time I was here. Calvin," Jenna surmised. After all, she lived at the McMann ranch, where he'd worked. "It doesn't surprise me, then, that he's disappeared."

"With Dallas away too, Hadley must have his hands full."

"Grey Wilson's been helping. So have others. That's one great thing about this town. People pitch in wherever needed. I wouldn't have recovered so well after my divorce without my family here, my friends, including you." She tilted her head to study Elizabeth. "And how're you doing, friend?"

"Coping. The kids came home early, but they're not little anymore so we manage our days more easily than I used to. Once I nail down a regular sitter instead of the temps I've been using, we'll be fine."

"I meant you, personally."

Jenna was one of her best friends, and she always sensed when there was a deeper issue. Elizabeth resisted the urge to put a protective hand on her stomach. Dallas had been right about one thing. That spring afternoon in May she'd been a Lizzie, more herself perhaps in that one day than she'd ever been—or thought of being—in her life. Now that Jenna had opened the door, Elizabeth decided to share her secret. Like Becca, Elizabeth needed counsel from someone she could trust. "Jen, I can't keep this to myself any longer. Becca isn't the only one who works here at Olivia McCord Antiques and is, um, pregnant."

Jenna gave Elizabeth a high five that she weakly answered. "Olivia and Sawyer are having another? Did she email you from Kedar?"

"Not Olivia."

Jenna gaped at her. "You mean—*you*? *Dallas?*" Her eyes widened. "Are you serious?"

"You warned me this was possible, Jenna, but I didn't want to listen. Please, don't tell anyone else. You and Becca, her for obvious reasons, are the only two who know. It's early yet, and I haven't told the kids. I made the mistake of letting them know too soon about the baby I lost last winter...so, this time I want to be sure everything will be okay." She'd waited with Dallas, as well. Was still waiting, wise or not.

"You said you used protection."

"Expired."

Jenna's eyes widened again. "I have to say, this is mind-blowing, kiddo. I won't tell, of course. Are you okay with this?"

Elizabeth nodded. "I want this baby. So much."

"I understand." Her eyes brimming, Jenna drew her into a hug. "What did Dallas say?" Elizabeth's silence spoke volumes and Jenna eased back from their embrace. "You haven't told him. Oh, Elizabeth."

"I'm waiting for the right moment. There's so much going on with the rodeo, and he's out of town..." The excuse sounded weak, even to her, but she already knew Dallas's view of a wife and family. She doubted he'd changed his mind.

"I don't imagine it will be easy with a baby

in the house again," Elizabeth said, "and my three stair-step kids. Still, most of it will be familiar for me. For starters, I've given up sleep before. But Becca has no idea what she's in for, and since Calvin deserted her—"

Jenna glanced toward the office, where Becca could be heard sniffling and rustling the aluminum foil that had held her sandwich. "That girl must be out of her mind with worry." She hesitated. "Do you know what she plans to do?"

"That's what we were talking about when you came in. She's not sure. She's considering adoption, but the only reason she's worried is because she doesn't want to lose her rights."

A determined glint appeared in Jenna's eyes. "I may be able to help. As you suggested, Hadley and I have been having some serious discussions. He doesn't quite see things my way yet, but I'm hopeful. This wouldn't be the same as our using a surrogate, which I was reading about last night—my latest attempt to find a solution. This could be a way for us to have a baby that wasn't from a stranger, and for Becca to know her child will be well cared for," she said. "We'd be keeping the baby in our community."

"Like Finn and Annabelle adopting Emmie," Elizabeth pointed out.

"I'd have no problem letting Becca be part of her baby's life." Before Elizabeth could comment, Jenna headed for the office. "I'll talk to her."

WHEN DALLAS RETURNED from Denver the next day, he went straight to the McMann ranch, where he found Hadley mucking stalls in a foul mood. Maybe his argument with Jenna hadn't ended. Or he was mad because Dallas had been gone so long.

"Sorry you had to take over my job too, Hadley." He wrested the pitchfork from his brother's hands. Dallas preferred the chore to sitting by his mom's bed all day feeling helpless or trying to allay his father's anxiety, though he thought he'd helped some. "I would have come sooner. I wish I'd been able to, but I waited till Mom got out of the hospital." He'd been away for a week.

Hadley's scowl lightened a fraction. "She doing okay now?"

"Her heart failure's a constant issue. She seems much better for now, and before I left, I hired an in-home caregiver. We'll see how that works out. Should at least lighten the load on Dad. He looks run-down." Dallas pitched a forkful of soiled bedding from the empty stall. "I finally talked to her doctor at length, and Millie's condition is manageable so far. The doc says she'll monitor her newest medications closely—and that we should keep Mom's spirits up."

"I hope she does fine." And still, something with Hadley seemed off.

"She sends her best to you and Jenna. Again."

Hadley muttered, "Thanks, we're going to need that. I understand better how she feels about another child, but Jenna's come up with a new idea."

"What's that?"

"She spoke to Becca Carter. Came home from town yesterday all fired up. The girl's pregnant—Calvin's kid."

"Yeah, I knew."

Hadley went on. "I ever see him again, I'll wring his neck." He kicked an empty bucket, which clanged against the wall. Halfway down the aisle, Trouble startled in his temporary stall while his was being cleaned. Dallas heard the dun gelding whicker then spin around, as if hoping to escape whatever danger lurked nearby. A dull thud told Dallas the horse had bumped into the wall. "Easy, boy," Hadley called, then, "Get this. Jenna wants to adopt Becca's baby. I hate to dampen Jenna's hopes, but what if we took the baby, then Calvin turned up again—accepted his responsibilities—and Becca wanted to make a family with him after all? I can just see those two coming to the house, taking that baby away with the court's permission. That would break Jenna's heart." When the twins were smaller, Hadley had feared a similar outcome from his former in-laws, who'd wanted custody of their only grandchildren.

"Not likely to happen, Hadley."

He scowled. "How do you know? You spend your life driving from one rodeo to the next, never staying long any one place—"

"You mean the way you used to do?" His brother had been known as a drifter until he married his first wife, Amy, and even when he stayed, she'd probably expected him to leave. Then after she'd died, and he had the twins to care for, Hadley fell for Jenna. He hadn't said a word now to welcome Dallas back. He had something else on his mind, something that involved Dallas?

He pitched another forkful of hay into the wheelbarrow between them. "You got something to say, Hadley, say it. Unlike Calvin, I didn't want to leave here, but I had to deal with the emergency at home. You said you understood. What was I supposed to do, keep punching cattle while my mother slipped away in that hospital and my father lost his mind? They're *my* responsibility."

"Oh, yeah? I thought you were theirs." He paused. "Mine," he said.

Dallas tensed. They were coming too close to those last days together in foster care. His heart raced. Before he could stop them, the bad memories rushed from the far recesses of his mind. Dallas heard that click of the lock again. Heard himself crying, begging for Hadley on the other side of that bedroom door.

The words were torn from him. "I'm not a kid now. They need me. I already let them down by going on the circuit instead of settling down, giving them the grandkids they want so bad." Which produced an image of Lizzie, the kisses she and Dallas had shared.

His sense at the hospital that he'd somehow forgotten to have his own life, commit to someone, didn't slow his pulse now. Neither did his realization that, yeah, he was falling in love with her.

"What were you supposed to do?" Hadley repeated Dallas's question. "Take care of business, that's what. You and Calvin."

Dallas blinked. "What does that mean?"

"When Amy and I filed for divorce, I thought that was the end for us. Then, weeks after we'd spent one night together for old times' sake, she told me she was pregnant. I didn't leave, Dallas. I stuck by her, put our pending divorce on hold, took care of her until the twins were born. I promised her we could try again after that to make our marriage work, but then she…didn't make it through delivery and I was suddenly a widower, a single dad with two helpless little beings to raise."

"You've done a great job. I know that was a tough time for you."

"Yeah, but you know what? That's life. That was being an adult, little brother. I love being a dad. I love being Jenna's husband even when we don't see eye to eye. I have no desire to pack my gear and move on again while you and Calvin—"

"Me and Calvin? Whoa," Dallas said, dropping the pitchfork into the wheelbarrow. What did all this have to do with him? "Why lump the two of us together? Twice now?"

"You took care of your parents this past week—I admire you for that—but why haven't you stepped up to the plate with Elizabeth Barnes?"

Dallas's heart stalled. "Lizzie? What's happened? Is she still sick?"

Hadley aimed another kick at the empty bucket. "If this thing with Jenna and Becca hadn't come up, I would never have known."

"Known *what*?"

Hadley turned away. "We were arguing last night about Becca and Jenna blurted it out—Elizabeth had told her. I shouldn't lose my temper like this, but I just can't believe you didn't tell me."

Dallas swung him around with a hard hand on his shoulder. "No, you don't get to tar and feather me along with Calvin Stern—" He stopped and stared at Hadley, who stared him down. The implication hung in the air. What had Calvin asked him? *Is your girl-*

friend pregnant too? "You mean—Lizzie?" He swallowed, hard.

"She's not some buckle bunny on the circuit you'll never see again. Talk about responsibility." Hadley raised his voice. "What the hell were you thinking? I'm disappointed in you, Dallas." Hadley had played the big brother card. "What did you do to that woman?"

Dallas's jaw clenched. As if he'd had the wind knocked out of him, he fell back against the nearest stall door. He'd left town to help his mom, and he'd come back to this crisis Lizzie must have faced alone. Had she known before he left? And that was why she'd looked like she had some secret she never wanted to share? It was like Calvin's question was a prophecy come true, but Dallas wasn't about to explain that one afternoon in Lizzie's house, her tears... His own weakness had gotten them in this fix. Not the best way to think about it but... "Hadley, I swear, I didn't know. I had a right—and she didn't tell me."

THE CHILDREN WERE in bed at last, and Elizabeth collapsed on the sofa just as her cell phone rang in her pocket. She almost didn't answer. It wasn't her mother's name that flashed on the screen, though. Dallas's voice sounded as tightly strung as the wire on Clara's fences.

"Are you home?"

"Yes."

"I'm coming over." Dallas must have been right outside, because he opened her front door as she pushed the button to end his call. And her heart sank. She'd guessed by his tone why he wanted to see her. With all her dithering about timing, her fears, she'd waited too long. Someone had talked.

"I would have come sooner," Dallas said, "but after being away so long I put in a full day's work." He stood in the center of the room, hands on his lean hips, his eyes cool. "Hadley says you have something to tell me."

Elizabeth could see a muscle knot in his jaw. "Jenna told him," she murmured. In Barren, others might always be waiting for the next bit of gossip to spread, but she hadn't expected Jenna to betray her confidence.

"There was never any flu, was there?" he asked.

"No, but at first I wasn't sure about…the other." She pressed a hand to her forehead. "Dallas, I didn't want to think I was pregnant. Then I didn't want to trouble you until I had to."

"Trouble me?"

"I should have told you, I know that. But I…lost a baby last year, and I've been so afraid that might happen again. I wanted to feel more confident that it won't before I said anything. Before we go on now, how is your mother doing?" Elizabeth added.

The muscle in his jaw jumped again. "Better. Out of the hospital. I took off too fast to call you. Sorry, and once I was there, I never seemed to find the time." Or maybe he hadn't wanted to. He returned to the subject that involved him now as well. "I'm very sorry for your loss then, but yes, you should have told me. Instead, *Elizabeth*, I had to find out from my *brother* that you're carrying my baby?"

Dallas came closer, eyes blazing. *"Why didn't you tell me?* Or did you not want me to know?" He waved a hand toward the stairs. "I was here long enough to take care of your three kids. I watched rodeo tapes with Jordan, read books to Seth, tried to connect with Stella, who's having none of that, by the way. I was in this house for *days* while you hid the truth from me. That's the same as lying."

"By omission," she conceded. "Dallas, I didn't intentionally mislead you."

"I think you did. You kept on talking about our rodeo plans, but you could never even say a few other words? Like, 'Dallas, I'm pregnant. Help me.'" He stood in front of her and Elizabeth looked up into his angry eyes. "You trusted me with your children, but you didn't trust me with the truth. I have to ask—what am I to you? What do you take me for? Just some guy you made one *mistake* with last May, someone who's passing through and will be out of your life before summer's over?"

"You will be," she pointed out. "You've never made any secret of the fact that you can't wait to get on the road again." She understood the worry he felt about that and his parents. "So, no, I didn't expect you to be thrilled about the baby. And when you do go back to the circuit, have you thought about what would happen if you got injured again? How would that help your mother or secure your parents' future?"

"I won't get hurt." Except that hadn't worked so well for him before.

Elizabeth flung out a hand. Stubborn man.

"You shouldn't even ride in this local rodeo. The animals you've managed to acquire are inexperienced. No one's ever tried to stay on them. Am I right?"

"You let me worry about that. I promise not to get killed in front of you and your children."

His sarcasm made Elizabeth see red. "I hope not, but isn't it time you faced reality? Riding bulls can't last forever."

His mouth tightened. "No, and when that's over, I'll decide what else to do with my life. Maybe stock contracting, becoming a rodeo announcer on TV, getting more involved with a group that helps injured and disabled riders—I might even think about buying a ranch of my own. I'm not there yet. But right now my folks can't live in that house much longer, even with the caregiver I hired. Over time Mom will need more care—expensive care. When I'm through on the circuit, I can relocate them wherever I decide to settle or go home and find them a better situation in Denver, but I need to get back to rodeoing so I can afford to do that. I thought you understood why my first priority has to be my parents." He drew a sharp breath. "But about this baby…what do you need from me?"

Elizabeth stiffened. This wasn't going any better than she'd expected. "I don't need your money. And I haven't asked you to stay, Dallas." Her voice quavered. "Or to be part of this child's life. I'm sorry I didn't tell you before Hadley did. Just go," she said, "back to your rodeo career and all that prize money you intend to win. I have a job now too, and my three kids have support from Harry. If I need anything more, I'm sure my friends will help."

He gazed at her. "Know something? This isn't about what I do. It's not about me being the wrong guy for you, a cowboy who's like some tumbleweed rolling over the ground. Isn't that what you meant?" He didn't give her a chance to answer. "You don't much like rodeo, I get that, but it's not really about me. It's not even about this baby, is it? I've been wrong. I think you care more what the town gossips might say—"

"That's not true."

"—and about your standing in this community, including with your mother, than you do even about the children you already have."

Elizabeth winced. "That's unfair. I don't want them shamed—because of my behavior with *you* this time!" Her voice continued to shake. "But that's on me. I had a rebound thing with you, Dallas. I shouldn't have and that also wasn't fair to you. One afternoon with a woman you barely knew, and now look." She gestured at her still-flat abdomen.

"Lizzie, I—"

She turned her head aside. "I'll see this rodeo of yours through because I promised my children." She tried to steady her tone. "And hope the whole town doesn't find out about us before it's over." She was trembling now, a leaf blown by the wind. "By the way, you have an interview with a reporter from the *Barren Journal*, and our TV station wants you on air." She rose from the sofa, marched over to the door and flung it open. "I won't be there, so you're on your own. And so am I."

CHAPTER EIGHTEEN

BECCA LEFT DOC BAXTER'S OFFICE, ignoring the receptionist, his wife, on her way out. Her father was waiting for her in his truck around the corner from Cottonwood Street on Main where he'd parked, but Becca's footsteps slowed. She'd rather have done this on her own.

They hadn't exchanged many words since he'd learned she was pregnant, yet he'd insisted on coming with her today. Becca hadn't known how to say no.

Halfway to the pickup, she heard someone call her name. Jenna Smith had seen her and hurried along the street from the café. She crossed over in front of Olivia's shop.

"Becca, I've been meaning to call you." Her gaze lingered on Becca's stomach before sliding away to focus on the sidewalk. "Since we talked a couple of days ago, I've been thinking of you a lot." She gestured toward the medical office. "Everything okay?"

"Perfect," she said. "I've been thinking too about the right thing for my baby, but I know your husband isn't wild about another child."

"Hadley and I have been…negotiating. I mean, discussing. He knows what this would mean to me, for our family. He's said yes." Jenna forced a smile. "Do you know what you're having?"

"A boy," Becca announced, unable to keep the smile from her face. "You're the first person I've told. He's due in December." Two months before Elizabeth's baby. It amazed her that her new friend had confided in her. Becca might even call her a mentor, and she relied now on Elizabeth's experience, her common sense as a guide. Still, Elizabeth had said Becca should make her own decision to keep her baby or—

Jenna's gaze lifted. "Tell me everything, please. How big is he, what does he weigh? Has Doc done an ultrasound yet?"

"Today," Becca said and pulled the sonogram from her backpack. For a long moment she studied it, wondering if she should draw Jenna into her private world, before handing it over. Instead of sharing this special moment with Calvin, she watched Jenna's eyes widen in wonder. "See, that's his hand and, over here, this is a leg." The baby lay folded in a typical fetal position, making it hard to see certain parts.

Jenna's gaze fixed on the image. "Oh, you can see his face clearly, that little snub nose…" As if reluctant, she gave back the sonogram, one finger trailing over the image of Becca's little baby inside her. "I don't mean to push, but it would be the most wonderful thing if Hadley and I could give your child a home." Her features seemed to blur for Becca. "I promise, you could see him whenever you like. You'd be invited to his birthday parties, for Christmas, all the special times." She stopped. "I'm trying to sway you, aren't I?"

Becca had lain awake every night, but now she didn't have to think any longer. Jenna and Hadley had a good marriage, and Jenna's infertility must be an agonizing thing to live with. Becca thought she understood. In providing what was best for her own child, Becca would also be making Jenna's fondest wish come true.

Becca reached for Jenna's hand. "I've made

up my mind," she said, looking toward her father's truck. He sent her a curious glance as if to ask what was keeping her. "I'd like very much for you and Hadley to have him."

"Becca." Jenna pulled her close for a hug. "I don't know what to say."

She choked on her words. "I think you'll be the best parents he could ever have."

Now the tears were flowing down Becca's cheeks. She and Jenna stood in their tight embrace, both weeping, until Becca knew she couldn't stand here any longer or she'd fall completely apart. Of course, this was the right, the totally right, thing to do. Still, it hurt.

"I can't wait to tell Hadley," Jenna said. "He's such a great father. He will be for this baby too. Thank you, Becca, from the bottom of our hearts."

When they finally parted, Becca started for her dad's aging Ford pickup. She swiped at her tears. Her steps faltered before she squared her shoulders and opened the passenger door. Her father's hound dog eyes seemed to bore into her thoughts, the regrets that wanted to form. "Everything okay?"

"Perfect," she said, slipping onto the seat beside him.

"What were you talking to Jenna Smith about?"

"Just small talk." Her voice sounded strident to her ears. "Let's go home."

"But you looked sad." He hadn't twisted the ignition key. He cupped her chin in his rough hand, forcing Becca to look at his woeful expression, the one she'd come to know all too well from the moment her mother's diagnosis had been made. "Something's wrong. And I know I haven't been a very good father since I first knew about the…baby—"

Through a blur of fresh tears, she patted his hand. "You're always a good dad."

"If there's a problem, we'll deal with it, Becca."

Her stomach tightened. He'd managed her mother's illness with steadfast devotion.

"Nothing's wrong," she said, and, to Becca's relief, he didn't probe any further. "The baby should come at Christmastime."

He started the engine, the truck pulled away from the curb, and she took a shaky breath. Calvin didn't matter now. He could stay wherever he'd gone. It wasn't as if she'd gotten pregnant on purpose to keep him with her. Other people might see her as childish, but her decision to let the Smiths adopt her baby was the most mature thing she'd ever done. At the same time, her heart seemed to be breaking. For a minute she wanted to jump out of the truck, run down the street and tell Jenna she'd changed her mind.

Instead, she fixed her gaze on the road ahead. Her own future.

A road without Calvin. Or their baby.

FOR THE NEXT WEEK, Dallas felt as if Lizzie's words were some ghostly specter, drifting at his side and floating through his head wherever he went. He shouldn't have said what he had, especially about her standing in town, but for now it seemed wiser to steer clear of her. The day after he'd learned about the baby, he'd decided to enter a small rodeo an hour's drive from Barren. It would be his first event to test his renewed fitness—he'd been planning this since around the time he first thought about his own rodeo. Now he was ready.

After that, what if he just kept going? *You can't wait to get on the road again*, she'd said, which was true. He'd already failed to show up for the interview she'd mentioned, the TV spot. How had he gotten so careless as to make a baby with her? To put Lizzie at the forefront again of more damaging gossip that would threaten any chance to repair the reputation she so valued? He couldn't stop the thought. *The mayor's ex-wife with a rodeo bum.*

They'd both said hurtful things, and Dallas hadn't tried hard enough to discuss their options. As he carried his gear from his truck toward the outdoor arena in the little town of Serenity, he got a few steely glances from other riders that seemed to say what a jerk he was. "Don't you belong in Vegas?" one guy called, pitching a cigarette butt into the dirt between them like a gauntlet. "Big shot."

A second said, "Not much chance, Maguire, for us local boys with you around."

"I'd say that's hardly fair," drawled another.

At the sullen tone of their voices and the hard looks on three faces, Dallas shifted his gear bag from one shoulder to the other, freeing up his stronger left arm, his riding hand. These guys looked eager to beat him to a pulp. Another second, and he might be at the center of an all-out brawl. Wouldn't be his first fight. Maybe he had that coming to him, one way to work off his guilt about Lizzie.

The three rough cowboys had closed in and were circling him when Dallas heard another, more familiar voice. "Come on, now," the man said, ambling across the dusty ground. He tipped back his battered Stetson and, to Dallas's surprise, there stood Calvin Stern. "You never been busted up and had to get on the horse again, Horace? Jake? How about you, Dudley? Just to prove you can?" He half smiled at the group. "Let him be."

"He took second in the Finals two years ago," said the first man, practically spitting the words. "There won't be no competition here. Might as well save my entry fee."

The second guy motioned toward Dallas's truck. "I were you, I'd get in that fancy rig then floor it before we teach you a lesson about trying to grab another man's territory."

"Y'all need some manners," Calvin said, again in that same, unconcerned tone.

Dallas tensed. He hadn't asked for Calvin's protection, but the muscles had bunched in the other men's arms, their stances widened to intimidate. Two against three now.

One guy's fist was already raised, and as he charged, Dallas sidestepped the blow.

"No need for this," he told them, but each of them threw a punch, one landing on Calvin's shoulder. He winced but returned the insult with a swift uppercut to a jaw. One man shoved Dallas, another Calvin. The fight truly would have been on then, but Dallas put out an arm to block the next attack, then backed away, his hands in the air.

"We go on like this, boys, none of us will be able to ride. You three won't look nearly as appealing to all those pretty girls at the Saturday night dance."

The first guy feinted another assault but stopped without moving forward. A slow grin spread across his face. "Point taken. I'd rather ride than spend the rest of the weekend putting liniment on my aches and pains. Tell you what. We'll all ride and kick your—"

"You can try." A narrow escape. Hoping he'd read them right, Dallas turned his back to face Calvin. "Let's set up. Then I'll buy you lunch. You and I have some talking to do."

In Serenity, there weren't many restaurant choices. Dallas and Calvin took their fast-food burgers and fries to his truck. After the first few bites, he eyed Calvin before he launched his own attack.

"This where you've been since you left Becca Carter?"

"No, I just drove around the state, here and there, tried my hand at a rodeo in Burnside. Placed fourth," he said with the tilt of one eyebrow. "You were right. Kind of gets in your blood."

Dallas didn't smile. "I thought it might. But why'd you leave Hadley like that too? He's working double time now." Dallas had made that worse the week he'd been gone to see his mother. He was doing it again now. He blew out a breath. "I'm disappointed in you, Calvin." *In myself too.* And he sounded like his brother.

"I didn't mean to make things harder for Hadley. Becca either," Calvin added, "but, man, I panicked. Me, with a kid on the way? And her talking marriage again? I never thought she was serious. Then she lays the baby on me, and all of a sudden I was coming out of my skin." He dug another fry from the bag. "The open road looked mighty good."

"How do you think Becca feels?"

Calvin didn't answer, but Dallas knew that Becca, like Lizzie, had a reputation to uphold.

Dallas too had left Lizzie to fend off any town gossip, the thing she dreaded most. What to do? If he stayed in Barren with her, worked for Hadley or bought land of his own, he'd be giving up the championship, his endorsements. None of his sponsors would want a washed-up cowboy then. He'd have Lizzie, though, and had it been that hard to take care of her three kids for a few days? Seth was sweet. Jordan seemed eager to learn everything he could about Dallas's lifestyle, to see him as a role model. Stella…well, not as easy there. She might never accept him.

But as they grew, they'd all need more guidance along with Lizzie's love. On the other hand, if he went back to the circuit, he could better manage his parents' growing needs without the distraction of a ready-made family, but he might lose any chance he had left with Lizzie. And the thought of raising this child they'd made, together… He needed this time away to make some decisions.

The situation had tied him in knots more tangled than the thought of Ace signing another rider to replace him. He handed Calvin

the large bag of fries. Dallas seemed to have
lost his appetite. He slipped his half-eaten
burger into the other sack. "What are you
going to do after this rodeo?" Dallas could
have been talking to himself. "You made a
bad choice before, Calvin."

"Yeah, I did," he said, then shrugged.
"Guess I'm going back to Barren. Face the
music. See what Becca really wants to do—
if she'll talk to me."

Dallas could understand that. "Only way
to find out."

A FEW DAYS LATER, Elizabeth was watching
Seth play on the backyard swing set while,
on her knees, she weeded what she laugh-
ingly called her "garden"—most of the plants
were dying off this late in the summer—when
her next-door neighbor stepped onto his back
porch. Her heart skipped a couple of beats. A
minute later Dallas had crossed the grass between their houses and was helping her to her
feet. His hand felt warm, strong, but Elizabeth
pulled free. "Where have you been this time?"
She'd asked the question idly, she hoped, not
because she'd missed him. She'd been stuck
with his duties as well for the rodeo, that was

all. A glimpse of what life would be like if she and Dallas were really together.

He gazed around the yard. "In Serenity. Not much more than a wide spot in the road, but they put on a decent rodeo. Had to try out my rusty moves, but I wasn't exactly welcome there, especially after I finished first riding bulls. Thought about getting dumped on purpose but couldn't throw the event—or the chance to prove myself. I donated my winnings to their local senior citizens' group. My parents won't suffer the loss of those few bucks I won there, and I'll make that up to them." He frowned. "I, uh, came over to see if there's anything we need for our rodeo."

Elizabeth felt herself weakening. He looked wonderful, his face tanned and streaks of sun in his darker hair. Yes, they'd had words before he left, but there was no sense in giving him the cold shoulder now. They were adults. She'd had her time to feel furious, hurt, and soon his rodeo would be over. Then this sad tension between them would end. Dallas would leave. "I rescheduled your TV appearance—in the hope you'd be here for it. The *Barren Journal* will publish a write-up about you next week. You need to call them."

"Thanks," he said. "I didn't mean to leave you holding the bag."

Elizabeth said nothing, and they ran out of words that weren't charged by the issues between them, specifically the baby. She and Dallas hadn't been this uneasy with each other since May.

Fortunately, Seth filled the awkward silence. He'd been digging a hole under the swings but looked up, spotted Dallas—and tore across the yard. "Hi! Where did you go? My mom says our grass is getting too long. Did you bring me a present?"

"Seth!" Elizabeth said, blushing.

"You did say that, Mama."

"Your grass is pretty high," Dallas agreed with Seth. "I'll get right on that. And yeah, maybe I did bring you a present." He didn't seem to mind her little boy wrapping his arms around Dallas's legs. He *would* make a good dad—if he'd wanted to be one. Caring for her children while she felt ill hadn't fazed him; but she assumed spending the rest of his life helping to raise them and the new baby wasn't on his schedule.

I didn't ask you to make a lifetime commitment, Dallas had once said.

"Can we read another book?" Seth asked.

"Sure."

"I'll be right back!" He ran toward the house.

"I didn't mean this second," Dallas murmured, a smile tugging at his mouth. He cupped the nape of his neck, not quite looking at Elizabeth. "He misses his dad, doesn't he?"

"He misses his fantasy of what Harry—a father—should be." She winced. "That sounded bitter, sorry. Not your problem. You were saying about the rodeo...?"

He rephrased his earlier question. "Anything else left I need to do for you?"

No, except stand by me when this scandal breaks, be here for this baby, and doesn't that sound needy... Talk about an impossible dream, which probably wasn't in either of their best interests or, equally important, in her children's. The last thing they needed was another broken relationship if Dallas couldn't resist the call of the rodeo circuit—a second loss would throw them into fresh turmoil.

"I think you're all set," Elizabeth said at last. "Clara's been wonderful, taking charge of things I wasn't familiar with, and her enthusiasm is catching."

"That's Clara." His smile didn't reach his eyes. "Lizzie."

He didn't correct himself. She didn't mind the name as much as she once had, but she replied, "I'm not that person, Dallas. I'm still me, Elizabeth Barnes, uptight, proper and making another fool of myself, really."

"You haven't. You didn't. You aren't." He broached the topic that had kept this conversation awkward. "I don't blame you for getting mad. I'm sorry if you thought I ran out on you." He nodded at her stomach. "You feeling any better now?"

"Some," she said.

"Have you told your mother yet?"

She laid a hand on her stomach. "No. I should, I know, but…"

"I'll go with you if that would help."

Elizabeth's breath caught. Had he just offered his support? "She's not your biggest fan."

"Neither are you lately," he pointed out. "That doesn't mean we can't handle this."

What was he saying? As if they were talking about bull riding, not her pregnancy, she imagined his strong hand on the rope, his muscles straining for control of the huge animal. In spite of the angry words they'd exchanged, the hurt he must have felt, the resentment she'd nursed when he abruptly left town again, he was a decent man. He'd come back, hadn't he? Her anger was hard to maintain, especially when he said, "You're not on your own here, Lizzie."

Dallas seemed about to say more when Seth burst through the back door, then floated down the steps. "I brought all my books. You can choose which one to read first."

"Looks like a long afternoon," Dallas said, daring to brush her cheek with the back of his hand. He looked into her eyes. "Reading, mowing…and maybe we can talk later. You and me. Could all that earn this sorry excuse for a guy dinner?"

She supposed that was his way—charming at that, even dear—to apologize. Elizabeth held up a hand. Her little boy had charged up to them, books flying everywhere. "Seth, slow down." But she was also addressing Dallas, who wasn't any kind of poor excuse for a man. He just couldn't be the one for her, long-term. Could he?

As Seth sat cross-legged in the grass under the big oak tree and fanned the books like a deck of cards for Dallas's inspection, he and Elizabeth stared at each other over her son's head for a long moment before she said, "Yes, you can stay for dinner."

CHAPTER NINETEEN

DALLAS HAD SPENT that evening and most nights of the following week at Lizzie's house. That first dinner had broken the ice between them, for which he felt more than grateful. Tonight, they'd cooked hamburgers and hot dogs on her grill, then eaten at the picnic table in her backyard to the songs of crickets and a few late-summer cicadas. The evening hadn't cooled much from the day's earlier heat, but as the stars and mosquitoes began to come out, they moved inside. All five of them.

In the living room Dallas discussed rodeo with Jordan, who seemed beside himself about tomorrow's big event, and Dallas tried to talk Lizzie into letting the boy ride. Well, almost. She was still "reserving judgment" before she'd make her final decision. He hoped it would be the one Jordan wanted. Dallas understood her concern for his safety but thought she was needlessly prolonging Jordan's begging.

When he set up the video for him to watch again, Lizzie merely rolled her eyes as if she was about to give up on her son and Dallas.

Her youngest (not really the youngest now, he realized) lay in Dallas's lap, which seemed to have become his favorite spot. Dallas could get used to this warm feeling of being part of a family, especially when Hadley was barely talking to him since he'd let Dallas know about Lizzie's pregnancy. Wearing a smile that wouldn't go away, Dallas read a few more books to Seth, whose eyelids had started to droop. Lizzie and Stella sat on the sofa, perusing an issue of a children's magazine, their heads close together. Stella refused to look at him. "Seth would hear about *Janie Wants to Be a Cowgirl* all night," Lizzie said. "Believe me, I know. That book has been handed down, it seems, by every kid in Barren."

"Read again," Seth said in a sleepy tone, making her and Dallas laugh.

Minutes later, with his head on Dallas's shoulder, he began to snore lightly, clutching the spotted horse model Dallas had bought him in Serenity. Dallas glanced at Lizzie.

"I think he's out cold." He'd given Jordan a video of the kids' rodeo there. Stella still hadn't looked at the pretty patterned scarf he'd bought her with cowgirl boots on it.

"It's past Seth's bedtime. Everyone's bedtime," Lizzie said, reminding Dallas of the night the kids had come home from Colorado. Before he knew exactly how connected he was to her family.

He cradled Seth close, then carried him upstairs with Lizzie and Stella behind. He could feel Stella's glare boring through his back. He sighed.

"Jordan," Lizzie called down the steps. "Turn off that TV. You need to come up to bed. Now."

Grumbling, Jordan obeyed, but in the upstairs hall he grinned when Dallas gave him a fist bump and said, "Every good cowboy knows that rest is a requirement." A slight exaggeration, yet it seemed to work. Jordan was in bed before Stella. Finally, everyone was settled, and Dallas stood in the hall. Lizzie joined him after helping Seth say his prayers.

"Every cowboy?" she asked with a pointed look.

"Well, not all," he said, then slipped an arm

around her shoulders. Maybe she'd forgiven him for his trip to Serenity, if not his first reaction to her pregnancy. They needed to talk. Too bad he still didn't know what to say.

Together, they went downstairs. "Thanks for helping me put them to bed," she said.

"No problem." Dallas reached for her hand. They'd been dancing around each other all evening. If she thought he was going home now, she was wrong about that. "Didn't do bad for my first time." He drew her to the sofa and sat beside her, their fingers still clasped. "Maybe there's hope for me yet."

"Hope for what?"

"Something more," he ventured. He held her gaze, his eyes serious. This wasn't just about whatever relationship they could have, not about this pleasant evening or any other they'd spent with her kids. "What I said before about dealing with this? I don't know exactly how, but we can—if that's what you want too. Yeah, I was mad when I found out you were pregnant, but not because of that, just because you didn't tell me yourself. I'd never leave you to manage this on your own." He hesitated. "I, uh, know how that feels."

She stiffened. "I don't want you to feel obligated."

"I'm already part of this, but that's not what I meant. I mean I know how it feels—felt once—to be utterly alone."

Her gaze softened. "You mean when you were a little boy?"

Ever since he'd come to Barren to see Hadley last Christmas, the memories he thought he'd left behind years ago hadn't let him be. Each time he almost let them in, they seemed to draw closer, tighter around him, to become more vivid. They would never leave unless he took them out, looked at them, deprived them of their power, and it was Lizzie he wanted to tell now.

He ran a hand through his hair. "A while ago my mom said she thinks that, because of what I went through then, I've been standing in my own way. I told you Hadley and I got separated years ago, didn't see each other for a couple of decades, but before you and I go any further, I want you to know the rest." He cleared his throat. "Our folks threw us out like garbage when I was about five years old and Hadley was seven. The state took over," he said. "In foster care we moved around, house to house, family to family, and we stayed together, but we never belonged any-where." Except with each other.

"Were there good people who cared for you?"

"Some, sure. Others, not much." He stared down at his hands. "My worst was the last place with Hadley. They already had a bunch of foster kids, made a nice living off them. The couple drove fancy cars, wore fine clothes, ate well…we got the dregs. There was rarely enough to eat and I'm talking mac and cheese from a box, mostly. Stuff like that." Lizzie sat stone-faced, listening but not say-ing a word. "Pathetic, huh?" He swallowed hard. "The discipline could get rough. Their abuse scared me, but it made Hadley mad."

"He's a good big brother," she murmured, her voice tight.

He shook his head. "I'm not telling you this to gain sympathy. I just want you to know what *you're* dealing with here. My mom also said she can see the damage in me." The im-ages rolled through his head like an old film. "I never fought back, but Hadley did, so they often punished me for something—didn't have to be anything much—that my brother had done. That last time, they shut me in the bedroom we'd shared, locked him out. They didn't feed me for days. Hadley was afraid I'd starve to death. So was I. When he got desperate enough, my then ten-year-old brother took food for me from the corner store."

"Because he loved you," she murmured.

Dallas's throat ached. "When the store owner contacted the authorities, the state investigated then took us out of that house—that was the good part—but Hadley was sent to juvenile detention. After he got out, I don't know where he went. By then I was with the Maguires. His record was sealed."

She touched his arm. "Dallas, that's dreadful." Her voice sounded hoarse. "You were just little boys. Like Jordan and Seth." Lizzie hesitated. "My friend Annabelle had a similar experience except she was an only child. You should talk to her sometime."

"Maybe, but it's a miracle Hadley and I found each other again. Mom was right about me. I think, because of all that, I…freaked out about the baby. I've never liked being cornered, which is how that felt at first." Like Calvin. "But I take full responsibility. I'll gladly pay support, but I can't offer you the kind of life you thought you had with Harry, that you must still need now." He held up his hands. "So, where do we go from here?"

Her gaze held the sympathy he hadn't wanted. Her touch on his arm was like a healing balm. "I understand better now what you went through as a child. I think that's why you're completely devoted to the Maguires, why you want to see them cared for, even why you don't want a…wife and family." She withdrew her hand from his. "But for me, a part-time relationship would never work. If I needed proof, all I'd have to do is think of my divorce. Of how life was before that with Harry. Oh, Dallas. The timing is still wrong. For both of us."

He couldn't answer that. He didn't have those words either, only the soft look in her eyes that told him maybe there was a solution for them, even after he'd just spilled his darkest secret. Dallas held her gaze with his, knowing his eyes must show her how serious he was.

When he took her in his arms, she didn't resist, and he had the oddest feeling this was where she belonged too. "Ah, Lizzie," he whispered, then his mouth covered hers.

Dallas put a little more into this kiss than he had before, savoring the feel of her lips until it finally ended, and to Dallas's utter astonishment, she laughed. After he'd shared his worst time with her tonight, she'd stayed in his arms, that sheer, unexpected joy wrapped around them like another warm embrace. "We must be crazy," was all she said. And laughed again.

Dallas wished this tentative truce between them wasn't so fragile, but if they weren't straight with each other, they wouldn't have any chance at all. "We don't have the answers yet," he said. "But I think they're worth looking for."

Dallas couldn't say where this moment might take them, but the possibility had been there in her laughter, and for now it was enough. After the rodeo, they'd see.

"ARE YOU ALL RIGHT?" Lizzie asked Dallas.

"I'm fine. Why?"

It was Rodeo Day! At last, but his stomach was already tied in double knots. Even when he'd spotted her getting out of her car, the three kids in tow, and returned their waves, he'd felt close to running for the nearby Porta Potty.

Lizzie saw through his weak defense. "Really? You look very pale."

In Serenity too, Calvin had pointed out his pallor. It was always like that, and at the moment he couldn't even appreciate the uber-Western getups Lizzie's children wore today. Jordan and Seth flaunted plaid shirts with the requisite pearl snaps, jeans and shiny boots. Though Stella sent him a jaundiced look, she apparently had some rodeo spirit too with a tan fringed leather skirt, green cowboy boots and a Barren Elementary School T-shirt. To his surprise, around her neck she wore the patterned scarf he'd bought her. The children had scattered, looking for their friends and checking out the horses in the paddock.

"I've been working since dawn," he told Lizzie. "No breakfast. No time."

"Clara didn't feed you? I can't believe that. You're nervous, aren't you?"

"Stage fright keeps me sharp. Gets the adrenaline flowing."

Earlier, he'd helped Calvin and Hadley ready the horses and bulls, checked the makeshift gate they'd rigged up to the makeshift arena, even made a tour of the makeshift bleachers to test their strength, all the while he suffered from internal panic. *It's not as if this is the Finals*, he thought, but people had begun streaming in half an hour ago, and the seats were filling up. His rodeo had been an idea before, a fantasy that had now become real.

It looked like every pickup truck in town was here. He saw Sawyer McCord get out of his truck with Olivia. They'd gotten home from Kedar only the day before so Sawyer could ride, jet-lagged as he must be. Cooper and Nell were already here, talking to friends and showing off her baby bump. He spied Clara bustling toward the white tents on the lawn. Dallas searched the crowd for Ace O'Leary, even though he knew his agent probably wouldn't come. Dallas hadn't talked to him in a while.

Soon it would be showtime. Sure, he'd won first place at Serenity's local rodeo, this was not an official PBR event either, and he felt good today, but if he didn't ride well, he'd have to face an ugly truth. Never mind that his hip had fully healed. His career might well be over or on its way. Then what? He'd be looking at the plan B he'd told Lizzie about. Stock contracting, TV, a ranch of his own, maybe even staying in Barren but without rodeo in his life.

He wiped a hand across his sweating forehead. "Really heating up out here. Gonna be a hot one. Did you give any more thought to Jordan competing?"

Lizzie hadn't answered before her son raced out of the nearby barn and ran up to them. "Can I, Mom? Huh?" he asked as if he'd been standing there and overheard.

"May I," Lizzie corrected him with an absent look. "How many times have I been asked that question, Jordan?"

Dallas twisted his bull rope in his shaking hands. He shouldn't interfere. He wasn't the boy's father, so he should butt out. On the other hand, Lizzie was carrying his child, which ought to give him some rights. Might as well say what was on his mind. Dallas said mildly, "He's a kid, Lizzie. Let him be one."

She studied him, then Jordan, and let out a long breath. "I take no responsibility for this decision, but you may enter the mutton busting—"

Dallas interrupted her. "Looks like Jordan's

had a growth spurt this summer. His legs are long enough now, his feet would probably touch the ground. I'd say the sheep are out for him."

"Steer riding, then?" Jordan's eyes had all but popped out of his head.

"He's old enough," Dallas pointed out. "And the kids actually ride calves."

She threw up her hands. "All of my fears for both of you have fallen on deaf ears. I hope you're right. Okay, steers," she said, and Jordan let out a whoop. He jumped up to give Lizzie a kiss even though, because of his age, he must consider any public show of affection to be uncool. Certainly, Dallas had as a kid, even with his mom.

He toyed with his bull rope again. "Jordan, better get over to the registration desk. You too," he told Lizzie, wishing he didn't have to say the rest, which concerned injury. "There's a waiver you'll need to sign, and it's almost time for him to cowboy up."

Lizzie jabbed a finger in Dallas's chest. "If he breaks a leg, I will hold *you* responsible." Her brow knitted. "And how safe will you be? Those are real bulls, tons of muscle, and your hand is trembling."

His voice husky, he held her gaze. "That's not because of the bulls." Well, that too.

"All right, Romeo." Glancing around at the now-crowded stands behind them, Lizzie said, "I'd give you a kiss for luck but—"

He sighed. "I know. People will talk. You're right." They shouldn't jeopardize her kids.

Indeed, he spied Bernice Caldwell in the stands, and—was that Claudia Monroe? Did Lizzie realize her mother was here? Dallas turned his head and, through a gap in the bleachers, saw his own parents getting out of a taxi. He stared. Naturally they'd known about his rodeo, but he'd never expected them to actually *be* here. How could his mom travel?

His pulse, revved up by his closeness to Lizzie, settled a bit, but his hands still shook and his stomach rolled. He always wanted to ride well. Now his folks would be watching. So would Lizzie. So would Jordan. People were depending on him.

Stage fright or not, he really had to make sure his backside didn't land in that dirt.

ELIZABETH'S MOTHER DIDN'T stay long in the bleachers. As soon as the parade to kick off the rodeo began, and before Elizabeth took her seat, Claudia scrambled down to confront her, and for an instant Elizabeth thought someone had told her about the baby. "That cowboy has been making up to your children now," her mother said. "*My* grandchildren."

"Whom you rarely bother to see." Elizabeth's stomach tightened. But it seemed Dallas had been right. Her mother at a rodeo. "Why on earth are you here?"

"I've brought my prize-winning hydrangeas, the lavender ones. They won at the last county fair held in Barren. Bernice has entered her heirloom tomatoes." A likely excuse for both of them. She and Bernice were here to judge, all right, but not the produce or flowers.

Elizabeth didn't want this confrontation any more than she had at Olivia's shop, yet maybe the time, as Dallas once said, had finally come.

Claudia sniffed at the parade going on without them. She drew Elizabeth around the end of the bleachers to a quieter spot. "How anyone could like this…sport is beyond me."

"Something on which we agree," Elizabeth murmured, still fearing her day could end in the emergency room with Jordan's arm in a cast. She didn't want to think about Dallas.

The air, which was already full of dust motes, carried the gamy aroma of untamed animals. In the background the bulls paced in their pens, pawing the ground. The horses in the paddock whinnied among themselves, stirring up more dirt as they danced in place as if to the strains of the national anthem now being played. The scents of grilling meat and cotton candy wafted to her from the nearby food stands.

"Elizabeth," her mother said, "listen to me. You'd risk your reputation with this man? I did not raise my daughter to end up living in some hovel on a run-down ranch."

Elizabeth stiffened. She must mean Clara's, which wasn't true. "You didn't need to bring those hydrangeas. You and Bernice judge other people without any props."

Claudia gasped. "You have a perfectly good home in town, Harry's support…and your children's welfare to consider. Isn't that enough?"

Maybe, for Elizabeth, it wasn't any longer. In the nearby ring the kids were lining up for the events. Having received a quick lesson from Dallas, Jordan stood in their midst, grinning, talking a mile a minute to his best friend, Nick, Olivia's son. Elizabeth heard a lot of laughter and friendly taunts among the other contestants. Jordan's eyes shone, and Seth had picked a spot at the fence rail to watch, his face poking between the boards. Stella stood with him. Everyone seemed to be having a grand time today, except Elizabeth right now.

She spoke loud enough to be heard above the din coming from the arena. "I'm not going to 'end up' anywhere but right where I belong. Please don't bring Harry into this again." She took a breath. "Actually, he's making his own plans. He's been interviewing and, according to Jordan, has a job offer in Wichita." Far enough away to keep out of her hair, near enough for the kids. "He'll be spending weekends in Barren to see the children."

"Then, if you play your cards right, you'll have an opportunity to win him back."

"Mother. Harry broke my heart. He betrayed me. What do you not get about that?" To make her point, she spaced out her words. "I. Don't. Want. Him. Back. Is that clear enough? You may think I'm the loser in our breakup, but I don't. Our marriage was never the perfect union you hoped for—" she wouldn't stop now "—the marriage you didn't have because Dad walked out on us when I was six years old! I never saw him again. He was a stranger to me, and he's been gone from my life for decades, but you're still living with that history."

Claudia turned a paler shade of tan. Elizabeth had to hand it to her mother. She kept herself in good shape, belonging to a gym she visited regularly, getting her hair done every week, spending time in the salon's tanning booth, which wasn't healthy but her decision. For any age, she looked great. But she was still alone. Still bitter after all these years.

"I'm sorry to remind you of that unhappiness," she said, "but I've heard enough of your rules and regulations for *my* behavior. Stop trying to dictate how you think I should live."

Her mother didn't say a word, which gave Elizabeth the strength to continue. "I need to make my own happiness, Mom. You need to find yours. You're still a young woman."

To her surprise, her mother almost smiled. "Youngish, perhaps." She wasn't taking that declaration as badly as Elizabeth had expected. Then, unable to stay silent, she sniffed again. "And you think that happiness of yours will be with...what's his name?"

"Dallas Maguire," Elizabeth said, certain her mother already knew that. "Yes, I more than like him, but that's our business." She remembered being in his arms, their kiss and her laughter, then Dallas saying they could find their way somehow. "You've gotten ahead of yourself. I'm not the bright-eyed girl who married Harry—and, yes, that was a lovely wedding, thank you, which I know cost you a lot, but nothing in our marriage made the term *happily-ever-after* apply."

In spite of her best efforts to mend things, Harry's affair had destroyed their marriage. As town mayor he'd subjected her to undeserved public scrutiny, at least in Elizabeth's mind. Was it partly because of her father's abandonment that she, like her mother, had become so fearful of such exposure, of humiliation? Dallas had even suggested she might care more about her reputation than she did about her own kids.

That wasn't true. Worried that gossip might reach their tender ears, she'd cared more about protecting them than she did herself. And yes, some people in Barren had judged her harshly, but not all people, not her closest friends, and no one had ever said a word to hurt her children. Why hadn't she seen that before?

At the beginning of summer, wounded in spirit, she'd taken refuge in her house not to let Bernice, now waiting for her mother in the stands, see her grief. To guess at her dalliance with Dallas on the day of her divorce. Elizabeth took full blame for that. But then she'd agreed to work with him on his rodeo—their rodeo, he always said—and in the past weeks she'd valued his friendship and rediscovered the appeal of a new relationship, which she'd tried to resist.

"You're in love with that man," Claudia said in an accusing tone, "which can only lead to further ruin."

Her mother sounded like some scolding Victorian matron. Dallas deserved Elizabeth to be completely truthful, not to hide him in the darkness as she'd hidden herself.

She couldn't know whether she and Dallas would work out, or if all he'd meant by "something more" was to share some responsibility for their baby, but she knew one thing for sure. She did love him, and she had the perfect opportunity, perhaps never to be repeated, to declare her independence from her mother. Maybe to shock her a little too.

"Yes," she finally murmured, "I am." She ignored the stunned, ever-disappointed-in-her look on her mother's face. From nearby, she heard the roar of the crowd. The kids' events had begun, and Elizabeth wanted to see for herself that Jordan was really okay. But right now she had to face what she'd been fearing for too long. She wouldn't care about whatever outcry there might be in town when this news reached Bernice, then the rest of the local busybodies. Elizabeth had done her time in the stocks of public humiliation. She had nothing to feel ashamed about. She did, however, have an announcement to make to this audience of one. "Brace yourself, Claudia Monroe," she began. "You'll need to— because, actually, that's not all. I'm expecting again. Dallas Maguire and I are having a Valentine's Day baby."

Ms. Perfect was no more. Let the gossip begin.

CHAPTER TWENTY

GAME ON.

Like most—if not all—bull riders, Dallas had a clock in his head. In the instant the blocky Angus broke from the chute, it twisted to the left, and the last pangs of nausea deserted Dallas. *One second*, he began counting. Alert to the slightest shift of the bull's body, he corrected his balance. One arm high in the air, he settled deeper into his seat, his bull rope wrapped tight around his other, riding hand.

Dallas had drawn a good ride. This bull belonged to the Sutherland ranch, where Nell Ransom had suggested they keep the young animal for breeding stock. It was no rodeo bull—but, man, Gorgeous had gotten the hang of this. *Two*, ticked his inner clock. Few people, other than bull riders, could appreciate how long the full eight-second count could seem to a man on board.

As he got jerked around in a half circle, Dallas's gaze caught a glimpse of Nell, her expression half-delighted yet worried, as Lizzie might be, but *she* was nowhere in sight. Had she gone home? Her kids were still here, so she must be somewhere on the grounds. Maybe not watching him, though, as the bull bucked hard. Gorgeous wasn't Greased Lightning, Dallas's nemesis, but he was naturally talented enough for this local event. If Dallas didn't need to stay focused on his ride, he'd smile. Instead, he gritted his teeth and held on. *Three seconds*. If Lizzie couldn't bear to see him risk life and limb, she must care. He'd like to prove to her that he could do this and survive in one piece. Before he'd cowboyed up and the chute opened, he'd noted that his parents were seated in the front row of the bleachers. His mom had a hand to her throat and high color in her cheeks. His dad was shouting, his voice raw. "Ride 'im!"

Four. Halfway now through the allotted time.

"Go, Dallas!" someone yelled. He and the bull flashed by little Seth at the rail. His mouth open, Jordan stood fixed in place, speechless as he took in Dallas's every move, the ribbon he'd won affixed to the boy's chest. And—what do you know?—beside the boys, Stella was jumping up and down next to Nell, who hadn't competed after all.

Determined to knock Dallas to the ground, the young bull spun to the right this time, and Dallas swore under his breath. *Not gonna happen.* It wasn't over yet. His new local friends had already ridden, but a few of Dallas's professional rodeo pals remained still to compete, and Finn, the local sheriff, who'd never ridden a bull before, had scored surprisingly well. Dallas needed to keep his focus.

Five. People were now pounding the boards under their feet in the grandstand. Jordan, like Dallas's father, had yelled himself hoarse—but still, Dallas saw no Lizzie. He wouldn't let his disappointment ruin his ride. Or get himself hurt again and destroy his chances with her.

Dallas was in his element here, the bull his to command—until Gorgeous suddenly whirled on his hocks like some barrel racer's horse. Dallas's hand was so tightly wrapped in his bull rope, the resin so sticky, that if he fell, he'd get hung up, then helplessly dragged around the arena, his arm caught in his rigging, in clear sight of Lizzie's children, his parents...and her?

His molars ground together. All the muscles in his arms, legs and abdomen rigid, he fought the bull with every bit of strength he had left. *Six!* The veins in his temples, his throat, must be standing out like those in his forearm, and a thought crossed his mind as it always did in these last seconds—*Hang on, cowboy. Set an example here.* Otherwise, he'd be on his back in the dirt, hurting. Humiliated like Lizzie by all the gossip she'd suffered.

His memory of Lubbock, his time in the hospital then rehab, kept him on this bull's back. So did the promise he'd made to stay safe. Jordan had already proved that he could. Now it was up to Dallas. His hip might ache and throb tonight, tomorrow, for the next week, along with his whole just-healed body, but in these few seconds he felt fine, and he thought, *I'm coming, Ace.* Serenity and Barren would be just the start. *I've got this.* He'd be like the phoenix rising from the ashes of his career.

Then soon, Greased Lightning would meet his match.

Seven. He almost made the fatal mistake

of loosening his grip on the rope, ever so slightly, when he knew how dangerous that could be, and predictably the Angus took advantage. The Sutherlands' bull wasn't done with him yet. A sinuous spiral torqued his entire body in midair—*gotta hand it to him*—and he nearly unseated Dallas. The crowd gasped.

Oh, no, you don't, he silently told the bull. *We're in this together. All the way.*

And in that moment, he spied Lizzie at the rail. She'd stayed. The buzzer sounded at the same second Dallas did the final count in his head. *Eight!*

The bull rope slithered through his hand as he hit the dirt. Standing on his feet.

"IS HE ALIVE?" Elizabeth wondered if her own heart was still beating. Seconds before, she'd joined her children at the fence but had to cover her eyes. Still, in the last instant she'd seen Dallas almost fall then recover his balance, and as she opened her eyes again now, she saw him standing, whole and strong and manly, in the center of the ring. With a shout of victory, he tore off his hat then flung it high in the air.

Jordan patted her shoulder. "He's fine, Mom. I bet he won!"

Stella leaned against her side. "I didn't think he would."

Seth clung to Elizabeth's hand. "When I'm bigger, I can ride too. Like him and Jordan."

Her oldest had come in third in the calf riding, perhaps thanks to Dallas's coaching. Even with his stomach churning, anticipating his own ride, he'd found time to help her boy. Elizabeth told herself the rising dust in the arena had caused her eyes to water. She didn't realize she was moving until she'd flung open the gate, run into the ring and thrown herself in Dallas's arms. He smelled of the animal he'd ridden, conquered, but most of all he smelled like Dallas. "Oh. My. Goodness. You were magnificent!"

His mouth quirked. "The part you actually saw, maybe. Let's not get carried away. Thanks for trying, Lizzie." He gazed above her head to beckon to someone in the crowd.

Elizabeth was riding high too over the look in Claudia's eyes when she'd told her mother she was pregnant. Yes, she loved him, but how would today turn out for her and Dallas? With his rodeo coming to an end, nothing held him in Barren any longer. He'd be ready, eager for the circuit again—he'd just proved that. Could she trust in that *something more* he'd mentioned?

As Dallas took her hand and left the ring before the next rider entered, two older people approached, their faces wreathed in smiles, and Elizabeth guessed who they were— another powerful reminder of Dallas's priorities.

Grinning, he walked toward them with Elizabeth. "Hey, Mom, Dad. Not a bad restart, huh?"

"You're our son," his mother said. "We're always proud, but today you were spectacular."

Releasing Elizabeth, Dallas leaned down to kiss his mom's cheek, then shook his father's hand, but got pulled into the kind of rough male hug that involved a lot of back slapping. "The next Finals in Vegas will be yours for the taking," his dad told him.

Nursing her doubts, Elizabeth held back until their three-way embrace ended and Dallas turned to her again. "Now you're in it," he said. "Meet my folks, Millie and Joe Maguire. This is Lizzie Barnes, my neighbor and… friend." He added, "For the time being."

Did he mean temporary friends, as she'd always thought? Elizabeth's spirits dropped even lower. Perhaps since their kiss and her laughter he'd changed his mind about her. "It's nice to meet you, Mr. and Mrs. Maguire."

Millie glanced between Elizabeth and Dallas. Her warm eyes danced. "If you're brave enough to put up with this one, you have my full support. You'll need it." Her gentle tone seemed to say instead that Dallas wasn't a problem. At that moment Elizabeth's children ran toward them in a pack, like young coyotes, and talking over each other. Millie clapped her hands. "These must be your children." She shot a look at Dallas.

"Three of them, remember?" he said.

"Lizzie, do you know how long I've been asking your 'friend' here to give me some grandchildren?" She studied Jordan, Stella and Seth in turn.

Stella's mouth set. "I already have a grandmother."

"She's mean," Seth put in. "She doesn't like us."

Jordan stiffened. "Yes, she does. She just doesn't know how to show it."

Millie's gaze faltered. "Oh, my."

Dallas said, "Mom, you're jumping the gun, aren't you?"

A small frown darkened her expression. "You know time is not on my side, Dallas, and don't give me that look. I feel wonderful today, but none of us has forever. That includes you. Don't waste any more time." Her face brightened as she addressed the children. "Do you three like snickerdoodles?"

And with that, she herded Jordan, Stella and Seth across the dusty yard toward the food tents, where all sorts of delicious pastries would be waiting. Dallas's father followed, giving him a wry look over his shoulder. "I hope they're hungry."

"Here we go," Dallas muttered to Elizabeth, who was standing there, feeling dazed. "There'll be no controlling her," he said, but he looked happy. From the top of the grandstand, where Hadley held the microphone, came another announcement. With the last few riders now done, the awards ceremony would start as soon as the winners' tallies were checked, and the judges delivered their verdicts from the competitions held in the tents. "Gotta run," he said, "but after all that prize money gets put in the pot for Dusty's care, we need to talk again, Lizzie."

She was holding her breath now. Elizabeth had no idea how that would go, but his parents, her children…appeared to have bonded instantly.

She didn't even mind that his mother too had used her nickname.

"BECCA." IN THE big tent that had housed the competitions for baked goods, vegetables and fruits grown by local people, she thought she heard Calvin's voice and wondered if she was hallucinating. Not willing to believe her ears, she moved baskets of zucchini and yellow squash around on the table she'd been assigned to monitor as a volunteer helper. Many of the entries were gone by now, either purchased or the leftovers packed to go home. Becca didn't turn around. She couldn't seem to move.

"I know you're mad at me." Calvin stepped closer behind her. "But hear me out."

She managed to circle the table to its front where two containers of raspberries and blackberries still stood. When she would have walked away, Calvin stayed her with a hand on her shoulder. The warmth of his touch threatened to melt her inside. He was here. She'd never expected to see him again.

"I understand how you must feel," he began.

"No, you don't. I have nothing to say to you."

She hadn't seen him earlier, and she hadn't left the tent all day, not even to watch one of the rodeo events. Why had he shown up now?

Her shoulders rigid, she cast a look around, hoping Elizabeth was nearby. Becca could use an ally, the mentor she'd come to rely on. Otherwise, she'd look at Calvin and be lost again, hoping they could be together when she'd already made her choice. Hers, alone.

He said, "Give me a minute, will you? We never talked much about ourselves—I didn't anyway—but I need you to listen now. Maybe then you'll understand why I did what I did." His tone lowered. "When I was a kid, my life got pretty messed up. My dad took off, my mom went into a tailspin, and I never knew what I was walking into when I got home. As soon as I turned eighteen, I joined the army, the only real structure I ever had until I came to work for Hadley. You see what I'm getting at here? When you told me about the baby, Becca, I thought, what if I was like my father with my mom and me? What if I couldn't be what you need me to be? I was wrong to leave," he said. "Nowhere I went in this whole state seemed like the right place. You know where that really is?" He didn't wait for her to respond. "With you," he said, almost too softly for her to hear. To believe.

Gently, he turned her to face him, but she couldn't meet his eyes. How could she tell him she'd given away their baby? This was awful, worse than her worst day in Olivia's shop trying to do her job.

"I want us to do the right thing," he rushed on. "Once the baby comes—"

"So, you're ready to be a father." Becca shifted a basket of melons, then to her dismay saw her own father walking toward them. What if he said something about the adoption? "You'd better go," she said. "My dad's coming, and his eyes are like flamethrowers."

Calvin didn't budge. "I'm not afraid of him."

A second later, her father was standing

toe to toe with Calvin, nudging Becca aside. "Leave her alone. I won't let you hurt my little girl again."

"She's not your little girl," Calvin said calmly. "Becca's a woman. She can make her own choice, and I'm hoping she'll choose me."

Her mouth fell open. As he'd said, Calvin had never been the sort to talk about his feelings. She'd told him she loved him, but he'd never said as much to her. "Please, Dad. Calvin and I need to talk."

Her father stared at the ground, his hands fisted at his sides. "This guy is nothing but a hired hand. Here today, probably gone tomorrow." He'd voiced Becca's own misgivings. Calvin was here now, but he might leave her again once he knew what she'd done. "That's no future for you, living hand to mouth, having his babies every year."

Calvin's mouth tightened. "This baby's mine, and I'll care for it. With Becca." He glanced at her dad's fists. "Hit me if it'll make you feel better."

Her dad didn't move. He focused on Becca. "You've spent the past few weeks pining over this guy. Did you hear one word from him that might set your mind at ease in all that time? No," he said, "it was me who had to see your tears, take you to Doc's, and what about the adop—"

Becca squared her shoulders. "Daddy, don't worry about me."

Her father's fists fell open. For a long moment he eyed Calvin, and she feared her dad might still land a punch. Instead, as if beaten, he put space between himself and Calvin.

She kissed her dad's cheek. "We'll be okay."

She wasn't sure and that didn't help her dad, who, like Becca, still mourned the loss of her mother, but he needed to find his own way again too. No matter how much she loved and wanted to please him, Becca couldn't do that for him. Just as he couldn't protect her from whatever life handed out. It was *Calvin* who could help her to heal.

After her father walked away, she rearranged some jars of golden honey until his hand covered hers. "I wish you'd gotten time beforehand to say your piece, Becca. I don't know where I stand with you—"

She didn't hesitate. "I love you, Calvin." She hoped that was enough.

He smiled into her eyes. "I love you too. I couldn't admit that—until Dallas made me see I'd decided wrong. I'll tell you about that later. I didn't come back until last night and earlier I couldn't find you. Clara finally said you were over here, and by then it was my turn to ride bulls. I came as soon as I could." Applause still sounded from the arena.

"I would have rooted for you, only I've been in this tent." Calvin told her he'd come in fourth in the bull riding, yet right now she needed him to believe in them, in her. "I'm glad you won a ribbon, but if you hadn't, you'd still be my hero." As she looped her arms around his neck, her own worry must have shown in her eyes.

What would he say when she told him about the baby?

"Give your dad time," Calvin said, though that wasn't what worried her now. "Let's go ahead and find a place to live. I think leaving that house where you grew up will be the best decision. You weren't happy with the rental we saw, but there'll be another."

"I do like that little house and the yard," she said just as someone called her name.

Becca froze. She should have expected this.

Everyone in town had come for the rodeo today. It seemed only natural that Jenna Smith would be among them. She lived here at the McMann ranch. Becca turned, a lump in her throat.

Jenna stood there with Hadley, holding hands. "I just had to tell you, Becca. After I saw you last time following your doctor's appointment," she said, "I sorted through Luke's and Grace's things from when they were smaller—newborn outfits and toys, and their bassinet is still in Clara's attic." The words had tumbled out of her.

"Jenna—"

Her face glowed. "We can go over the legal stuff later, and we'll certainly cover all charges for prenatal care, delivery. When you're ready to go home, we'll make the exchange as easy as possible for you. We're so happy you decided to let us have your baby."

Her pretty speech, like the one she'd given on the street before, went through Becca like an arrow. But she and Jenna weren't alone now. Calvin was here, staring at her too. He'd heard every word.

Jenna's excitement had blinded her to anyone else, and she seemed to notice Calvin for the first time. She tightened her grasp on Hadley's hand. "Calvin. I knew you had come back, but I didn't realize you were in this picture again."

"Well, I am," he said, searching Becca's face with an expression that practically shouted, *What's going on? What have you done?*

Hadley was frowning too, as if he knew Becca was about to destroy their hopes.

She wouldn't have Elizabeth's counsel now. Becca had to handle this herself.

She swallowed. "I know I promised, Jenna. I wasn't lying then…"

"Please." Jenna darted a look at Clara McMann, who was hurrying across the yard, her skirts flying as she tried to catch the twins before they reached the open gate to the arena, where the last of the prizes were being handed out. "Please don't."

The bleachers had started to empty as some of the townsfolk headed toward the food tables, and the scents of barbecue and hot dogs permeated the air. The growing look of confusion, then sorrow on Jenna's face demanded an explanation. And still, Becca remained motionless, not hearing the final announcements from the arena, the applause—Dusty Malone had come forward in his wheelchair to receive the donation check for him and his family—or seeing the cloudless blue sky.

But she had to think of Calvin. He and Becca were their baby's parents. She wanted more than anything for them to be a family.

"I'm so sorry, Jenna, Hadley. But Calvin and I are going to keep our baby."

DALLAS STRODE ACROSS the ranch yard in search of Lizzie, his progress hampered by people who offered congratulations for his win. Even the guys he'd competed against on the circuit seemed happy for him. "Glad you're back, Dallas." For those few seconds in the ring, he'd proven he was still on his game, and leftover adrenaline coursed through his veins. With another feeling he couldn't quite name. He could go back to the circuit now, and one of his first calls would be to Ace. His problem was what to say to Lizzie. What to do about them.

Lost in thought, he almost walked right past his brother. They hadn't exchanged an unnecessary word since he'd learned about Lizzie's pregnancy. Since Serenity, they'd been keeping out of each other's way. Hadley put a hand on his shoulder. "Hey, that was some ride."

"Thanks. You didn't do so bad yourself."

Hadley scanned the area, obviously distracted. "I need to find Jenna. We've just had a nasty blow and she headed for the food tents, probably to have a good cry." He told Dallas about the baby—Becca's child—they'd hoped to adopt.

"I'm sorry, man." Dallas didn't know what else to say.

Hadley rubbed his neck. "Yeah, well, Becca's choice. We'll be all right. Now that I see Jenna's point about a brother or sister for the twins, we'll work something out." He eyed Dallas for a moment. "You off to the road again? Or is there some way I can get you to stay here?"

"I'm not sure what to do yet." It wasn't the first time Hadley had asked, but those surprising words of acceptance from his brother gave Dallas courage. He'd hated feeling estranged again. "Look. I'm sorry I disappointed you, but I want you to know I'm going to do what's right by Lizzie."

"Okay," Hadley said, taking another look

around. "I figured you would. I need to apologize for telling you about her pregnancy. That was a rough way to find out and a mistake on my part."

Dallas stared at him for a moment, trying to find the other words that had lived in his heart for so long. "There's something else, Hadley. For over twenty years I thought I'd overcome any damage from that last foster place we shared. But Millie—Mom—says I'm still that scared little kid. She should have said a guilty kid. Because I failed you."

"What are you talking about?"

He lowered his gaze. "It was my fault you got caught after stealing that food."

"While you were locked up in that room? How could that be? I told you last Christmas you should have blamed me for not protecting you."

Dallas shook his head. "You went to that store because I couldn't stop crying. Screaming, actually." Which shamed him to this day. His cries had echoed off those walls.

"Didn't I tell you before?" Hadley asked. "You were *my* responsibility, Dallas. You were only *eight years old*." Lizzie had pointed that out too.

LEIGH RIKER

He barely heard. "And after they sent you away, what happened? The Maguires adopted *me*," Dallas admitted, "like I was getting some reward for what I'd done when that should have been you." Those words had been trapped inside him for a long time, as if he were still locked in that room. "I didn't... I don't deserve their love."

"Wait a minute. You really think a few tears caused all that? You're wrong." He hooked an arm around Dallas's neck. "You idiot." And he ruffled Dallas's hair, the way he always had. "Forget all that other stuff. To the Maguires you're their son, and you're okay with me too...for a kid brother. I love you, Dallas."

His vision blurred. Hadley had never been one to admit emotion. "I love you too."

"Are we square now, then?"

"We are," he said. The uneasiness that Dallas had felt since his return last Christmas—that he'd felt inside forever, really—had finally faded. From here on, he and Hadley would be as close again as they once had been.

Their shoulders brushing, they walked to the food tents that had held the domestic competitions, then his big brother went to look for

Jenna. As Dallas walked between the tables, now mostly empty, he finally spied Lizzie bagging up some brownies. He brushed dust from his jeans then snatched one off the table. "Energy bar," he said, catching her eye. "You done here?"

"Almost." Automatically, she glanced around to check on her children. In the nearest field, Seth was playing tag with some other boys. Sprawled on a blanket, Jordan and Nick Hunter, his best pal, were deep in conversation over a video game. Stella was helping Clara sort through a bunch of purple flowers for any still-fresh blossoms, which he heard Clara say would be donated to the local assisted-living home. In the west, the sun was sinking toward the horizon, spreading pink and red and orange across the big Kansas sky.

Following Lizzie's gaze toward her kids, he murmured, "Mother hen."

"That's my brood." As she'd once said, from six to nine they were similar ages to Dallas and Hadley when they'd lived in foster homes. Though Lizzie's kids enjoyed superior care and love, even from Harry, they were vulnerable too, and Dallas needed to keep in mind the little kid he'd been years ago when Hadley took care of him. Such good care.

He reached for her hand. "Let's find a quiet spot, okay?"

Dallas headed outside for a line of cotton-wood trees, a screen that hid the pasture from the house. That had been Clara's idea; she claimed she saw enough cows all day, didn't want them to take over her view at sunset. Which was probably baloney. She loved this ranch as much as Hadley did. His brother and Jenna, their heads close together in conversation, were strolling now in the direction of their house. *Thank you, Hadley, for always being here.*

In the cool shade, Dallas sat with Lizzie under a tree. She seemed pensive as they discussed today's events. Dallas had won the bull riding, but something didn't feel right about his win. "I couldn't have done this without you," he said.

"Our rodeo was a huge success. We made a ton of money for Dusty's medical expenses. I'm glad he's finally out of the hospital and will finish recovering at home. I'm so proud of you—first place, Dallas!" She didn't say anything else for a moment, then, "In fact, I'm

proud of myself too. I talked to my mother."
She explained her own declaration of independence. "I told her about the baby." Lizzie
grinned. "Frankly, I think it was kind of a
gotcha moment, but well worth that look on
her face."

Dallas stared at her. "What did she say?"

Elizabeth said lightly, "Oh, she's not happy
with me, but you know what? She'll get over
it." Or not. That was her choice.

"No wonder I saw her roving around the tables over there with an extra-mad look on her
face." He squeezed Elizabeth's hand. "Good
for you, but I wish you'd waited till I could
be there when you told her about the baby.
You're not worried about what people will
say?"

"Let them talk. If bringing our baby into
this world is another scandal, people really
need to get a life for themselves." His opinion too. "Where are your folks?" she asked.

"I sent them to my house. Mom had a
blast today, and her meds are working, but
she should rest. Jack's sending their dinner
over." Dallas studied her face. Twice now,
she'd said *our*, and he traced a line with his
thumb across her palm. "Lizzie. I'm not much

good at this kind of thing but—I shouldn't have said you care more for your reputation than you do for your kids."

"If I need to defend them from now on, I will, but they'll be fine, Dallas." Her smile turned wistful. "The kids *and* me. When I was married to Harry, he was often so absent from our lives, I was practically a single mom anyway. I hope now that he'll be working in Wichita, he'll spend better quality time with them here." She paused. "You shouldn't worry about us."

Dallas's stomach clenched. He was the absent type too. Was she about to reject him? She didn't need him to protect her, yet he wanted to be there for her anyway. What was it Hadley had said? *Is there some way I can get you to stay?* Dallas ran his thumb lightly over her palm again. Lizzie seemed newly centered in her life, but he was not. And his win today didn't seem like enough. That was what had felt wrong.

His mother was right again, as she usually was. Dallas had been wasting time on the road, in hotels, even in the arena. Of course, he hadn't known Lizzie then. "You know, I've worked real hard riding bulls, and a championship would be nice—"

"Is that what you call it? Nice? Dallas, that's been your goal for years."

"And to take care of my parents," he agreed, "but do I really want to spend my years piling up endorsements? Sponsors? Healing from broken bones and bruises? Sweating my brains out in rehab? Is that what I want— what I need most—after all?" From the instant he'd landed today after the eight-second buzzer, he'd felt uncertain, unsettled when everything should have been a green light. Get back on the circuit, work even harder next season. Dallas answered his own question. "No, it's not."

Lizzie seemed speechless. Then she said, "You're— You can't quit."

"Why not? Sure, today was fun and I'm glad you saw me ride, sort of, but you were right too. My life on the road is no life for a woman with three kids—" he glanced at her stomach "—and a fourth on the way."

"You couldn't be more wrong. Why give up what you love when you're this far—" she held up two fingers an inch apart "—from that championship? Where's your grit, Dallas?

"If I can hold my head up in this town," she said, "even if a single person never speaks to me again—which I doubt because I do have friends, enough loyal ones to counter the rest—you can go back on the road until you reach that goal. And keep winning to care for your parents' needs."

"But is that all I've been trying to do? Busting my backside riding bulls to win the money I thought they'd need? Maybe I've had this all wrong. When I met Millie and Joe, I was this skinny kid who'd never had a real home, and I always felt guilty that Hadley didn't have the same chances I did."

Yet his brother had found happiness with Jenna and the twins. It was too bad they couldn't have another child, but that wouldn't destroy what they already had. As he'd said, they'd work that out. Dallas tried to explain. "Maybe I saw rodeo as a way not only to help my parents, to repay them for what they've done for me, but to prove I'm worthy of the love they've given me all these years. Like I had to earn that too."

"But you don't, Dallas. Just as I don't need to prove anything to my mother. The Maguires' love for you is unconditional. You've always had that." She said, "Your parents won't care what you decide as long as that's the right choice for you."

He took a long, deep breath. She was right, but the next words weren't easy to say. "Maybe because of all those hard years in temporary places… I believed I didn't deserve anyone's love."

"Oh, Dallas." Her eyes had filled.

"I don't want to mess this up either, but my parents—and you, definitely you—are more important to me than any career." Who had he thought he was kidding? He hadn't been *falling* for Lizzie. He was already *in* love with her. "You and I said things we shouldn't, but people who care about each other have such power, they end up hurting that person they love most."

Her voice trembled. "Is that your way of saying…you love me?"

"Yeah. It is." *And what about you?* he wanted to ask. "See? Told you I wasn't good at this."

"Neither am I. After Harry and I divorced, I didn't want to even think about another relationship. When I met you, I felt so wounded, and then, somehow, we ended up… Well, you

know, that day before we were even friends."
Her face had turned an adorable pink. "Why
couldn't I see then that there could be so
much more? Even when I didn't feel the timing was right. Last January you didn't just
move in next door, cowboy." She blinked.
"You moved into my heart. I love you, Dallas, and I'm ready to trust again. In you."

"In us," he said, holding her gaze. "There'll
never be a perfect time for me to settle down,
have a family. That time has to be now. I love
you," he said, "so much. I want you to be part
of my life, I want to be part of yours, your
kids' lives. And this baby's."

Before she could answer, three wild children charged across the lawn right into the
serious discussion Dallas had been about to
tie up for Lizzie in a pretty bow. She would
really put up with his rodeo career? He wasn't
down on one knee yet, but…

"Mama! I'm going to marry Emmie's
friend when we grow up!"

Lizzie smiled, her free hand brushing back
his sweaty hair. "That's a long way off, Seth."

Jordan snickered. "Baby, baby, love and
marriage…"

"Jordan, don't tease your brother."

Wearing his ribbon from the steer, or rather calf, riding event, Jordan looked as if he were about to taunt Seth even more, but then, with a glance at Dallas, seemed to think better of it. Obviously worn-out after the exciting day, Seth dropped onto Dallas's lap and nestled against him as if he'd been doing so all his life. Lizzie was a great mother, and he'd have to rely on her experience, but it was Stella he still wasn't sure about.

Lizzie's little girl stood over him, scowling, which didn't make her face look any less pretty, and a fresh surge of protectiveness washed through him. He'd have to try especially hard to win her over. But to his astonishment, Stella suddenly plunked down nearby. She studied Dallas for a moment, as if trying to decide if he was a bad guy or a good one.

"You're a really cool bull rider," she finally said.

"The high mark of approval," Lizzie murmured.

In the years to come, Dallas would guide Jordan, who wanted to follow in his footsteps, in rodeo or any other walk of life. Seth too needed a father figure in the house. And so did Stella, whose vulnerability spoke to him. "Let's do this, then," he said. He made an all-encompassing gesture at their circle. "You and me. Them," he added, his heart pounding like a huge drum.

Lizzie held up one hand like a traffic cop. And laughed, the way she had before. He could listen to that sound forever and he planned to do just that. "We're going to take this slow, Dallas. We need to get it right."

"As slow as you want," he told her, "as long as you know my mother will be on your case every step of the way. She already hears wedding bells, and so do I." Dallas leaned over to kiss her, and Jordan predictably groaned at their public display of affection, but no one said a word in protest, even Stella. Dallas thought it couldn't get any better than this, but he was wrong again.

Lizzie said, "We'll manage, Dallas." Her green eyes looked clear, unclouded, and her dark hair could use a comb right now, but she was the most beautiful woman he'd ever known, inside and out. "This will be a partnership. I can oversee your parents and work around your demanding schedule on the road until you're ready to hang up your bull rope. And you can…keep mowing our grass."

Did that mean he was expected to move in with her? He'd take that as a yes. But… "That's not an even trade," he pointed out.

She whispered in his ear. "Neither is one baby with my three." She pulled back to gaze with love at her children. "You do know what you've signed on for?"

Dallas grinned. "I'll learn," he said. "What did I do to deserve you?"

Lizzie didn't have to answer. She slipped deeper into his embrace, Seth stayed curled in his lap and Jordan leaned against Dallas's shoulder. Stella sat slightly apart from them, not quite ready to join the group. Still, he felt accepted just as he had years ago when he'd walked into the Maguires' house for the first time and known he was home. Now, however fast or slow things might happen, he knew he'd made the right decision. They had. Dallas looked forward to sharing the rest of his life with Lizzie, her children and the precious baby they would welcome.

It was like a thousand blue ribbons, and a gold belt buckle, when the woman he loved looked up into his eyes and said, "Dallas, from now on I think everyone should call me Lizzie. Because that's who I am now."

Dallas kissed her again. Yes, she was.

But most of all, she was *his* Lizzie.

* * * * *